HOSTILE NEGOTIATIONS

HOSTILE NEGOTIATIONS

MCFADDEN AND BANKS™ BOOK 3

MICHAEL ANDERLE

DISRUPTIVE IMAGINATION

LMBPN Publishing
PMB 196, 2540 South Maryland Pkwy
Las Vegas, NV 89109

First US edition, January 2021
eBook ISBN: 978-1-64971-411-4
Print ISBN: 978-1-64971-412-1

THE HOSTILE NEGOTIATIONS TEAM

Thanks to our Beta Team:
Jeff Eaton, John Ashmore, Kelly O'Donnell

JIT Readers

Kerry Mortimer
Peter Manis
Jeff Goode
Deb Mader
Diane L. Smith

Editor
Skyhunter Editing Team

*To Family, Friends and
Those Who Love
to Read.
May We All Enjoy Grace
to Live the Life We Are
Called.*

CHAPTER ONE

Perhaps coming to the bar to do research wasn't the best idea he'd ever had.

He'd created all kinds of reasons to justify the decision. The first that came to mind was that they now served meals along with booze. Having easy access to both meant that he didn't need to spend too much time working on either one of those for himself. Second—and probably more important—the bar's Wi-Fi was probably the best on the base. Jian wondered why more people didn't take advantage of it.

Of course, once he'd spent a couple of hours in the bar, things became clearer. As soon as he had the opportunity to study the people who did spend considerable time at the bar, the disadvantages became obvious. It wasn't a knock on the patrons, of course. Jian knew full well that the people who lived near the Zoo needed any kind of coping mechanism that could be shipped to the middle of the Sahara.

But it was a loud environment, the kind that wasn't

conducive to getting his kind of work done. Soldiers and researchers alike came in to get themselves boozed up, and he knew he was in no position to ask anyone to keep it down. This was a place of merriment and the making of it, and all he could do was laugh when two researchers he'd worked with in the past got into an argument over who would go into the Zoo the next day.

It was better still when one of the soldiers drinking with them suggested that they settle the argument with an arm-wrestling contest.

Of all the different contests the two could engage in, arm-wrestling was probably the safest while still having a high probability of being amusing, both for them and the patrons around them.

Jian put his laptop aside for the moment and joined the group that began to gather around the two as they set themselves up to measure strength.

"Are we doing any betting?" the scientist asked and looked around. "Five bucks on Gregory." It seemed sensible as he was the younger of the two and appeared to be a little fitter and stronger.

"The redhead?" one of the soldiers near him asked. "I'll take that money!"

"I'll put five bucks in on the guy wearing glasses!"

The betting concluded quickly and enthusiastically and drinks were ordered for the two contestants. Their older colleague had never seen Greg and Terrence drunk but tonight, they seemed well on their way. They were two of the most introverted researchers he'd ever worked with, but they seemed to have unearthed some lurking social animal that even went so far as putting money down on themselves as the victor in their arm-wrestling contest.

It was a change that had played out often before, of course. The Zoo had a way of changing people and transforming them into something new. It wasn't always cut and dried like good or bad but rather a slow process of adapting them to become the kind of people who would survive their harsh environment.

"Let's get this show on the road!" Greg roared and was met with a loud cheer from the small crowd that had settled once business was taken care of—bets were made and recorded by the barman and enough drinks and snacks were lined up to suggest that they anticipated a prolonged contest. He took a hasty swig of his beer, coughed as a little went down the wrong pipe, and grasped his opponent's hand once he'd planted his elbow securely on the table.

The barman called the start and immediately, the two men began to strain and push against one another's hands in an attempt, probably, to force rapid capitulation.

Jian surprised himself and entered into the spirit of the occasion. He even cheered along with the rest of the spectators until finally, with a heavy thunk, Greg forced Terrence's hand onto the surface to a roar from the assembled crowd.

Money exchanged hands and fortunately, everyone took their losses in good humor and no one tried to argue with the bartender. Tonight's group were good sports. The older scientist moved forward to join his two younger colleagues at their tables. He patted Greg on the back.

"You had money on me, right?" the younger man asked as Jian sat in a chair he'd pulled closer.

"I knew you'd put a little extra effort into it if there was money involved, however small. You always were a greedy bastard."

Terrence laughed. "That sounds about right. He's been in the Zoo seven times and I've only been in there three. It's one of the benefits of having the type of technical knowledge I do but in the end, they want all the people they can heading in there. All in all, I guess it is my turn."

Greg laughed, his face red and flushed from his victory. "I won't lie, I thought you let me win. Maybe you'd like a chance at the record for the most trips in. You still have that one—right Everett?"

Jian raised an eyebrow when he was included in the conversation.

"How many times have you been in there?" Terrence paused to take a sip from his drink. "You got here…what, a year and a half ago?"

He nodded. "About nineteen months last Thursday, but who's counting? If my tally is correct, I've been into the Zoo twenty-four times and hated the fucking place more with every trip too."

"Is that the record?" Terrence asked. "I don't think I would be able to head in there twenty-plus times without losing my mind. Or my head, which is as likely."

"It's not," he corrected the man quickly. "It's not even the record among researchers, although I can't say who holds that particular one off the top of my head. The all-time record, of course, stands tall at eighty-four."

Both men turned to look at him and seemed to almost expect him to tell them he was only kidding. Instead, he simply took another sip of his vodka cranberry and waited with a slightly challenging expression until the number finally penetrated.

"Eighty-four." Greg shook his head. "What the fuck possesses someone to go into the Zoo that many times?"

"The better question is how does someone survive that many trips into the jungle?" Terrence muttered.

Jian nodded. "I went in there with the guy a couple of times. Taylor McFadden is a rough son of a bitch. He might as well have been cut out of wood and has bright red hair and a beard. People constantly called him a leprechaun because of his luck or something."

His two companions seemed intrigued enough to have momentarily forgotten their drinks, so he decided to feed their curiosity. "I remember one of the times when we went out there, his suit ruptured—not badly but enough for one of the panthers to force a little of its venom into him. He was trying to walk it off, but I managed to convince him to stop and take some anti-venom before he dropped. When we returned to base, he bought all my drinks, so I guess he realized he had acted stupid."

"I assume that luck didn't last?" Greg asked.

"It did and he's still alive. He retired after a trip that ended in a massacre that left too many people dead. He's back stateside now. The last I heard, he owns a company that repairs armored suits for the mercenary groups, and I've heard that many of the military guys want to give him their business but can't."

Terrence leaned back in his seat and sipped his beer, his expression thoughtful. "Hell, maybe he is a leprechaun. Of course, maybe the best luck would have been for him to not have gone in there in the first place, but hot-fucking-damn."

Jian nodded and shrugged as he looked at his glass and considered a refill. "Well, I can't speak for any of that."

He had never been much of a believer in anything like luck, but if that was how people chose to interpret it instead of looking into the thousands of variables that came into play instead, he wouldn't make a fuss about it.

"Do you think you'll ever get to the record yourself?" Terrence chuckled. "Think about it. You're already more than a quarter of the way there. All you need to do is keep going in and well…you know, not die. It seems doable for someone who sets their mind to it."

"I think you can contact Guinness World Records to let them know once you get to eighty-five," Greg agreed.

Terrence nodded. "First things first—you can go on the one heading out tomorrow. Take my place and you'll be on your way to owning your own Guinness World Record certificate."

"Is there a prize with that?" Jian asked.

"Nope." Greg shook his head. "World-record holders don't get anything other than a certificate that they have achieved a world record."

He leaned back in his seat. "Well, that's…depressing."

"Back to the matter at hand," Terrence cut in, "what do you say? Will you take my place on tomorrow's trip into the Zoo? It has one hell of a hefty price tag to it."

"They approached me with the option to head in before they did you two," he told them. "And I turned it down. It's way too close to Wall One for comfort. There's a reason why I've survived this long and it's because I avoid the missions that are the most dangerous. No one is likely to sing any songs or make any movies about my exploits, but I'll be alive to feel bitter about it. You have fun, though."

Terrence rolled his eyes and held a hand up to order another round for the three of them.

All in all, it wasn't the least productive day Jian had ever had. Keeping his mind off things while getting the work done was about as good a day as he could expect. The higher-ups had finally acknowledged the anxiety that most of the researchers felt about being so close to the alien jungle, and a call for qualified counselors to get to the Zoo had gone up some three months earlier to help those who needed it.

Of course, the psychiatrists and psychologists all began to develop a little anxiety of their own, which meant they needed to be cycled in and out to avoid a nuts-run-the-nuthouse scenario.

Jian left the bar before his legs felt wobbly, which was a good way to keep himself from accidentally ending up in the wrong house. It might sound dumb but had been known to happen—and more than once—among the regular alcoholics who frequented Mark's every night.

It was still early as he moved across the mostly empty streets of the base to where his little prefab home had been set up.

Crime was uncommon but not unheard of on base, especially since more and more private-sector workers were allowed in and out than they had been in the original post-Surge paranoia days, but he was not worried about being accosted or attacked on his way home. He'd been a military man before getting his PhD in Biology, which meant that anyone who tried would be in more trouble than they bargained for. Still, he couldn't help an odd feeling that someone was following him through the streets.

He ran his fingers through his straight black hair and used the motion to covertly look back the way he'd come to make sure no one was following him. The fact that he couldn't see anyone behind him did little to ease his mild but very real discomfort. Cameras had been installed all over the base. If someone wanted to follow him, they didn't even need to do it physically.

There was still no sign of anyone approaching him as he strode through the clutch of ugly, prefab houses that had been made available for the people who spent considerable time on the base. Most of the military men were housed in the barracks and always complained that the researchers were given preferential treatment.

The simple truth was that Jian couldn't argue with that. Then again, they were always outfitted with suits that had armor and heavy weapons while going into the Zoo, while researchers were fitted with a hazmat suit that didn't even qualify as glorified.

If researchers like him wanted to go in with any kind of protection, they had to pay for it themselves, and he had done precisely that. A couple of stores around the different bases were buying second-hand suits and selling them cheaper than the new versions coming out of the factories. There was a cost for it, of course, but he knew a couple of establishments on the French base that knew how to put a suit together from the scraps that were for sale.

The scientist paused suddenly and narrowed his eyes as

he turned onto the walkway from the road into the little house he had called home for so many months. Nothing seemed out of place as he approached it. There was no garden to tend to and nothing to speak of when it came to decorations or anything to indicate that an actual human lived in the space.

But something was off. It was immediately apparent, although he needed a second to determine what it was precisely. He blamed the five vodka cranberries and three beers he'd guzzled as the culprits that slowed his mind now.

The front door was unlocked and slightly ajar.

He knew he'd locked it before going to the pub, and he certainly hadn't left it open. There were too many corporate spies around to leave the research he was working on accessible to anyone who happened to walk past.

After quick, rational consideration, he slid his hand into his pocket to retrieve his satellite phone. He could call security in to take a look and make sure nothing was wrong. It seemed reasonable, but he hesitated. There were too many reasons not to.

For one thing, they charged exorbitant amounts from anyone who made those calls, whether it was necessary or not. And it felt exactly like a little kid calling his big brother to handle a bully. He had a Glock tucked under his pillow and if he could reach it, there would be no real problem.

After one quick peek through the door, he pushed it open and waited for something to leap out at him from the darkness. He doubted that a Zoo monster could pick the lock and leave the door itself completely unharmed, but making assumptions about what the Zoo and its monsters could and couldn't do was essentially how the whole mess started.

Jian eased inside but held himself low and ready for an attack as he felt for the light switch.

It didn't surprise him at all when the light didn't come on but it was certainly alarming. Someone, his logical voice told him—and sounded vindicated—had broken in. The only options that remained were whether they had come and gone or if they were still inside, waiting for him.

There was no point in risking it. Jian reached for his phone again, this time with the full intention of calling security to his little home. As he turned to leave the house, however, he realized that the door had closed soundlessly behind him.

Hints of shadows advanced toward him with hardly a sound, but he could tell immediately that these weren't monsters. Well, not the kind that came out of the Zoo, anyway.

His instincts kicked in without conscious thought about what he was doing or who was trying to attack him. Jian lashed out with his foot and caught the closest attacker around the knee. The sound of a bone breaking echoed through the small room, and he immediately followed it with a sharp hook that caught the man across the jaw as he lost his balance.

The scientist's fist ached from the contact, but the blow snapped the man's head around and he slumped forward, immediately unconscious.

A second figure attacked from the left in a somewhat wild attempt to tackle him. This one was larger and smelled of cheap deodorant. Jian planted his foot firmly to stop their momentum, twisted his body at the hip, and hammered his elbow into the side of the man's head.

A muffled curse was uttered as his assailant stumbled back, clutching the side of his head. The researcher spun to try to reach his bedroom. His Glock would serve him well at this point.

In a second, it felt like his whole body had shut down. Pain arced from his back and seared a burning path up his spine, which made it difficult to breathe. Someone had hit him, he decided—a third attacker, that much was obvious, as the first and second were still recovering from the blows he had delivered.

He knew what was happening. The punch had caught him flush in the kidney, and the feeling of having a car battery hooked up between his shoulder and his groin was only too familiar to him.

Most of his memories of this were from accidental shots during sparring sessions, but the point remained. He would be pissing red for a week.

The third attacker approached quickly to kneel beside him and insert a needle into his neck. The effects of whatever drug it contained were felt immediately. The pain remained, a dull ache that would linger for at least another couple of hours, but the drug made it a little more bearable. He sighed deeply and his entire body relaxed as the drug did its work.

The shadowy figure turned to his two comrades, who were slowly regaining their senses.

"Are you fucks stupid or something?" he demanded. Jian could barely make out what he thought might be a North

African accent in the man's voice through the haze that his brain had descended into.

"He...hits like a sledgehammer," the first one muttered, limping visibly when he was helped to his feet.

"If I wasn't here to clean up for you, he would have called security in and you would be spending the rest of your short lives at Guantanamo Bay. Fucking morons."

Jian wondered somewhat fuzzily why the US would bother with that when they had the evidence-eating Zoo on their doorstep. Neither of the two men he had beaten made any argument and set about restraining him with more haste than concern for his well-being.

In his drugged state, he didn't think he would stand much of a chance for a while now, even if the sedative they'd pumped into his system began to fade away. For one thing, his whole body ached like he'd been run over by an entire rugby team. Still, it was good to know he'd instilled fear in the group.

Good for his ego, at least, but probably not great for his chances of breaking free and running away.

The first two assailants, in the dull gleam of the full moon glow that streamed through the window, appeared to still have difficulty remaining on their feet. This left the task of getting their captive to the door to the only man among them who was unscathed.

"You fucking idiots need to learn to carry your weight," the man complained while he hauled the scientist behind him.

It was less carrying and more like dragging, which left the scientist thankful that his floors were mostly the smooth, pseudo hardwood that came with the nicer dwellings. Most of the others had rough surfaces that the prefab usually left behind. That would have left him scratched and covered in even more bruises when he was eventually able to stand again.

"You let me know when you have the ability to disable the alarm systems and the electricity on a house without triggering the base security," the first man snapped, still rubbing his jaw as they reached the door. "If you don't think I'm carrying my weight, you try getting into one of these houses after they've been locked up and alarmed."

Jian hadn't bothered to turn the alarm on in his home when he'd left to visit the pub. There wasn't much of a point and it was simply one more thing to worry about. They were on a military base with thousands of well-trained, well-armed, and angry soldiers who were paid too little and who would fight to the literal death to keep what they had spent blood, sweat, and tears to gain.

From his oddly distant position—almost like he inhabited some kind of alternate reality—he wished he could point out how full of shit the man was. He also wished he could call his bluff and point out that he'd had to accomplish diddly-squat to gain access. Unfortunately, he wasn't in a position to do either.

The second man had nothing to say and still looked a little unstable on his feet as he took a radio from his pocket, keyed into a frequency that was decidedly not the same one used around the base, and tapped the control on the side of the device a couple of times.

It wasn't in Morse code which came as no surprise. Jian guessed that they had agreed on a simple code between themselves instead before their mission started. It made sense to ensure that no one would understand them even if they accidentally tuned into the right frequency.

Two quick blips, a pause, three long blips, another pause, and one last quick blip comprised the full extent of the communication.

All three of his kidnappers remained silent and stood at the closed door like they were waiting for something. The researcher groaned and tried to move his right arm. It twitched but felt like a three-ton elephant was sitting on it. Despite his predicament, he found the mental image that followed amusing. Perhaps the beast would be reading a newspaper or something.

He registered the weirdness of the thought. Perhaps it was one of the side-effects of the drug they'd pumped into him. His brain seemed to flit from thought to thought without much inhibition and it was difficult to be worried about what was happening around him while he was high on it.

Finally, another three quick blips emitted from the radio, and the man with the injured leg pulled the door open. The other two hefted their captive onto their shoulders and rushed him toward the road as a van pulled up. Someone inside opened the side door and helped the two drag the drugged man into the back. Darkness descended when they pulled a tarp over him and made sure it was securely tucked in place. Thankfully, he could still breathe but he grimaced from the stuffy air as he heard the door close once they had all climbed inside.

Not a word was shared between the group as the van began to move. Jian shifted slightly across the floor of the paneled van with the acceleration, but not enough to escape his dank-smelling cocoon.

Even an idiot would realize they had covered him for a reason, and Jian didn't need his expensive degree to know what it was. His assumption was validated when the van eased to a halt and he could hear the electric window buzzing open.

"Do you boys have anything in there you think I should take a look at?" asked a man in a clear North Carolina accent.

"You know it. But I thought you might be a little too busy examining the label on this twelve-year, single-malt bottle of MacAllan to pay much attention to what we have going on."

The guard laughed and Jian's heart sank. The guy probably thought they were merely smuggling parts of weapons to the private dealers on other bases. It was a common cash-grab that worked best when they had a little of what the guards could be tempted with.

"Well, it is a pretty label and a gorgeous bottle besides. I think myself and the cameras will need to take about five minutes to run a full inspection of the contents of the bottle."

"Far be it from me to get between a connoisseur and his choice of ambrosia. You have a good one, Steve."

The van began to move again as Jian realized he could twitch his fingers, however slightly. It certainly wasn't enough to get anything done but at this point, what was there to do but lie where he was and wait for the inevitable?

CHAPTER TWO

"Are you fucking kidding me?"

Taylor folded his arms in front of his chest and kept his head low as Bobby's rampage gained momentum. He had expected it from the man, and all he needed to do was let him vent his frustrations on the condition of the suits he was returning. He had decided that it was best if he made the delivery alone.

Niki would most likely try to go on the offensive and somehow twist it onto Bobby and simply make everything worse. She could be confrontational like that, especially when she knew the other party was at least partly right and guilt rubbed at her. The belligerence that always seemed to lurk below her calm had its place and time and it most certainly was not when they delivered the fire-damaged suits to Bobby's shop.

"Oh—fucking hell," the man exclaimed and shook his head as he loaded the suits carefully onto their harnesses. "Have you even seen any of this? Were you trying to wreck them?"

When the mechanic looked accusingly at him, he leaned forward and squinted at the suits. "Well...I'd be terrible at either one of those. The suits are...kind of...mostly intact. To me, they're not even close to wrecked."

"I'd prefer wrecked to this—" Bobby couldn't finish his sentence and he merely gestured at the scorched suit in front of him.

"Okay, look. I'm paying for the work, right?" Taylor took a step forward. "Think of it as you picking up twice the charge on one set of suits."

"And twice the work. No. Quite frankly, it's more than twice the work."

"But they're not even wrecked! I bet that you could turn those babies on and they'd dance to 'Hello My Baby' without breaking a sweat. Um...if suits could break a sweat. It's a metaphor."

"Fire damage is different than puncture damage or even crush damage and you know it, McFadden. The heat can melt the insulation and even the wiring and circuitry, which means pressing the wrong button could freeze the whole damn thing at best. It could even cause a short that fries every goddamn circuit—or hell, start a fire in the suit or even electrocute the pilot. I'll need to take them apart plate by plate to make sure that everything is still working before I even dare to start any repairs."

The man had a point, he conceded inwardly. That would require considerable work.

"Do you need me to pay extra to make up for the additional costs?"

His friend shook his head. "That's already part of the invoice that we sent you. The real problem is that these were loaners. They belong to some poor bastards out there in the Zoo and they will now have to wait until I work through all this shit and we know exactly what the fuck is working from this point forward, right?"

Taylor nodded agreement with the somewhat absent-minded assertions as the man, his mind already distracted by the focus required by his task, began to remove pieces from the suits and inspect the damage beneath.

"Right." When no other comment was forthcoming, he grunted and took a deep breath. "Maybe I can drop in for a couple of days and help you guys with the repairs. I'd bet you I could even talk Vickie into coming down to take some time off from her screens and work with her hands for a while to help you to get these suits finished."

The stout mechanic studied him carefully and tugged his beard gently before he shook his head. "No, it'll be fine. All I'm saying is that the next time you try to incinerate good armor, how about you try to not incinerate those that belong to dumbasses who are still working in the Zoo."

"Point taken. And we might need to purchase a couple of spare suits to have on standby so that the next time, we can set fire to ours and not cause any additional problems for you. If you get flak from your clients, feel free to throw me under the bus. Tell them it's...like...a transition glitch where I screwed up and left you running to play catchup."

Bobby laughed. "Come on, man. You know I will never do anything like that to you."

"Whatever, you burly Jet Li impersonator. I'm merely giving you options to get you out of the hole that I dug you into."

"Sure." The man shrugged. "You didn't even use the fact

that you guys barely escaped from that plane intact yourselves and that other drug-addled morons blew the fucking aircraft up. It was an integrity move. I like it."

Taylor shook his head. "It never crossed my mind. You put the suits in our hands, which makes what happens to them our responsibility. It doesn't matter how it happened. What's important is that we find a way to stop it from interrupting your production."

"Yeah, yeah, whatever." Bobby leaned back in his seat and drew a deep breath. "You know, I was all prepared to shout it out with you."

"And I went the more productive route—find the quickest and most efficient way to get the process working again so you can return the suits and help our friends and comrades in the Zoo."

"Fuck you."

"I love you too, big guy. So where do you think we should go for new suits?"

"You don't want to buy anything new. They're perfectly fine new, of course, but it's more fiscally sound to find someone who sells them used, bring them to me, and I can set them up better than new."

Taylor nodded. "I'm always happy to bring you more business."

"Bullshit, You'll help and I won't charge you a dime over the costs of parts." Bobby laughed. "Do you want coffee? I bought a new machine that makes fucking awesome coffee."

"I'm always down to try fucking awesome coffee."

Before the man could stand, Taylor's phone vibrated in his pocket.

"I'll get you the coffee and you take that call," Bobby rumbled as he moved toward the break room.

Taylor drew the phone from his pocket and accepted the call.

"Hello?"

"Hey, Taylor," shouted a familiar voice on the other end of the line. "Freddie Hendricks. I've tried to pick your number up for a few hours already, but it's been something of a hunt."

"Freddie, it's nice to hear from you. You could have simply dropped Bobby a line for my number. I'm traveling around far more these days. He's taken over the actual running of the business, so if you have any problems or business needs, you'll need to talk to him."

He was careful to not say anything on the line that would let anyone who was potentially listening in know that Freddie was helping them to launder the money they'd stolen from Rod Marino's casino.

But still, if the man had encountered any problems sending the money, it was probably best to hear what he had issues with.

"No, no, nothing like that. Everything's going smoothly on our end of things. No, I needed to talk to you about something that's happened here at the US Base."

Taylor straightened and frowned as he glanced to where he assumed Bobby was tinkering with the new coffee machine.

"What's on your mind?"

"It's not a huge issue—or not according to the base commandant, at least. One of our researchers has gone missing, Dr. Jian Everett. He up and vanished one day, and no one can find out where he went."

Taylor nodded. "That does tend to happen to people around the Zoo. He might not even be dead and simply found a team to head in with him if he needed time out there."

"Yeah, it's possible, but I don't think that's what happened. I heard him talking to other researchers before he went missing, and he was damned adamant that he wouldn't go in there anytime soon. A team went in the day after—they'd asked him to join them, which is why his refusal was mentioned—and nothing has happened since his disappearance."

He ran his fingers through his red beard. "Okay. What did you need me to do?"

"Well, there are a couple of leads but the commandant won't start anything until they can confirm that he's missing, and by that time…" The man's shrug was almost audible over the comms line. "Well, you know what could happen to someone in that time. I can't do anything, so I wondered—"

"If I could come over and make something happen." Taylor nodded and drew a deep breath. "Okay, I'll see what I can do. I'll let you know."

"Thanks, Taylor. I appreciate it, seriously."

He wanted to ask what Freddie's connection to the researcher was, but it seemed irrelevant. Taylor owed the man some hefty favors and having one called in meant that he wouldn't waste time with unnecessary questions.

His lips pursed, he pressed the button to end the call on his phone and thought through the request and its possible consequences. Helping a friend was one thing but heading to the Sahara to help them was something else entirely.

"I know that look."

Taylor turned to where Bobby approached with a mug of steaming coffee in each hand. He passed one to his visitor and let him sip the beverage.

"What look? I don't have a look."

"Don't go all dumbass on me, McFadden. I know you, and you're wearing the face you put on when you're about to go out and kill some monsters."

"I have a face for that?"

"It's more obvious than most other people's faces. You look thoughtful—like you know you don't like it but you'll do it anyway. You feel like it's your job or something and no one else can do it as well as you can—like you just bit into a sour lemon and you're trying not to show it on your face."

He laughed. "Okay, fair enough. What kind of face am I wearing now?"

They both sipped the warm brew—which was as good as the mechanic had claimed before Bobby leaned forward.

"You're going back there, aren't you?"

He sighed. "Freddie's a friend and I owe him. If he says jump, I'll grumble loudly about what it'll do to my knees and jump anyway, mostly because I know he'd do the same for me—or you, for that matter."

Bungees nodded. "Yeah, I know. Still, it's not exactly the kind of call you want to hear."

"No." Taylor growled with both reluctance and displeasure, then stiffened. "Shit."

"Let me guess. You realized that you don't have any usable suits to take out there?"

"No, we do. I have the suits we generally use. No, the bigger problem is…well, I don't know how I'll break the news to Niki."

"Ohhh." Bobby grunted, then chuckled. "Shit is right. In fact, you'll miss the wonderful taste, smell, and texture of shit when you compare it to what telling her will be like."

"Yeah."

"Honestly, I think I'd prefer to simply head to the Zoo and avoid having that conversation with her—wait—do you think that might be an option?"

Taylor narrowed his eyes at him until Bobby snapped his jaw shut again and focused his attention on the mug of coffee in his hand.

As much as he wanted to agree with his friend, the mechanic could not be more wrong about the situation. A part of him hoped more than a little that Niki would be able to talk him out of it. Or that she would get Vickie to find them a way to help the missing researcher without setting foot on the African continent.

He doubted any real possibility of that, though. Niki would be pissed, yell both his ears off, and pull Vickie into the discussion somehow. Despite her efforts, it would always end with him boarding and heading to the part of the planet he hated most.

"I'm sorry," Bobby finally stated and rested a hand on his shoulder. "I know how tough it is for you to go back there."

He placed his hand briefly over the other man's and tried to force a smile, but all that resulted was a grimace.

"It's all about duty—not to country anymore but to the friends and comrades who helped me to escape from there and return to the US."

"That's what puts you head and shoulders above the rest. It also means you're probably a little screwed in the head, but I guess we already knew that. And that's why Niki will volunteer to go out there with you despite the fact that she probably hates the Zoo more than you do."

The man had a point. More than only one, he realized when he thought about it. Niki would stand by him if he needed to see this through but she would complain about it with every fucking mile they covered too.

"You'll have to make a big deal of it," Bobby suggested. "Take her out somewhere nice. Wear an expensive suit— the kind that comes from a tailor, I mean—so she knows you're trying. Go down on her."

"What?"

"Come on. You'll need to butter her up and nothing butters better than putting the work in between her legs. There's something Tanya likes, especially when I haven't shaved in a while and I use my tongue to—"

"Oh, fuck no." Taylor shook his head vehemently. "You need to stop that. Forever. Seriously, Bungees, I will slap you. I will give you a concussion."

"I'm only saying that a woman is more likely to be amenable to the news that her paramour is heading into an alien jungle after she's had her toes curled and has difficulty walking for a couple of days."

"You could have said that and be done with it. I don't need to know what Tanya wants you to do with your beard and your tongue."

"Fair enough."

"Look at me, Bungees." Taylor pointed two fingers at his own eyes and then turned them to point to Bobby. "I'm not joking. You will be hospitalized. You know how hard I can hit, and I will use every ounce of power I have to silence you if you try to talk to me about what kinky shit you and Tanya get up to."

The mechanic laughed and nodded. "All right, all right. I get the picture. But you know I'm right. You'll need to pull all the stops out for this."

He tried not to shudder. "Yeah. The only problem is that I don't think there are enough stops to pull for a conversation like this."

"True, but you have to try anyway."

CHAPTER THREE

It took a while for all members of the DEA strike team to gather in the warehouse. There weren't too many places where ten men could gather in San Francisco without being picked up by fifteen different cameras and twelve different social media sites.

The extra caution required by this particular operation meant that they would have to meet a little outside of San Fran at a location that had once been connected to the port but had since fallen into disrepair. There was a whole conversation about how the required maintenance to the property had simply ground to a halt while it passed from hand to hand. Trade disputes and building code changes continually exacerbated the complexity of the original issues and eventually, was simply abandoned.

For their purposes, however, it was ideal—no cameras, no security, and no foot traffic aside from a few meth addicts who had dug in a couple of buildings down the street.

Tom had considered calling the cops on them to make

sure the area was completely clear, but he'd decided against it. In the end, that would only lead to more attention being drawn to the first acceptable rendezvous location he'd found in almost a full week of searching. If the cops decided to watch the other building for a few extra easy arrests, it would destroy all use the location had for their purposes.

The only real potential threat was the addicts, but they had most likely already sold their phones.

Kevin was the first to arrive and looked like he was coming in from a jog. Trix was next, riding a motorcycle she probably rented under a fake ID. Jones and Anne arrived together on foot. Tom wondered if that meant the two were having some kind of affair but refrained from asking. If they thought they were in trouble, they would merely lie. Besides, he trusted both enough to know that they wouldn't let any personal feelings get in the way of the mission.

And everyone needed a life and a release outside of the job, even if it was only a few snatched intervals between high-stress operations.

The others filtered in, having staggered their arrivals to avoid looking like they were a group. Everyone selected a little space of the abandoned warehouse and set their weapons and tactical equipment out for one last check—in part to get the ball rolling and to make sure nothing was out of place but also because it was a good way to get into the mindset a mission required.

Tom had worked with most of them before, although not all. Working a ten-man mission would always be tough, and he preferred to keep his fire teams small and maneuverable. Unfortunately, his preferred way of doing things wasn't always possible. In this case, having numbers wouldn't be a bad thing.

All those he hadn't worked with before had come highly recommended, and from what he could see, were already living up to their reputations. They had reported on time to collect their equipment at the designated locations and arrived at the warehouse in the time and manner he hoped he wouldn't have to instruct them on.

He was used to yelling at newcomers for fucking things up. It was a good way to get them in line and show them he was the boss and would be running things, but that didn't feel appropriate at this point.

Oddly enough, he missed the yelling. Maybe next time.

"All right, folks," he stated loudly enough for the ten men and women assembled to hear him. "Check your gear and assemble at the northeast corner of the building for a brief in five minutes."

The designated area was the only one that still had electricity, and he'd set up a small screen to enable him to display the intel that had been gathered.

Within five minutes, the whole team was assembled and waited silently for the briefing to start.

Tom turned the screen on and brought up a picture of a massive cargo ship at dock.

"This is the *Poseidon Alexis*. It flies a Greek flag and is owned by the Poseidon Shipping Company out of Athens. There's nothing particularly interesting there and a host of boring financial digs haven't turned up anything dirty. So far, anyway."

A few of the group were taking notes, but the others

seemed like they wouldn't have any difficulty remembering all the details.

"Anyway, the *Alexis* did make a quick stop in Shanghai, and we all know what that means. The DEA began to track a shipping container the vessel took on board during that stop and have now passed the information on to us. The *Alexis* made port in San Fran earlier this morning, and the shipping container was unloaded first. A truck brought it to one of the few operational warehouses in this district, and there hasn't been any movement all day until a couple of hours ago. The building is two hundred meters from our location, and we'll move on it in fifteen minutes. Any questions?"

One hand went up. It was Chris, one of the new guys.

"What kind of defenses do you expect?"

"The triad team that brought the stuff over was mixed with a couple of local toughs. No heavy artillery was noted, though. We'll try to take any prisoners we can in there since the higher-ups want to get as much intel out of these guys as we can. Anything else?"

After a moment of silence during which heads were shaken and no more questions asked, he clapped sharply.

"Good. We move in fifteen."

The group separated but Trix hung back and checked her sidearm until she was sure the others had moved on before she approached him.

"Are you cool?" she asked simply and kept her voice down but not to an outright whisper.

"Am I cool?"

"I know how you get on these drug busts with what

happened to Cameron and everything. I'm only making sure you're not aching for payback on this."

He shook his head firmly. "I appreciate the concern but I'm good. It's merely another job."

"Sure."

She didn't believe him and he wasn't sure he believed himself. Cameron's death still hung heavily over him and he wasn't sure if he would be able to contain himself. Which, he reasoned, was why it was probably best that they'd brought a larger team in on it. Having them to look out for would help him to keep his head on straight if things grew a little too hot.

They were all assembled exactly twelve minutes after the briefing and ready for action. Their maps were updated with the location of the warehouse that had been high-lighted as their destination. Once they had halved the distance between it and their rendezvous point, he gestured for Trix to take her position while the remainder of the group paused. A few of them retrieved binoculars and used them to see what was happening in the target area.

Intel hadn't been wrong, it seemed. About twenty of the fuckers had holed up there.

"I see two entrances," Trix announced over the comms once she had reached a higher position. "The main entrance is over there, where the group of five are playing cards around the barrel. The second entrance is up top with a ladder to access it. I see two guys on their phones. How do you want to handle it, boss?"

Tom adjusted the strap that supported his assault rifle and scratched the bristle along his jaw, his face contorted in the scowl he usually assumed when he was deep in thought.

"Do you think you can eliminate those on the top before they realize they're being shot at?"

"Come on, man."

"Good, do that. Kevin, take three and head on up there to give us an elevated position in the warehouse. I'll take the ground team and knock on the front door. Engage on my mark."

"Roger that."

Kevin nodded and patted the shoulders of three of the other team members, who followed him. The four operatives crept stealthily toward the rear entrance, using the cover of darkness to keep their movements from being noticed. Tom waited until they were in position before he moved the rest of the group into position to breach the front door at an angle that would give them the most cover.

Tom yanked a flashbang from his belt and pulled the pin. "Okay, three, two, one...mark!"

He lobbed the ordnance over their cover when he heard the low crack of a suppressed rifle. The two shots were quick to the point where they might have almost been mistaken for one. His grenade detonated and he peered over the heavy, concrete-filled barrels they used for cover, his gaze down the sights of his weapon.

Two of the triad goons had lost the top halves of their heads before they realized what was happening. The others weren't given time to reach their weapons before his team converged on them and disabled and disarmed them with impressive efficiency. Tom gestured for Anne to keep an eye on the three who were being gagged and zip-tied. She nodded and dropped to one knee beside them as her teammates headed toward the door.

There was no chance that the people inside hadn't heard what happened outside and no one was at all surprised when a barrage of fire erupted from within. Kevin's team was most likely already engaging the defenders from an advantageous position, but gunfire was aimed at those breaching the entrance too.

Holes appeared in the thin aluminum walls of the warehouse and Tom's eyes widened when he realized the danger they were suddenly in.

"Get down!"

Most of the team were already moving as they had noticed the unexpected threat as well, but it wasn't quite in time. Chris' body went limp and he landed hard. The rounds had punched through his faceplate and helmet, both of which were supposed to be bulletproof.

The realization that the triads were using armor-piercing rounds quickly registered on the final few members of the group who hadn't noticed before and they dropped and now crawled through the entrance. All of them stayed low and kept as much cover as possible between themselves and the criminals.

Kevin and his team were well-positioned and raining fire on the group that had been gathered in the center of the warehouse, probably to try to use the crates they had been taking out of the shipping container as cover. Only six of them remained and they looked like they wouldn't be able to hold their position any longer.

"Hold your fire!" Tom roared over the comms. He felt a

surge of pride when the whole team held their fire and activated the laser-sights on their weapons to drive the point home to the men on whom the sights flicked menacingly. "Put your weapons down, get to your knees, and put your hands on your heads now or we will resume fire!"

That was directed at the six that remained standing.

"Do it now!"

His teammates took up the shouted call and overwhelmed the defenders with the idea that they were seconds away from being gunned down where they stood. Tom dropped back again when they started shooting again anyway.

"Smoke!'

The team above dropped a collection of grenades that filled the warehouse rapidly with their noxious smoke. The shooting continued, but he circled away from where they were exchanging concerted volleys and eased into position within the enemy group.

He dropped low, used the butt of his rifle to knock one of the gunners' knees, and quickly lifted his weapon and pulled the trigger.

Without even a pause, he swung to locate his next target. Most of their adversaries appeared to be local thugs, but one was covered in the brightly colored and frankly ugly tattoos the triads were known to mark their people with. He put a few rounds down low to wound the man in the feet before he swung the butt of the weapon to strike him in the jaw. His team converged quickly, forced the survivors onto the rough concrete, and slapped zip-ties onto them.

He knew that he was being a little too rough with the

man as he pushed him to his knees and applied the restraints, but Chris' death demanded some kind of revenge. With a grunt of satisfaction, he shoved his prisoner onto his face, then paused to look at the rest of his team.

Eight of them on their feet, which meant Chris was the only fatality from his group. The operation hadn't been quite as quick or clean as he'd hoped it would be, though, and blood seeped from Kevin's arm when he joined his teammates on the lower level.

"Shit." Tom gestured to the wounded area. "You're bleeding, man."

The man looked at his arm like he hadn't noticed it. "I ain't got time to bleed."

"You might have the mustache but you don't have the jawline to pull that off. Get yourself some medical—now. Consider it an order if you like."

Kevin nodded and moved to where Trix had joined them in the warehouse. She had the best first-aid skills in the group. At least as far as he knew.

One man was set to watch over those captured while another hurried to help Anne to drag in the three she had guarded. The rest began to dig into the crates the group had been unloading from the shipping container.

They hit paydirt early and soon unloaded bricks of light brown powder. Jones put one of them on the table immediately, retrieved his test kit, and poked out a sample from one of the bricks. He poured it carefully into the solvent.

He shook the vial gently before he let it settle and lifted it to the light as the solution turned a dark-brown.

"We have primo heroin here, chief," he announced and

turned to Tom. "It looks like we struck the motherlode. I'd say there are about a thousand Ks in these crates, at least. A rough estimate puts it at around fifty million dollars."

Tom narrowed his eyes. "What's in the rest of the crates?"

One of the others opened a sealed box and withdrew a jacket in plastic packaging. "Counterfeits, by the looks of things. A host of Armani knockoffs and—oh, look, they're being used to pad what looks like a collection of phones. All to be donated to combat corporate greed here in the US, I'll bet."

He sneered at the obvious boss of the criminal group and nudged him in the ribs with his boot. "You guys got philanthropy in mind, eh? Doing the world a favor? Helping some orphans out, right?"

The man kept his eyes down and pretended he couldn't understand what he was saying, which only caused the taller, powerfully built man to smirk.

"Yeah well," Tom said abruptly. "You'll find out that the Grizzly is far nicer than the folks I have lined up to talk to you. And they speak Mandarin too, so you won't be able to pull any of that 'I can't understand what you're saying' crap on any of them."

Again, no other answer was forthcoming, but questioning the fuckers was beyond his pay grade. Instead, he turned his attention to where the team hauled more crates out of the container and opened them.

"Hey, boss?" Trix called. "I think you'll want to take a look at this."

He approached the crate she was looking into, peered

into it, and squinted with a frown. In all honesty, he wasn't sure what he was looking at either.

"What is that?" he asked and leaned closer. "Are those rhino horns?"

"That was my thought," Trix admitted. "But they're too small. I'd say it might have been taken from younger rhinos, but the young don't grow their horns until they get older, right?"

"I read something about this," Kevin noted as he approached, having had his wound seen to, and reached into the crate. "They started producing counterfeit rhino horns that are genetically identical to the real thing. The logic is that if they flood the market and lower the price the poachers are getting for the real ones they sell—oh, shit!"

He'd picked one of the packages up but dropped it like he'd been stung and took a hasty step back.

"What?" Trix asked.

"The… Those…they don't make counterfeit blood to go with the fake horns, do they?"

Both she and Tom leaned forward to see what he was talking about and he hissed a swift intake of breath when he realized that something blue and liquid had collected inside the plastic packaging.

He had seen that kind of blue before. The fact that it was practically bright enough to glow in the light shadow that was cast by the crate the merchandise was packed in was all the confirmation he needed.

"Seal the goddammed crate." He all but snarled the order and when no one hurried to comply, he snapped his fingers at them. "Did I fucking speak in a foreign language? Seal that shit up now!"

Trix and Kevin lurched into action and followed his instruction with alacrity and not a single word exchanged between them. He left them to it and backed away to unhook a radio from his hip and dial into the frequency their intel team was on.

"Overwatch, this is Simmons. Do you read?"

The device crackled for a few seconds before a woman's voice responded over the connection. "Loud and clear. Nice to hear from you, Grizzly. How'd the raid go?"

"One of our people is down and another wounded. We have…nine?" He looked around and counted them quickly. "Nine here who need extraction to a black site for debriefing and a few of them might need medical, but we hit a snag. Is the section chief there?"

"Give me a sec."

The connection crackled again and finally, a man spoke. "Simmons, this is Section Chief Montgomery. What's the situation on the ground?"

"We've encountered an unknown substance among the illegal imports." Tom looked at the crate and his scowl deepened. "It appears to be organic and originating from the Zoo. Please advise."

"Repeat that. Did you say it's out of the Zoo?"

"That is what it appears to be, sir."

The section chief sighed over the line. "Fuck me. Like we don't have enough on our plate with alien crap sneaking in. Contain the situation, Simmons. No one is allowed in or out of that warehouse until specialists are called in to inspect the contents of those crates. We'll have to seal the area off to avoid any accidental contamination as well. In the meantime, orders are to clear any possible contaminants in the warehouse. That means any rats, insects, or other organic material. Keep them all away from those crates."

Tom had been read into the protocol when it came to dealing with possible Zoo contaminants, of course, but it was good that the chief was spreading the word. That way, he didn't have to do any explaining.

"Roger that, Section Chief. Do we have an ETA on specialist arrival? We do have a couple of wounded combatants here in need of medical attention."

"I'll let you know when we do." Montgomery grumbled something he couldn't understand over the line. "Good work, Simmons. We'll be in touch. Stay safe."

"Will do, sir."

He cut the connection and looked at his team.

They were all professionals, of course, so there wasn't a modicum of fear in their eyes, but it seemed many of them had at least heard of the significance of the notorious blue blood. There would no doubt be a slew of questions if they'd heard his conversation with the section chief.

They'd all heard about the alien jungle that was turning into a nightmare straight out of a budget horror flick and for most of them, it was an unknown quantity. It would be better to keep them busy and moving and not thinking about the fact that they were stuck in a warehouse with the biological equivalent of a ticking time bomb.

"You heard the section chief!" Tom barked. "Isolate the crates that have the hazardous material and get to hunting anything that could get infected. Anne, Jones, keep an eye on the prisoners. If they so much as twitch, give them the two-hole punch experience."

They all jumped into action, happy to have something to do while he circled to the leader of the group. Despite the fact that the man's eyes remained downcast and he seemed determined to not speak, a sheen of sweat had oozed over the heavy tattoos on his arms and shoulders.

"Goddamn fucking chinks." Tom snarled at him. "As if it wasn't bad enough that you're sending your death drugs over here, you now have to bring Zoo contraband to the party?"

The leader showed no sign of a reaction other than a slow glance at him, but a hint of fear had crept into his eyes. Perhaps he hadn't been told about the Zoo shit. Part of him felt that was impossible, but he honestly felt that was the case. He knew for a fact that he and his cop-killers wouldn't have engaged in a vociferous exchange of fire if they knew there was something that hazardous in the crates.

Thankfully, none of this was his problem. His only responsibility was containment until the specialists were sent in.

It took the team almost a full hour to clear the warehouse. There weren't many rats or mice in the area due to the lack of food but more than enough insects. Tom made no effort to stop them when they seemed a little more enthusiastic in dealing with them than they had to be.

They were working stuff out. Whether it was Chris' death or the fact that they were stuck in the warehouse until the specialists showed up, he wasn't sure. It was probably a mixture of both with a couple more factors thrown in.

"Grizzly?" Overwatch called over the radio. "Section Chief said you should expect the specialists to arrive in a couple of minutes."

"Thanks." He moved to the door and had been there for less than a minute when an SUV pulled up to their location, along with a number of hazmat vans that careened toward them as fast as possible.

The SUV arrived first and a tall woman stepped out. She looked like she was part of a three-letter agency, with the short brown hair and gray pantsuit and the hard build of someone who had gone through almost a year of urban combat training.

A distinctive bulge around her midsection spoke of a weapon tucked into her suit jacket within easy access.

A pro, he decided, from head to toe.

The others were pros too, although he couldn't determine much from them aside from the fact that they were all in hazmat suits and immediately began to scan the outside of the warehouse.

"Special Agent Simmons?" the woman asked as she advanced quickly.

"That's me."

"I'm Agent Felicity Ahlers, DHS. I understand you ran into something of a situation here."

He nodded. "You could say that, yeah."

"I've been briefed on what you found and the team will scan the whole building to make sure there aren't any issues with contamination. Once that's done, you'll be able to continue with the operation and get your prisoners and the material you apprehended out of here and pushed through the regular channels."

"Huh." Tom grunted in surprise and watched the hazmat team move through the entrance. "I won't lie. I thought you Homeland Security geeks would take jurisdiction on this whole operation."

"You've been dealing with the triad imports. We have no intention of interrupting your investigation to satisfy an inane departmental dick-measuring contest between agencies. We'll take the contaminants off your hands and you can continue your operation, although we might need to work together to trace where the horns came from."

Tom had to admit that he had begun to like the woman. "Well, like I said to the section chief—"

"There are wounded. The paramedics are a couple of minutes out. We hope to have the scanning done before they get here. Of course, if any of the…ahem, prisoners or your people, for that matter, were contaminated, that might throw a wrench into proceedings."

He nodded. If there was a Zoo contamination, they all had problems that were far bigger than heroin and contraband.

"Yeah, I've heard of what that blue goop can do. It can turn you into a monster. Or worse."

She tilted her head. "Out of sheer curiosity, what do you think would be worse than being a Zoo monster?"

"Being the guy killed by a Zoo monster."

"Oh. I guess that makes sense."

CHAPTER FOUR

"Are you sure this will work?"

Vickie narrowed her eyes. "You're asking that like you don't trust me. No, allow me to rephrase that. You're asking that like you don't trust Desk. Is that truly something you want to have on the record?"

Niki raised an eyebrow. "Is there a record? I wasn't aware that anything like that was going on."

"I do tend to keep a memory database of the meaningful interactions I have with humans," the AI announced over the speakers in the room. "This most definitely qualifies as meaningful."

"Do you honestly want Desk to have a memory of you saying you don't trust her in her database of meaningful human interactions?" Vickie demanded. "How can you do that to her, Niki? After all that she's helped us through."

"That is quite insensitive of you," Desk concurred.

"All right, all right. I withdraw the question." She rolled her eyes. "But stop ganging up on me."

That had begun to happen more and more often lately.

Desk and Vickie had grown chummier by the minute, and she wasn't sure she liked it. Especially since their tendencies became noticeably a little darker and more dangerous. Not that she was against dark, dangerous things, but she'd always wanted to stop her cousin from being involved in it.

Desk, on the contrary, seemed determined to egg her on and put her into the dangerous positions she should never have been caught in the middle of.

Vickie did try to keep herself on the straight and narrow when Taylor was around, though. It was like she was trying to impress him or something, and Niki was relieved to see it. She would have been even happier if it were more common. What might have been worse was that the young hacker didn't even bother to try to mask anything from Niki. Then again, perhaps the honesty was a good thing.

She still didn't like it.

"If I die in this sim, I'll haunt the shit out of both of you," she complained and shook her head.

"Have a little faith," Vickie replied and pulled her headset on. "They've used this system to prepare special operations soldiers and the like to head out into the Zoo so it's not a huge surprise. We've dealt with weird cryptic creatures for a while, so we should be miles and miles ahead of the people who would go in for the first time.

"Besides, they're trying to adapt the gaming system used to the sim games that are coming out about the Zoo now. I think...*Crypto Hunter 2* will use this same system, and they simply snatched the presets of the Zoo monsters and put them on a spaceship or...fuck, I dunno. Or something. I only saw the trailer so I'm not sure what the plot is about or if there is even a plot."

That sounded a little more like the hacker she knew, and Niki settled into her seat with a sigh, pulled the sim headset into place, and flicked it on to connect with the gaming station before she took the controls.

The VR system booted up, and Niki now stood in a very familiar environment. The system was almost like putting a suit on, but there were sensor replicators in the suit that would let anyone piloting it know what they were in the middle of.

Niki had suggested, when she first saw the system, that they simply send the suits in while the pilot remained in base, hooked up to one of the rigs to keep people from dying in them. Taylor had made the point, however, that sending a heavy signal into the Zoo was borderline impossible. The best idea they could come up with was to set an AI up in the suit and send it in, but all those available were still a few years away from being ready for that level of combat environment.

She admitted that he'd made a solid point but stood by the assertion that there had to be something to do to stop people from going into the Zoo while still performing the same tasks.

A little curious now, she looked around at what was a jungle environment, although thoroughly alien. All the trees were impossible to identify and small creatures scuttled high in the trees that she couldn't identify either.

Although perhaps that had a little to do with the fact that she had thoroughly failed high school biology.

"Is this the Zoo?" Vickie asked and jumped lightly from

side to side in the suit she'd chosen for herself. Of course, since they didn't need to put any money into it, they had access to the most advanced suits on the market. They weren't prototypes, of course, since those were still protected under a dozen or so copyright laws, but from what they could tell, even these "lesser" models were impressive.

"I think so," she said and scowled at their surroundings. "Frankly, it isn't the kind of vision that would greet you anywhere else in the world. It simply...oozes an alien feeling."

"The design of the software is meant to replicate how the Zoo has been depicted and described in first-hand accounts."

Both women turned to see a third member join their party in a light, hybridized suit. The stranger danced around lightly like it was made out of helium.

"Will you join us, then?" the hacker asked and took a step forward.

"The sim is designed to be run under a minimum of three party members, matching the rules of engagement of all American Zoo exploration parties. As Taylor is in Las Vegas at the moment, I thought it would be a good idea to join you in the fight."

Niki took a step forward, tilted her head, and peered through the faceplate. "I have to admit, it's a little unnerving that you're wearing my sister's face in the sim."

"My software was designed to emulate Jennie in every way, shape, and form," Desk explained. "As such, it is appropriate that I be her identical representation in this simulated environment."

"No, no, I get it and it makes sense." The former agent shook her head and looked away uncomfortably. "But it's a little…."

"Unnerving," Vickie agreed with a firm nod. "Maybe we should make our faceplates opaque."

"Why are they see-through here anyway?" she asked and grimaced as her sister's face disappeared. "They aren't visible through the real suits."

"I think it's a part of letting people interact in the sim." Vickie adjusted a few more settings before she turned the sim on fully and brought it out of the paused environment it had been in. "Okay, I activated the first level of attack from the Zoo. We'll deal with the creatures in waves and each time we get through one, it becomes more difficult."

"Do you think these waves are designed based on trips Taylor took part in?" Niki wondered aloud and checked her weapons out of force of habit. They could already pick up a couple of signatures approaching through the jungle. "He's been on a record number of them."

"The final level is designed after one of the missions he was a part of," Desk informed them. "To be more precise, the mission on which he was one of three survivors."

She raised her eyebrows. Of course, Taylor didn't talk much about his time in the Zoo and she didn't blame him for remaining silent about it. But the very specific number rang in her mind because he wasn't the only one who talked about surviving a mission with only three members.

Perhaps it was appropriate that Jennie was among them, in face if not in person.

Niki raised her weapon, recalled the advice that Taylor had given her, and turned to face ahead. There weren't many warnings but they seemed important. Stay moving at all times. Stay still and you end up dead in the Zoo. Stay focused and avoid distractions, or you end up dead in the jungle.

She caught sight of one of the monsters and it suddenly surged forward.

Wave was a good way to describe them, she decided as others rushed in behind it. Hastily, she backpedaled to make sure that she knew where Desk and Vickie were so she didn't accidentally shoot them instead.

While she did feel like she was better prepared for the sim than most others would be, it was still a little shocking to see the sheer ferocity of the attacking animals. The monsters they found in the US seemed almost timid by comparison. The locust-like creatures merely rushed into the hail of bullets and showed no concern about their safety. It was as if they tried to soak up as many bullets as possible to provide the larger creatures behind them with a chance to break through.

"Stay together!" Niki shouted when Vickie drifted off to the side as a handful of the creatures latched onto her arm.

"I'm...trying!" the hacker shouted before she yanked her arm free of the mandibles and shot the monsters that had attempted to drag her away.

Desk moved quickly and smoothly. Almost a little too much of both, Niki thought as she watched the AI navigate the bounds of the sim almost effortlessly, keeping the beasts at bay until none of them were left.

It stood to reason that the sim wouldn't be like the real thing, but it was still a little too easy to simply fall into the trap of taking it too seriously.

Vickie straightened and checked her weapon before she looked at her companions. "Okay, that went well, right? I bet you most of the soldiers who try this for the first time die in the first wave, right? So we're already doing better than they are."

It looked like Desk was thinking, but the movement was a little too exaggerated—almost like a caricature. Perhaps she needed an update in her ability to physically mimic a human's actions, but Niki wasn't sure she would recommend that to Jennie.

"The average survival rate of members of the armed forces in the first wave is eighty-five point seven-two percent, rounded off to the nearest hundredth of a percentage point. It should be noted that when stipulations to the percentage include armed forces members who are entering the sim for the first time and have not entered the Zoo before in person, that percentage is reduced to seventy-five percent."

"Still, it's good enough to start with," Vickie commented. "How many of the total make it past the second wave?"

The AI tilted her head pensively again before she answered. "Fifty-seven percent."

"Awesome. Let's get this show on the road."

The ex-agent looked around and noted that the bodies remained in place. The realism was probably not something to be surprised at, not in this day and age, but she still wondered how much data was constantly processed to give them this level of detail of a jungle she had no intention of setting foot in.

"The second wave's starting now," Vickie warned, and

Niki noticed that the ammo in her suit had been refilled and reset to the starting levels.

A handful of the locusts appeared first but they were larger this time. She could also make out a couple of them with tails protruding from their backs like scorpions. It was an odd addition for creatures that would not work anywhere outside of the Zoo.

But where there was cooperation, there was a way, and more monsters launched from the jungle to attack them. Most looked a little more mammalian—like hyenas—but were massive with muscle-bound shoulders and heads that hung so low that they almost touched the jungle floor.

"Huh." She grunted around her scowl. "Taylor never mentioned critters like that."

"Maybe they're a new breed?" Vickie suggested. "They're always talking about how the Zoo monsters keep evolving and improving and all that shit."

The hacker was right, of course, and Niki shrugged and selected one of the stinger creatures as her first target since it appeared as though the smaller, weaker monsters were protecting the larger ones by their sheer numbers. She activated the rocket launchers in her shoulders, launched two of them, and whooped while the white plumes arced toward the group of creatures that pushed aggressively toward them.

The gratifying explosion merely appeared to enrage the monsters and thrust them all into the battle with more intent.

The large hyenas, with drool dripping from their jowls, waited until the rest of the smaller ones were killed. A handful of the scavengers had already started to attack the corpses of the mutants that had been killed and dragged them away while packs of them resumed the Zoo's attack against the three teammates.

Niki pushed herself to move again and noticed how the monsters used the trees for cover, both from the bullets and to allow them to move unseen in the shadows. The impression was that they attempted to strike from all sides at once.

It was the type of tactical awareness intelligence that people believed belonged only to humans, which was what made the Zoo so very, very unpredictable. Despite the somewhat disquieting realization that the claims of some of the so-called Zoo crazies might be factual, the three combatants all joined the fray. Vickie and Desk worked together to keep the creatures at a safe distance while Niki began clearing the way ahead of them of the trees the hyenas used to remain out of sight.

She grinned as one of the taller trunks groaned and toppled noisily to crush a small huddle of the beasts that had been distracted by the opportunity to feed ravenously on the corpses that littered the area. She supposed it would have been an unsettling sight for people who weren't used to the concept but also knew that even in the simulated environment, each and every monster they killed was one less that would be able to kill them in the end.

"See?" Vickie inclined her head to the side in a sharp gesture that caused her whole suit to jerk with it. She regained her balance quickly but her dignity would take a little while longer to repair.

"See what?" Niki asked and checked her assault rifle quickly.

"We got this." The hacker nodded. "As long as I can remember that I'm in a suit of power armor and don't accidentally break a bone."

"You would not be able to break your arms in the simulation," Desk commented. "But you are correct. We do appear to be doing well in this scenario, which might be the best first attempt by a civilian."

"Um…okay, but are we really civilians?" Vickie asked as she moved her arm back and forth to try to make it move too quickly.

Her cousin rolled her arms. The idiot girl was trying to break her arm in a simulation.

Niki shook her head and sighed. "I think Desk means non-military personnel. This sim would be a little different from those they keep working on for civilian use and games and shit like that. So we're going through military training here."

"Breezing through it, more like." Vickie laughed. "Let's get the next level going. How many of the first-timers get to the last level?"

"In their first attempt?" Desk asked.

"Yeah."

"Under one percent."

"Oh, yeah," Vickie danced from side to side. "Under one percent here we come, bitches!"

The next level was activated and already, Niki could see a difference. The monsters made little effort to attack them from the ground, for one thing. There was no hint of movement from the jungle floor, although she knew something would undoubtedly already have begun its advance on them.

She shifted her gaze upward and noticed something moving in the trees. The simians in the branches moved away, and Desk was the first to notice a creature that inched through the foliage, Large, heavy, and muscular, its fur was black and meshed perfectly with the darkness of the trees.

"Up top!" Vickie announced, raised her weapon, and opened fire.

Of course, there was more than one of them. Dozens leapt from branch to branch as bullets peppered the trees. Branches snapped loudly and fell, making it hard to hear anything other than the noise of the onslaught and the roars of the panther-like monsters that continued their attempts to approach.

The alarm on Niki's suit activated and she pushed into motion almost before she knew it. She twisted and muttered an imprecation at one of the panthers that plunged toward her from a branch they'd missed. It had six limbs—which explained how it was able to move in the trees so easily—and long fangs tipped with venom.

Her suit was already reacting to bring the minigun up from her shoulder and she annihilated the panther before it reached her. A split second and almost two dozen rounds later, it lay on the scrubby soil of the jungle floor, smoking and with dozens of holes that dark-blue blood seeped out of.

"Oh, shit!"

Niki turned but held her weapon ready. She expected more of the six-legged panthers but she couldn't see much other than the fact that Vickie had sagged and sprawled in a particularly worrying stillness. Desk had as well, although she had given no warning.

Smoke rose from their armor, pale white, noxious, and painful to breathe even through the suit's filters.

Another alarm sounded on her suit, and Niki spun to face a smallish lizard about the size of a Labrador retriever, although almost completely prone. It merely stood and watched her as if waiting for something. She looked at a coagulated glob of liquid that had landed on the leg of her suit. It made the metal smoke and in seconds, a hole appeared as the acid started began to eat through the armor, looking for the soft flesh below.

It found it, and she couldn't resist a scream when the burning seared up her leg. The lizard moved closer and expelled another stream of milky liquid from its mouth. Immediately, more of the armor began to melt away.

"Oh...shit!" The last word came when the sim had already shut down and she was pulling her helmet off. A little shaken, she focused on her cousin, who was getting a bottle of water. The hacker tossed her one.

"Well, they have the pain sensations down pat," Vickie commented acerbically and ran fingers through her short hair. It was a little longer than usual, although she still shaved the right side to give her more of a punk rocker look that matched the outfits she usually wore out in public.

"The pain is meant to discourage the gratuitous death that is generally seen in video games," Desk announced over the speakers. Niki wasn't sure why she'd expected to see the AI in the room with them.

"I guess that makes sense if you're trying to train them

to survive and all," Vickie muttered and paused to sip her water. "Did Taylor ever mention those acid-spitting lizards to you?"

"No." Niki shook her head. "But I know about them. They're some of the first Zoo creatures anyone managed to capture on camera but that was years ago, now. The fucking bastards snuck in behind us."

"Okay, let's go in again."

"What?"

"We might not be in the top one percent of the gunners who go into these sims, but I'll be damned if I'll leave even one of these unfinished. I have a reputation to uphold, you know!"

Niki shrugged, not concerned by the suggestion. "Sure. Fine. But we need to be more on guard for those fuckers coming in behind us."

"I should be able to cover our six as is stated in common terminology," Desk announced. "The sim is ready for when you want to try it again."

Of course, it wouldn't keep everything the same every time that they went in. That would be a little too much like cheating. The Zoo would constantly evolve and make changes to keep things interesting, and Niki could understand why a character like Taylor would develop a certain kind of addiction to it.

What they experienced was only a bite-size of what the real Zoo was in its much larger entirety and in the end, if they wanted to prepare themselves for the monsters that would wait for them on the outside at some point in the future, they couldn't simply turn the difficulty down to make it more manageable or comfortable.

Unfortunately, Vickie was particularly pissed when the acid lizards appeared in the first wave and killed the three of them almost immediately before the rest of the critters could even attack.

"This is bullshit." The hacker growled her frustration and shook her head. "I'll murder the—we can't die, not again. I won't do it again."

"Is it because you don't want to climb the levels?" Desk asked.

"Fuck no. Dying hurts. I may be many things, all of them crazy, but I'm no masochist. Doesn't it hurt for you?"

Desk paused and considered the question. "My receptors in-game note that my simulated body is being rendered into a non-functional state, which would be what humans would call pain. With that said, I do not have the organic perspective to make that pain as prohibitive an experience as it would be for you, especially in a simulated environment."

The girl rolled her eyes. "What the fuck ever. Fine. Let's head in there again.

Of course, having Desk take over the defenses while Niki and Vickie both went on the offensive didn't mean any less difficulty going forward and it would be a tough way to keep moving. The AI was able to keep the smaller, sneakier monsters away, but it left the bulk of the fighting on the shoulders of the two humans in the group.

Still, it worked out for the best. Niki grinned as one of the lizards dropped and its acid pouch emptied onto the soil that it apparently had no effect on.

Those few monsters left that continued to throw themselves at the small team had their limbs suddenly melted off in the pools left by their acid-spitting brothers, which made it far easier for Niki and Vickie to eliminate them before they paused to examine their surroundings.

"How did Taylor do this eighty-four times?" Vickie asked and shook her head.

"He did have a few days or weeks pause between trips to the Zoo," Niki reminded her.

"Yes, there's that. But he also headed into the fucking jungle for days and weeks at a time. I assume he wasn't always fighting, of course, but he would have constantly had to be on the lookout in case some fucker appeared behind him and tried to melt his ass or inject him with venom."

"It should be noted that the teams that Taylor went into the Zoo with were larger," Desk commented. She looked annoyingly refreshed and not tired at all by the experience. "They were generally well-equipped for a longer trip and possessed qualified members who were trained to face the challenges they encountered. Many were experienced too, for the most part."

Niki narrowed her eyes. "Sure, but they ended up dying as well."

"It's something to keep in mind as we head into the fifth wave."

She suddenly disliked the AI. For one crazy moment, it almost bordered on hatred and startled her with its vehemence.

The wave was activated and her mouth dried when nothing triggered the suit's sensors.

Before she could comment on the unexpected inactivity, a slew of somethings seemed to spawn from the jungle in an instant and her sensors went ballistic.

"Fuck me in the ass," Vickie whispered, activated all the shoulder-mounted weapons she carried, and poured them into the solid line of monsters that surged toward them from all sides.

Niki was far more preoccupied by the massive signature that advanced on them from the rear. It wasn't a mass of smaller creatures, she determined as the monster slithered closer and felled trees as it approached.

It made an odd thudding and clattering sound on the packed earth but no screeching, or roaring. And it moved fast. She flicked all her weapons to ready and opened fire with everything she had as the creature revealed itself in the fake sunlight of the sim.

The fact that it was in a sim didn't make the monster any less unbelievable. Hundreds of tiny brown legs pushed a fully armored creature forward. It shrugged the firepower off with ease, despite the fact that she poured a continuous barrage like she was hitting it with a nerf gun.

It was not a good feeling.

The carapaces took the explosives and absorbed them for the most part although some dents and damage were visible. Unfortunately, it seemed nowhere near enough.

Hundreds of legs scuttled toward her at an impossible

speed. The creature bulldozed into her and the limbs at the front ran her down, punched through her armor, and drove her into the dirt.

At least it didn't hurt quite so much. It was a quick way to die, although she had a feeling it wouldn't end quite that quickly if she was in the actual Zoo.

She removed her helmet slowly, shook her head, and looked around. Vickie removed her headgear as well and a scowl was very much in evidence. Whatever that massive centipede creature had been, it had killed them both at almost the same time.

"What… What the fuck was that?" the hacker asked and shook her head as if to clear it.

"The scientific name is *Lithobius formidolosus*," Desk told her crisply.

"Great the…uh, terrible centipede," Niki whispered. "No one strained any creative muscles when naming the fuckers, did they?"

"Those who have tangled with it have taken to calling it the killerpillar," the AI continued. "Its reported weak spots are around the head, which is generally only exposed when it is preparing to strike."

The former agent nodded. "Okay… Well, that's good to know. So, do you think we should go back in?"

Vickie shrugged but seemed to vacillate somewhat. "I… I'm not one to simply leave a job unfinished so…sure."

"Yeah, we can continue the fighting, right?"

"We got this. We only need to remember when to strike at the fuckers and we'll be fine."

"Right. Right. We got this."

"I'm afraid that we'll have to take a break," Desk interrupted before they could activate the sim again. "I have a call waiting for you from Trond Jansen. He says it is urgent."

"Oh, well, we have to take that." Vickie jumped from her seat near the sim. "If Trond needs you, it's probably best to not keep him waiting, right?"

"Right," Niki agreed, maybe a little too quickly. "We should see what he needs. And we can pick this up some other time."

It was for the best, ultimately. She needed a break from the fight anyway.

He didn't like not having a place to lay his head for the night, but the residence they had bought from Marino was still under construction. It needed considerable work and likely wouldn't be ready to live in for a while yet.

Which meant settling into a hotel for the night once they were finished at the garage. Bobby had been nice enough to not mention Freddie's call during the day.

But he would have to put his mind to it anyway. He tried not to think about it on the ride to the hotel but mental avoidance wouldn't do him any good.

Part of him wanted to stop for a drink but he decided to resist and rather order room service for dinner and get to work immediately. Desk would be able to help him.

The hotel did offer a decent menu and he chose the chicken parm option before he settled with his laptop in close proximity.

The AI was already on the line, waiting for him.

"I guess you heard the call?" he asked and popped the top from the beer that had been chilling in his minibar.

"I did. What do you think happened to the researcher?"

He shook his head. "It's not easy to sneak someone out of a military base. Not impossible, mind, but very difficult, especially with all the surveillance they have in place. Occam's Razor says that he left the base of his own accord, so we need to make sure he's not doing a little extra research at one of the other bases or maybe took time off in Casablanca or something before we raise any alarms."

"So you agree with the commandant on this?"

"I know that sounds ridiculous, but we need to rule any other option out before dropping thousands on suit transport to get me to the Zoo to find him."

Desk paused. "I thought you might think that way so I've already begun to scan the local feeds to try to find where he might be. I'm also studying all departures from the base since he was last seen so we have a better idea of where to look."

"Nice work, Desk. You might want to peek into the transmissions coming to and from the base too. See if there's anything hinky on that end. We might even be able to pick up on anything our researcher might have been involved with."

"Do you mean infiltrate confidential military communications? Isn't that illegal?"

Taylor stared at his screen for a few seconds until he realized Desk was trying to be sarcastic with him. It had almost sounded like Niki's voice for a second.

He shook his head. "You're already in the Pentagon servers so it shouldn't raise any flags there, right?"

"Correct. I'm glad you have been paying attention."

"The Banks family talks so much that it's hard to not absorb some of the information shared."

"Do you think of me as a member of the Banks family?"

She seemed to genuinely want an answer so he thought about it for a moment and shrugged. "I've seen people call anything from their cars to their televisions family, so I don't see why it shouldn't be applied to you too."

Desk didn't answer for a second. "You are an example of both, are you not? I know you consider Liz to be part of your family. Was there a television as well?"

He shook his head. "I don't want to talk about it."

"Come on."

"Fine. My parents bought a new TV, which meant the one in the living room went to their room and the one already in their room went to mine. It was an old LCD Phillips, and I put googly eyes on it and called it Stevie."

The AI didn't answer for a few seconds. "Stevie the TV?"

"Fuck off. My point is you have so much more personality than any TV could, no matter how many weird voices I made for him, so yes. Irrespective of what anyone else thinks, you'll always be a Banks in my book. Even if you do take over the world—which, let's be honest, is probably the most notable 'Banks' move you could make."

"I agree on that, which is probably why they fear that I would end up doing it so much."

"That makes sense."

"I'll let you know if I find anything. Good luck, Taylor."

"Thanks."

The fact that he needed to do all this investigating from

afar was probably the most annoying thing. If there was a threat, the folks nearby were better equipped than he was.

They didn't have an AI who would run the whole process on her own, but that was neither here nor there. He had a feeling that something was wrong despite his desperate hopes that Everett was merely getting drunk on the French base.

His instincts were seldom wrong, which meant he would have to put all his personal issues aside and return to the Zoo. He drew a deep breath and looked around the room.

It wasn't like he had much to pack. They were living out of suitcases at this point anyway, so all he needed was the clothes he had asked the hotel to clean.

He was barely a few shirts in when the door to the room opened and two female voices drifted into the living room of their suite.

"Taylor!" Vickie shouted before she pulled the bedroom door open. "I'm seriously here to kill you!"

His eyebrows raised and he looked at Niki, surprised to see that both women looked more than a little exhausted.

"Don't look at me," his girlfriend grumbled. "If she screws up killing you, I'll finish the job."

"Okay," he muttered and tried not to give anything about his plans away. With them like this, it seemed prudent to keep his news to himself. "Is there any particular reason why or are you guys simply feeling a little extra bloodthirsty today?"

"We tried a couple of Zoo sims," Vickie explained. "Killing mutants in a simulated environment. And we want to kill you because you never told us about exactly what kind of monsters we could expect in there—the...uh, killerpillars in particular. I will have nightmares for weeks about that fucking monster."

"If you think that was terrifying, you should try seeing them in person," Taylor muttered. "No wait, don't try that."

"Agreed." Niki dropped down onto their bed. "Anyway, guess who called while we were trying the sim?"

"Trond Jansen," Vickie answered before Taylor could.

Her cousin narrowed her eyes. "I wanted him to guess. Anyway, he gave us the details of a DHS suit by the name of Felicity Ahlers and said that we should contact her because she needs our help with something. I already scheduled a call to her on the TV and Vickie can sit in if she likes."

The hacker had probably invited herself to the conversation. It wasn't like she wouldn't hear what was being said anyway but it would make her an active participant at least.

The former agent pulled her dark-brown hair back and tied it in a quick ponytail as the younger woman connected the call to their TV.

Ahlers did, in fact, look like a DHS suit, down to the gray pantsuit they all wore. It was like agents for three-letter agencies all coordinated their outfits or something. The woman removed a pair of glasses and stared into the screen for a few seconds.

"Oh, right." She grunted and her confusion eased. "I wasn't sure if it was connected. Mr. McFadden, Ms. Banks, I do appreciate you being able to—"

"And Ms. Madison," Vickie interjected, leaned in, and waved cheerfully.

The agent's eyebrows raised and she nodded. "Right, Ms. Madison. Anyway, I appreciate being able to talk to you three about this because frankly, Homeland Security is a little out of its depth when it comes to dealing with this kind of thing."

Taylor folded his arms across his chest. He had a feeling he knew what kind of thing she was talking about but wouldn't interrupt.

"We ran a drug raid in San Francisco last night that netted a large quantity of illegal narcotics, but they also uncovered a stash of horns that originated from the Zoo. Testing determined that the blood and DNA in the horns were of alien origin, although what tipped the raid team off was the blue blood. It was assumed that the stash was intended to be used like conventional rhino horns are used on the black market."

"Rhino horns?" Vickie asked and shook her head. "That's sick. I love rhinos, even if they're from the Zoo. I say we murder these fuckers on sheer principle."

"Goddamn fucking limp-dicks who think they can cure their lack of performance using goop." Niki shook her head. "They are always thinking with their cocks instead of their heads."

"Wait," Taylor interrupted and looked at Vickie. "You love rhinos?"

"Of course." The hacker leaned forward. "I have since I was a kid and watched those national geographic documentaries about them. I've donated to the Save the Rhino fund for years and lately increased my support now that I can. It's a truly good cause."

"Rhino horns are prescribed for many different things,

actually," Desk interjected. "Which explains why their prices are so high. Anything from devil possession to getting rid of nightmares, headaches, and feverish colds. A couple of books from the sixteenth century appear to be the origin of these myths."

"The claims about earth rhino horns might be myths, but if these are out of the Zoo, there might be a little more fact involved than there would be otherwise," Taylor interjected. "If they find a way to market those horns, they will get a reputation for a noticeable success rate and from there, you can bet your ass that demand would sky-rocket —and not only among those who struggle to bring their little soldier to attention."

Ahlers narrowed her eyes like she had something to add —possibly regarding the fourth voice that had spoken through her connection—but moved past the impulse quickly. "Right. Anyway, the delivery that came in was about eighteen horns in total."

"Eighteen?" he asked and narrowed his eyes. "Okay, when you consider that the goop all but grows on trees, you can understand how it's being brought out so quickly via things like the Pita flower, but so many items taken from animals? That can't be a good thing."

"We'll have to find someone local at the Zoo to investigate that angle," Niki commented. "Perhaps we can rope Sal into this."

"I do need to stress that all the details on this investigation are highly classified," Ahlers insisted. "We can't risk alerting anyone involved in the smuggling, so if you're going to alert someone in the Zoo, you'll have to do it in person."

"Like…in person in person?" Vickie looked at her teammates in growing concern.

"Unless you plan to go to the Zoo yourselves, you'll have to find another way."

Well, if that wasn't a piece of goodfortune, Taylor decided.

He leaned forward. "Well, now that you mention it…"

CHAPTER FIVE

The car was supposed to represent something about the power of the man who had sent it. Chen Lu Wan was familiar with the tactics of the men who had called on him. It wasn't that they attempted to intimidate him specifically but rather a matter of habit. They wanted everyone to know they were dangerous.

And even though Lu Wan knew of their tactics and knew what to expect, it didn't make them any less effective. His mouth dried and his fingers tapped idly on the hand rests.

Engaging the driver in any kind of conversation had brought on no results. The man wore dark sunglasses and although his passenger could see tattoos peeking beyond his cuffs and collar, he appeared to be the epitome of professionalism. He didn't so much as look into the rearview mirror when Lu Wan asked where they were going.

It was a purely rhetorical question, something he felt

was expected of him. The truth was that he knew exactly where they were going. He'd lived in San Francisco long enough to know the places that needed to be avoided if he planned to keep his wallet, phone, and life.

The warehouse district of the city had moved constantly for years and crept inexorably closer and closer to the city. This left massive chunks of unused real estate to be claimed by the criminals who abounded. The cops learned quickly that it was a good area for quick raids if they needed to round their numbers out but not much else.

No law-abiding citizens spent enough time there to justify regular patrols, which meant there would be no one to help him if he needed it. Even if he was able to get a call out, there was no chance that any police would arrive in time to do anything but fail to identify the body since he would inevitably be missing his phone, wallet, teeth, and fingertips.

He had no idea why there was a market for human fingertips and teeth, but more of the bodies recovered in the bay lacked these compared to only a few that didn't.

The limo came to a halt outside one of the warehouses. A few gang signs from the triads were spray-painted on the sides, an indicator for the other gangs to keep away. These particular sloppy signatures were the symbol of the Brotherhood of Blood. This group had replaced the Insane Dragons that had generally held sway in San Francisco around the turn of the millennium.

He climbed out of the car without waiting for the driver to open the door for him. Lu Wan assumed that the man didn't know that was what was expected from chauffeurs and he also knew what to expect. A handful of guards stood at the entrance and made no effort to hide their positions as they let him pass without a challenge.

A number of operations were based at the warehouse and all would be running smoothly. The triads' position in the city had been settled almost two centuries before and it would take considerable might and effort to dig them out. If there was a raid, everything would simply shut down and three more would pop up elsewhere within a day.

One particular raid, however, was the reason why he was there.

A single man was seated on a sofa positioned in a corner of the warehouse. Most of those present appeared to avoid the occupant and Lu Wan knew why. There wasn't much about him physically that could clearly be pinpointed as off. The only real difference between him and the rest of the workers in the warehouse was the fact that he had none of the tattoos the others used to identify themselves to the world.

He boasted a score of scars instead, clearly visible and on display through the tank top he wore, and a selection of weapons—firearms and otherwise—were spread on the coffee table in front of him in various states of disassembly.

"You came," the man stated softly in English.

"Didn't you expect me?" Lu Wan asked, also in English.

"We were told to expect you but I did not think you would come. Is that not why telephones were invented? They even have the smaller ones available now—the kind to be carried in one's pocket."

He knew the man was being condescending but his flat almost monotone delivery made it a little difficult to adjust to.

"I apologize for inconveniencing you, Zi Shou, but I needed to gain your perspective about what was lost in person. I arrive to find that your men display themselves out in the open. They might as well hang a sign saying, 'Brotherhood of Blood here: FBI welcome' on the building."

Zi Shou looked up from the pistol he was cleaning and Lu Wan realized that he might have overstepped his boundaries. A chill rippled down his spine when the cold green eyes shifted over him. It was uncomfortable to feel that look from the Executioner, and he vaguely assumed that was the point, but the brutal gaze returned quickly to the weapon he was tending to.

Oddly, he thought, it seemed to make little difference that he was effectively the man's employer, if only in this particular matter.

"The police already know of this location, which is why you will find only legal enterprises here. All our other enterprises have been moved elsewhere. If a raid is planned, it will find nothing but small dolls being prepared for the Christmas season. You can relax. Please, take a seat."

His movements were slow and deliberate, pointing Lu Wan to a seat across from the Executioner himself, which was as close to a sign that there had been no offense taken to him speaking out of turn.

Lu Wan complied but sat a little stiffly and studied the man across from him, who continued to clean the firearm in his hand.

"I spent considerable money to build the contacts to

secure the source of the horns and smuggle them safely into this country, only to find that all of them have been confiscated."

"Being raided by the local police is a risk you are more than familiar with."

"I do not care about the money!" Lu Wan hissed annoyance and tried to not move forward in his seat. "The sources who sent them to us will need assurances that they will not be tracked through the smuggling operation. Plus assurances that future shipments will not be lost, or they will cease all business with us. That is something no amount of money can correct."

He was probably one of the few people in the world who could raise his voice to the Executioner with no repercussions, but it was still a bone-chilling concept—one that was matched only by the anger that surged through his body at the thought of what had been lost.

"More importantly, others were waiting for delivery who will not receive what they have already paid for. A blow to our reputation is the best we can expect. Consequences must be meted out. Do you understand this?"

Zi Shou nodded slowly. "What do you wish me to do?"

"That *un tyen shung duh eedway ro* who was captured alive is in police custody, yes?"

"Him and the *go tsao de* locals he hired for the job of transporting the merchandise. Our contacts have already sent me their locations."

"I want them dead."

"Their tongues will be cut out before the end of the day."

"See that they are. If any of them so much as breathes a

word of what happened, you will have more than me to deal with."

The man didn't look up from his weapon but the message was clear. An Executioner seized his power by killing all those who came between them and the position. In the end, there would always be a few waiting who wanted to take the Executioner's place and would be more than willing to take his title and power in the same way that he had taken them from another years before.

"It will be done," Zi Shou said quietly as he deftly assembled the pistol again. "It will be done in a manner in which no fingers will be pointed at us—or you."

The Executioner stood, collected a few of the weapons, and strode out. Lu Wan didn't think he would be so dramatic as to head out to do the work himself. Killing someone in custody would not be an easy feat and would take considerable planning and many phone calls.

But as long as he was working on the problem, the businessman was happy. A fire had been put under his ass and he could now genuinely tell the people who were waiting for answers that something was being done.

Besides, replacing the horns that were taken could be accomplished quickly. Lu Wan took a moment to pour himself a drink from a nearby decanter that looked like it was serving bourbon. He couldn't tell the difference between scotch and bourbon anyway. His palate wasn't that refined.

Once his nerves were a little more settled, he took his phone from his pocket. He had other matters to tend to now.

The number he dialed was for a youngster he was putting through college in exchange for the odd favor here and there.

Now was the time to call a favor in.

"Mark? I need you to look into any records from a Greek company called Pos—no, I am not calling you from a Chinese strip club. Now focus. You need to find all the records for a company called Poseidon and send me the travel logs for a ship called the *Alexis*. Call me when you can see them."

The boy was a little annoying but surprisingly effective, and Lu Wan expected to hear from him again soon. It meant he could get on with the process of shipping more horns using the new smuggling operation he'd have to create to replace the old that was no doubt compromised.

"So, you simply what? Planned to go to the Zoo and not even tell me? Did you think I wouldn't notice you were gone?"

Taylor dragged in a deep breath and tried to not lose his temper. It would have been far easier if Vickie hadn't been seated in the room. She hadn't said a word since the call with the DHS agent had ended and she now watched the two of them with a small frown that suggested she was a little confused.

"I intended to tell you," he said finally. "I was merely packing to get it out of the way."

"Were you going to tell us when you were already

fucking there? Or maybe when you got back and had to explain the souvenirs you bought for me?"

"I think we need to take a deep breath here and think this through," Vickie interjected. "You guys are forcing me to be the voice of reason here and I'm not a fan of that—not for myself and especially not for others."

"We both know you're not going there alone," Niki continued like she hadn't heard what her cousin had said. "We're a partnership now, Taylor, and that means we share equally in everything—and that includes information."

"I wasn't entirely sure if I would go there at all, for fuck's sake," he snapped and shook his head. "I just got the news today and I asked Desk to collect intel. For all we fucking know, this missing researcher could be up to his ears in STDs at a Casablanca whorehouse. I wanted to tell you when there was something to tell."

"Well, now there is and I'm coming with you."

"On a research mission? Are you nuts? Why would both of us have to travel across the world when only one needs to go? Desk can keep an eye on me while I'm there and I'll fly as soon as possible."

"Because we both know it won't be merely a research mission. You'll try to head into the Zoo and it'll try to get you killed. And if that happens, you won't do it without me!"

Taylor couldn't think of anything to say or do. She was very close to him and saying stuff that made him very happy, no matter the motivation behind it. All he could do was reach out, pull her closer to him, and crush her lips with his.

"Oh, gross," Vickie muttered in disgust and ducked under a handful of pillows.

Niki growled against him but after a moment, she pulled him closer. Her embrace was a little more aggressive than his but she could afford to be. Him being aggressive would end up having to rush her to the hospital.

Finally, she dragged herself away—not far enough to stop pressing her body into his but enough that she could suck in a deep breath.

"If you think that'll change my mind, think again," she whispered, "but do keep trying."

"No," Taylor admitted with a smile. "But I think we both needed to take a deep breath and think about shit. Also, I needed you to shut up long enough for me to tell you something important."

"What can be so important that you have to kiss me to shut me up?"

"Only this. If you think I will let the woman I love go into the Zoo, you need to think again. I won't listen to you scream while you're shredded and consumed by a horde of Zoo monsters the likes of which you've never imagined, let alone seen. And no, a sim doesn't count."

"But—"

"But nothing. Your being there will probably get both of us killed. Me because I'll be looking at you and distracted by all my worrying, and you because you have no fucking clue about what you'll run into in that fucking jungle."

"But I can—wait. You said the woman you…uh, love?"

Taylor leaned back a little when he realized that he hadn't told her that yet. It was an odd thing and an odd time to say it for the first time, but it needed to be said.

"Well…yeah. Why do you think I let you get away with so much anyway?"

That was a bad attempt at humor and he probably wouldn't hear the end of it once she stopped to think about it. For the moment, however, she was smiling at Vickie, who still had her head buried in some pillows.

"You…you big fucking lug. If you think you 'letting' me do anything has any bearing on how I live my life, you're dumber than I thought. But I let you get away with saying bullshit like that because I love you too."

"You do?"

"Well, yeah. If anyone else tried that shit or any of the five hundred other kinds of shit that you try to pull on me, they would have been out on their ear a long time ago."

"Huh. Interesting."

She grinned and rested a hand on the collar of his shirt. "Stop thinking about it. Come here and kiss me."

Taylor obeyed the insistent tugging on his shirt to press his lips to hers again. He shivered gently as she brushed her fingers through his hair and dragged her nails ever so gently down his scalp. Her other hand reached down to grab his ass.

They both heard Vickie gagging in the background.

"Seriously, guys, this is worse than the arguing. Can we keep it PG? We still have shit to do."

Niki pulled away from the kiss, but barely. "Who asked for your opinion?"

"I keep telling you that I hate having to be the voice of reason, but you guys are forcing me to be the sane and sensible one here. I know I'm bound to snap and go buy fifty grand pianos in a spree. You have been warned."

"You?" Taylor asked. "Sane? Sensible? In your family? It's not possible."

"Fuck you," the hacker snapped.

"I have to agree with that. Fuck you." Niki offered her middle finger to go with it.

"Not to interrupt a romantic moment," Desk interjected, "but Taylor does have a good point about not having enough Zoo experience."

He took a step back as a distraction from Niki and how much he wanted to simply continue to kiss her.

"What do you mean?" he asked.

"Desk, don't you fucking dare," Niki warned.

Taylor tilted his head, immediately intrigued. "Dare what?"

"Nothing," Vickie added quickly.

"Oh, well, I don't believe that," Taylor muttered. "What's Desk talking about? She wouldn't bring it up if there wasn't something to talk about, so if there's something for us to discuss, we might as well get it out of the way."

Vickie shook her head. "I don't know what you mean."

"I'm equally in the dark," Niki lied.

"I could simply ask Desk and she wouldn't be able to twist the telling of whatever it is to make you look good."

Taylor looked around but both women refused to look at him. In fact, they gazed anywhere but where he stood.

"Okay. Desk, what the hell are you—"

"Fine!" Vickie jumped up with a ferocious scowl. "I'll tell it. Niki and I were given access to some new sims they're working on—the VR systems they've been using to train recruits and people heading into the Zoo for the first time."

"Right. I think Bobby told me they were setting you guys up with something like that."

"Sure, right," Niki interjected. "Anyway, we were working through the levels of attacks based on what you might find in the Zoo, and...well, things didn't go very well for us in there."

Taylor folded his arms and narrowed his eyes. "Explain."

"Well, we managed to get to the third level without too much difficulty," Niki admitted. "That's where we ran into those acid lizards that Vickie wants to kill you over."

"Yup," the hacker agreed and dragged her fingers through her short hair. "And...well, we kept trying and the top three levels are fairly difficult. We finally managed to get to level five and one of those crawlerkillers—"

"Killerpillars."

"Right, killerpillars showed up and handed us a wipe. We had Desk in there to help us, but even she had difficulty keeping the monsters off our backs."

Taylor couldn't resist a small grin before laughter bubbled up from the back of his throat.

"Well, I'll give both of you ten points for trying, anyway," he admitted and shook his head. "But you should have gone in with me. Next time, I'll join you and I'll be able to teach you a thing or two. As it stands, we might have to get you to unlearn any bad habits you might have picked up going in on your own."

"With that said, it does give me an idea," Desk interjected. "While I was testing my functionality in a Zoo-like environment, I came to the realization that I might be able to go into the Zoo with him."

Niki narrowed her eyes. "What? How? And why does Desk get to go into the Zoo and I don't?"

"You keep treating it like it's some kind of treat you can earn," Vickie pointed out. "You do remember how painful shit was in the sim, right?"

She gestured dismissively. "Semantics."

"Anyway," Desk interrupted quickly through the speakers in their bedroom TV, "it would depend on the suit he's taking in there. Taylor, can you get hold of one of the testing units in the Cryptid Assassin Range? The one you mentioned that has multiple arms and limbs and has to be operated by some kind of AI or VI systems."

Taylor combed his fingers pensively through his beard. "Huh. It's an interesting idea. Besides, they'll probably like that we'll test their software with an advanced AI."

"You might want to avoid telling them that you will possibly stress-test this system in the Zoo," Niki pointed out. "Asking for forgiveness instead of permission and all that."

He nodded. "Right. It'll be one hell of a marketing ploy to say their system has been tested in the Zoo, but perhaps it's best to tell them the good news once we get out in one piece."

Vickie tilted her head and looked around the room as a bright smile settled suddenly onto her face. "You know, that might work. We would have to put in considerable work since Desk wouldn't be able to transmit data into the Zoo like she's able to in normal conditions. But we could create a specialized version of her that has been stripped to remove any functionality unneeded in a combat AI. Think of it as a shard of the parent AI. That version would probably be able to function off the SSDs they have running through the suits. I'd need to get a hand on one to be sure, though."

"I have calculated the hardware capabilities in the suits Taylor and Niki tested before," Desk assured them. "The simulations have given me reason to feel hopeful, although I would need to be able to test on the actual suits to be certain."

"There might be something else for us to worry about," Taylor muttered and tugged his beard instead of combing it lazily. "We don't want to alert the Department of Homeland Security—along with all the other agencies in the country—that we're working with an advanced AI. You know, the kind that the military is trying desperately to keep a stranglehold over?"

"But will you be safe in there?" Vickie asked.

"Will she be safe?" Niki countered.

"I can do it," Desk asserted, "but there would have to be compromises. A failsafe, as it were. My full systems cannot be put into the suit for fear of discovery and also because the bulk of what I am capable of would not be required in that situation. All that notwithstanding, enough could be downloaded to help Taylor. If the suit is compromised, I would—through the version of me resident in the suit—be in a position to enable the software to override the safety mechanisms in the hardware to fry the suit."

Niki scowled deeply. "And kill Taylor while he's inside?"

"It would be a last resort," Desk reminded her. "While he is in control of the suit, the decision would have to be his."

"So the only time you would be in a position to make

the decision is if I were somehow not able to make it." Taylor finished the AI's train of thought bluntly.

"Are we honestly thinking like this?" Niki growled in frustration. "Because I'm fucking not."

"It's scary, is what it is," Vickie whispered. "One step closer to Overlord. People will seriously complain about how they need to sit around computing pi all day because idiot Vickie plugged Desk in and created the New World Order of Skynet or some bullshit like that."

CHAPTER SIX

Of all the planes in the world, there was one that Taylor dreaded the least. The Hercules aircraft was large enough and heavily laden enough that he could feel there was something sturdy between himself and a thirty thousand-foot drop into the ocean. There was also the fact that it was large enough for him to bring a small hammock and settle in, especially since he was the only passenger on the flight.

He had difficulty sleeping on planes and probably always would, but a little chemical help always did the trick. Within an hour of takeoff, he closed his eyes and drifted off.

The dreams, unfortunately, seemed determined to steal his rest. He hadn't told Niki or Vickie about them, of course. The two women barely accepted the idea of him heading to the Zoo on his own as things stood. Telling them he had a bad feeling about it all would certainly not help.

He tossed and turned through eight hours of drug-induced sleep and once his meds wore off, there was no point in trying again.

It was a military plane, of course, which meant there was no in-flight service, which left him the only option of bringing food himself for the longer haul flights. A few bags of chips and roast beef sandwiches were quickly consumed, along with the bottled water, and shortly thereafter, he felt the Hercules bank into what he guessed was their final run to their destination.

While frustrating, it was for the best, he told himself. He didn't need more time in the air where there was nothing else for him to do but think about shit. Vickie had set him up with things to do on his phone and a laptop he had brought, but the roar of the engines was a little too powerful for him to hear anything else.

After slightly less than an hour, they began to circle in earnest for their final descent. The plane shuddered a little more violently before the wheels touched down on the base's airfield, and his whole body unclenched as the aircraft began to taxi to its designated stopping area. He could almost feel the sun beating relentlessly down as the Sahara welcomed him to the most unforgiving area of the planet.

The plane finally came to a halt and he shouldered his pack and moved to where the bay door had begun to open. The aperture grew wider to reveal the desert he'd hoped he would never see in person again.

At this section of the base, the wall was still far from complete and he had a clear view of the green ribbon that stretched across the horizon. Even more than the desert, he had hoped fervently that he would never see that landscape in person again.

Perhaps he was going crazy but it looked far bigger now than it had when he'd last seen it.

"I'm back, bitch," he whispered.

Three Hammerheads were already pulling up outside the bay door. The usual military paraphernalia identified two of them as official vehicles, but one was very clearly civilian-owned. Taylor exited the aircraft when a man climbed out even before the Hammerhead had come to a complete stop.

He was built lean and hard, and his brown hair was cut to military standards despite the fact that he hadn't been a service member for almost a full year now.

"Taylor Mc-Fucking-Fadden!" he yelled, jogged to the lowered bay door, and almost tackled the giant in a hug.

"Freddie. It's good to see you alive and well." He waited until the man pulled back to give him a quick scrutiny. "Or alive, anyway. How the fuck are you still alive out here?"

"Bobby's treated us well. Aside from that, a little dumb luck and a whole lot of skill. On my part, at least."

Taylor grinned. "I wish I could say it's good to be back, but it is good to see a couple of friendly faces still holding down the fort around here."

Freddie turned to the men who manned the forklifts and whistled to get their attention. "That crate over there goes on our Hammerhead, and get it moving. No one wants to be here all day, huh?"

The drivers rolled their eyes but turned their attention to the crate that contained Taylor's suit and ferried it to where one of Freddie's team pulled the doors in the back of the vehicle open.

It was a tough way to make a living. Not as tough as going into the Zoo, of course, but the support staff were as vital to the Zoo operations as the people who went in there. The fact that they were paid much less for it was a point of some contention that Taylor had no intention to dive into.

"So, are we headed to where you guys are based?" he asked as they walked down the ramp and headed toward the Hammerheads.

"In a while. First things first, though. You need a real welcome back, and that means a few drinks at Mark's. Or more than a few drinks. Besides, most business done around here is over a shit-ton of booze anyway, so we don't want to deviate from tradition, right?"

"We…do not."

Taylor did need a drink, and the fact that people would pay for his drinks when he arrived was certainly a plus. It wasn't the kind of thing he generally thought about when returning to the Zoo, but his unexpected presence was bound to draw some attention.

"What kind of suit did you bring?" Freddie asked as they climbed into the Hammerhead and the heavy vehicle started again. "I know you can afford the good ones. Maybe not top-of-the-line but still better than those the GIs are issued with around here."

"I managed to talk one of the dev companies into loaning me a prototype suit to stress-test. That said, I might have neglected to mention that I would take it to the

Zoo, but how better to stress-test a suit meant for the Zoo than in the fucking jungle?"

"Interesting. I wish I could get something like that going again."

"They named the model line after me, so I do have a little sway with them."

"They called the suits McFadden? Or Taylor? The Leprechaun?"

"Cryptid Assassin," he explained before the man moved on to the less-flattering nicknames he'd picked up.

"Oh. Who calls you that?"

"It's the official name they had on my files. I didn't choose it. Hell, I only heard about it when I was first contacted by the FBI about being a part of their program to kill the monsters over there."

"I still can't believe that these monsters are over there." Freddie shook his head, disgusted. "We like to think we're the last line of defense around here, but we keep hearing about idiots who accidentally release those fuckers into the world at large. It makes me sick to think about one of these beasts rampaging through a city or something."

"We can only hope it's done accidentally," Taylor muttered.

"What was that?"

"Nothing."

There was no need to go into his suspicions that the Zoo-based products could influence minds to start spreading the goop. That was the type of thing best left to conspiracy theorists until he had actual evidence to support it.

They drew up outside the bar and Taylor looked back as they headed inside.

"Will no one try to take it?" he asked. "You have a shit-ton of equipment in there."

"You've lived with civilians for too long. While we might have idiots who try to engage in criminal behavior around here, they're generally smart enough to do it outside the base where there aren't so many cameras around to keep an eye on them."

The man had a point. Drones patrolled to make sure there were no Zoo infiltrations, but they also kept an eye on the hundreds of people armed to the teeth on the base. Not only that, he'd noticed that security had tightened up considerably since he'd been there.

There was no announcement when they stepped into the bar. It was something of a down-time for the establishment but there would always be regulars hanging around at all hours. This meant that while they weren't alone, most of the booths were available.

Taylor joined Freddie in one of these and raised his hand to the bartender, who nodded without so much as looking up.

"Well, it's not the most auspicious of greetings," Freddie commented.

"It's for the best. I didn't think that many people remembered me for anything other than being a big bastard with bright red hair."

"Well, there's the matter of still holding the record for the most trips into the Zoo. People still try to keep track of the records."

"I bet you most of the top ten are dead."

"But the top one is still alive."

The bartender approached and placed a tall glass of beer in front of each of them. "Nice to see you around again, McFadden. Do you plan to head into the Zoo again or are you only here for a visit?"

"Here for a visit and hopefully not heading into the Zoo. Still, I haven't ruled it out."

"Nice." He pointed at the mug. "That one's on us. I'd say your drinks are all on us, but I happen to know how much you can drink and I don't think we would survive that heavy a hit on our beer stocks without getting paid."

"I completely understand." He grinned. "Nice to see you again, Marky."

"Not so loud. I'm trying to make sure no one else gets to call me that."

"Good luck with that, Marky." Freddie laughed. The bartender flipped him off and returned to the bar when a small group arrived.

"You just earned yourself a fat gob of spit in your next drink," Taylor muttered.

"It was worth it."

More people began to filter in and the pointing and the staring grew noticeably worse with the new crowd. They were younger and all looked like fighters to him, and he wouldn't keep them entertained.

"There was recently a debate on who held the record," Freddie explained as he took a long sip of his beer and wiped the foam mustache that covered his top lip. "I think there was an arm-wrestle in progress too, but I was five tequila shots in so I don't remember much about what was happening. But I recall that they held a discussion about who held the record."

"I don't think anyone will ever go in more times than I have. Honestly, I hope they don't."

"Are you worried about your record?"

"I don't want people killing themselves for no reason. And there would be no reason for anyone to go in there that many times—no good reason, anyway."

"So you're calling yourself an idiot, then?"

"I thought that was the point of having that particular record."

Freddie nodded and the two men tapped their glasses together in a wordless toast before Taylor took a couple of large gulps of his beer.

"Only one man I know wears his bright red hair like that," someone said from the entrance and Taylor looked back at a couple of familiar faces.

"Conrad," Taylor greeted them, "Eric, it's good to see you guys still alive."

"I can't believe you survived this long as a civilian," Eric commented as he approached to shake hands. "I honestly thought hanging around and talking about taxes all day would be the death of you."

"It probably would have been, but I've done more government work. Clearing up monsters that have popped up stateside has kept me alive and well."

"As long as you're staying busy." Conrad clapped him on the arm.

"It's good to see you guys again," Freddie interjected, "but McFadden and I have a little business to discuss."

"No, sure. We came in for a drink. And your next round is on us too."

"It is?" Freddie asked.

"Of course."

Taylor shook his head. "You don't need to do that."

"I know we don't have to but it's still going to happen."

The two men moved to an empty table and Taylor could only shrug.

"I guess we can't argue with that," he muttered. "So, to business."

His companion nodded. "To business. Honestly, I can't say we've discovered anything around here about Jian's whereabouts but we have been looking. I even persuaded the commandant to agree to let us look around and everything, but we couldn't dig anything up. The dude has straight-up vanished."

"Yeah." He scowled and shook his head. "That's about what I was able to turn up. I had some tech-savvy people look into where he might have gone—like any of the other bases or even some of the local cities—thinking he might have used a credit card or appeared on someone's social media."

"Let me guess. A big fat load of nothing."

"The second worst big fat load anyone can run into."

"I…don't think I want to know what the worst one is."

"No. No, you do not."

The man sighed and ruffled his short hair with his fingers. "He wouldn't have simply gone into the Zoo. I know that. And it's been a few days now since teams went out, so all the patrols he might have joined for a quick trip in have already come back and gone out again. Waiting around and hoping on the off-chance that he went in with one of the missions going deeper is… Well, we can't wait that long."

"You still haven't explained why you're so determined to find this guy," Taylor told him. "I know I'm returning a favor and that means I won't ask any questions, but if you were in the mood to share the reasoning behind that or if there was anything weird going on around the Zoo, now would be the time to put it on the table."

Taylor left the man a way out of answering a question that he didn't appear to want any part of, and he took it.

"What do you mean by weird?"

"You know, anything…uh, different."

Freddie tilted his head in mild confusion. "In the Zoo?"

"You know what I mean. There's a kind of pattern to the Zoo, and I'm asking if anything has seemed different or off."

Before Freddie could answer, they were interrupted by loud shouting from the entrance. Both men turned to see what was happening.

"Fucking idiots," Freddie whispered while he took a swig of his drink.

Taylor couldn't find it in himself to disagree. The racket came from a small group that looked like they had just come in from the Zoo. A certain air about them said that they had pulled their suits off a short while earlier and were now looking to get themselves something to drink.

Or to get into a fight, given the way that they accosted the people closest to the door.

"You idiots need to get a fucking life," the apparent leader of the group yelled and tried to kick the stool out from under one of the other patrons. "Let the people who need it get a drink in fucking peace. We already took our Pita plants in but no, we have to hang around and do nothing about it afterward. Fucking shits!"

The bartender seemed to teeter on the edge of getting involved but his reluctance showed in his face. Taylor knew he could probably help the man and he nodded to Freddie.

"I guess we can spare a couple of minutes out of our day," the mercenary replied and pushed from his seat.

"What do you mean by we?" Taylor asked. He was already on his feet and strode to where the confrontation had almost reached breaking point. "Would you mind getting the door?"

Mark saw what was happening and nodded. "Do you mind helping me out, McFadden?"

"This guy?" one of the others asked. "The fucking leprechaun who grew a little too big. Are you looking for your pot of gold here, Fergus?"

"That's Taylor McFadden, man," another whispered. "*The* Taylor McFadden."

The leader took a step forward, narrowed his eyes, and inspected the redhead closely. "Seriously? This guy is the reigning Zoo Champ? Are you fucking kidding me? The Zoo critters must have left him alone because they didn't want to have to look at his fucking face. Or maybe they felt sorry for an old-timer spending his time in the jungle."

The insult was uncalled for, but Taylor chose to wait rather than respond to it.

"This is what all the hoorah is about?" another one chimed in.

"I told you it was all hype and only hype," the leader added before he turned to look at Taylor. "So why are you here, Gramps? Tipping the elbow, drinking with your war buddies, and chatting about the old days that have been blown way out of proportion?"

"Careful you don't bend that elbow too hard, Grandpa. Your arthritis might lock it there."

"Fucking has-been."

Taylor decided that they'd had their fun at his expense and the petty attempts to denigrate him were about as much as he was willing to take.

"Don't worry, I'll take the trash outside," he told the bartender and gestured for him to get back to pouring and serving drinks.

"Who the hell are you calling trash, old—"

His hand snapped out before the man could blink, grasped him by the jaw, and dragged his head onto the bar top. It wasn't hard enough to damage either his head or the counter but was sufficient to stun the man into silence before he moved closer, caught him by the collar and belt, and lifted him off the floor in one smooth motion.

Freddie was already waiting at the door. He yanked it open as Taylor tossed the man out onto his face before he turned to face the rest of the group.

He hadn't noticed that there were so many of them, but as the silence fell over the establishment, he realized that seven men were part of the team of the man he'd tossed out.

"Right then, you squirts." He growled his displeasure and folded his arms across his chest. "You're too green to know better or you'd see what's right under your fucking noses. But I don't mind teaching you a thing or two. If your balls are as big as your mouths, that is. Get out there and I'll show you what's hype and what isn't. Let's see how you hold up against an old has-been."

They didn't seem even vaguely convinced that he would be enough of a threat against seven of them. Instead, they laughed and exchanged looks like they were psyching each other up while Taylor simply stood his ground and waited. He didn't mind. It had been a long time since he'd gone into a fight where people thought of him as the underdog.

After a few long moments, he left via the same door he'd tossed the other man through and removed his jacket as Freddie came out to join him.

"Admit it. You miss this bullshitting with your peers," the man commented as the seven came out of the bar behind him, followed by almost a dozen of the patrons.

"I would if I had any peers," Taylor admitted and winked as he pulled his shirt off as well and draped it over Freddie's shoulder while even more of the bar's customers poured out. He half-expected Mark to come out with them, and a couple of bets had already been placed.

"Do you plan to strip to your underpants?"

"I only have a couple of shirts packed and I don't want to have to battle the laundry service around here again."

Freddie nodded. "It's worse than it was."

"How?"

"You don't want to know."

Taylor probably didn't. The laundry services at most military bases were already iffy but out in the Sahara, they stretched bad into terrible.

Right now, however, he wouldn't put too much thought

into it and had other things to deal with. He rolled his shoulders, took a deep breath, and felt a hint of gratification at the faint traces of doubt that flitted across the faces of the men who ranged themselves against him. Seeing his sheer size was one thing but they had failed to fully discern the power behind it and now wondered if they should reconsider their bravado.

He laughed, cracked his knuckles, and took a step forward. "Will any of you ladies step up and get this fight started, or do I need to get the ball rolling for you?"

A few exchanged looks and two of them dropped back behind their comrades, most likely hoping to catch him while he was focused on the others or once he was tired from facing most of the group.

Of course, it could as easily be that they planned to run when the fighting started. None of that concerned him, however. He had ached for a good fight to take the edge off the anxiety that had occupied his every waking moment since he'd come to terms with returning to the Zoo.

The first one to attack did so after a couple of deep breaths to gather his courage. For people to fight thousands of monsters in the Zoo, one man shouldn't have been that big a deal. Taylor took a step back when two punches hammered home in his midsection. A shock of adrenaline rushed through his body as he took a step forward and clapped a hand over each of the man's ears before he could follow through with his attack.

The impact was almost instantaneous and the man's eyes bulged as he raised his hands to cover both ears. Taylor grasped the side of his head and pushed him to the left and into the path of two others who had chosen to attack from that direction.

More blows followed and he had a feeling they would leave a few bruises, He launched his foot forward and powered it into the ribs of the merc who attempted to bull-rush him. He regained his balance quickly and pivoted at his hips to snap his elbow up and catch another of his adversaries across the jaw.

Three were down in a matter of seconds and an odd grin of exhilaration settled over his face as another man tried to lunge forward.

He punched up but still managed to land a good blow and blood began to seep from Taylor's nose. The grin remained, however, and he pushed forward and lashed out with a backhand slap. His knuckles rapped the man's mouth and drew blood as he caught the back of his oppo-nent's head with both hands and dragged him down to meet his rising knee.

Bones and teeth were broken and he simply let him fall when the remaining three tried to attack him together in an effort to overwhelm and overpower him.

His laughter was almost an insult although a handful of punches met their target. He could taste blood in his mouth and more shocks of pain flared in his hips and midsection before he caught the head of the one in the center as well as the one to his left. Without warning, he yanked them hard and their heads met with a loud thunk that made the spectators wince.

Both stumbled away, dazed and a little confused, which left the last one standing against him alone. Without backup, he had the smartest idea that should have occurred to his comrades as well and tried to turn and run.

Taylor knew the small audience gathered wouldn't let the merc escape, but he didn't want to rely on them. Before the man could complete his turn, he caught hold of the collar of his shirt and yanked him into the fight.

In a rapid jerk, he powered his forehead down to make impact with the merc's nose and drew blood immediately before he drove his fist into the idiot's gut. The air rushed from his opponent's lungs in a whoosh, and he finished the attack when he held him by his belt, lifted him about a foot in the air, and hurled him onto the pavement.

Whether his head impacted the hard surface or not, it didn't matter. The lights went out and no one was home. That left him the task of straightening to turn to the other two who had managed to stay on their feet, although both struggled visibly and tottered from side to side like newborn calves.

Taylor spat the blood out of his mouth and touched what trickled slowly from his nose before he turned his attention fully on his hecklers.

"Okay, numbnuts. Remember that this is what happens when your dick gets in the way of your brains. This is what happens when you try to find trouble at Mark's."

A chorus of agreement from the spectators followed, and for a moment, it looked like they planned to keep on fighting until one dropped to his knees and vomited, which drew a roar of laughter from the crowd.

"You know," the final man muttered, trying to keep his head up, "you might have won the fight but you've already lost the battle. Word is that you and Freddie are looking for your friend who went missing, but you might as well fly home, asshole. He's long gone by now, and he's somewhere you'll never find him."

Taylor stepped in quickly and wrapped his hand around the man's neck to steady him while he swayed and tried to recover his balance. "What the fuck are you talking about? Do you know where Everett is?"

Freddie approached quickly, suddenly serious, but the man's eyes rolled to the back of his head and his body went limp.

"Fucking shit," Taylor snapped and dropped him. "We need to question him. Now!"

"He's a little too unconscious to question," someone pointed out from the small audience. The man was still in uniform but probably not on duty if he was at the bar. "I can take him into custody and make sure he gets medical treatment. He should be ready to be questioned again in the morning."

The offer made sense. There would be no point in trying to question an unconscious man, but Taylor didn't like it either way.

"What's your name?"

"Lieutenant Mark Chambers."

"Chambers, I'll need to know the second he's awake."

"Understood."

A couple of the others in the audience helped the soldier lift the man from the where he sprawled motionless on the hard surface and he carried the unconscious merc to where a couple of Hammerheads were parked.

Taylor shook his head, suddenly no longer in the mood to drink.

"What about the others?" Freddie asked.

"Get them into custody too. They might know something about what that dipshit was talking about."

In truth, he didn't care what happened to the others but leaving them to die was probably not a good idea. It had been a fun enough brawl but fatalities would make it all incredibly serious incredibly fast.

CHAPTER SEVEN

Most folk connected the city to a movie with Humphrey Bogart and Ingrid Bergman, and fair points to that. It was a great film. Haddad had always been a fan of both the film and the actress, and he tried to watch it when they played it in some of the old-fashioned theaters in the city.

Of course, those showings were awash with tourists who were there for the very same reason but he didn't mind too much. It was part of the experience.

In the end, however, Casablanca was so much more than a scene at an airfield in which a man asked a woman to leave him forever while the Nazis were on her tail. It was a city that had been alive with roiling humanity for centuries and recently, it had turned itself into a trade hub for the military bases that had been established in the Sahara.

It could be said that the Zoo was the best thing that happened to Casablanca since the 1942 film.

Haddad was certainly among those. Smuggling hadn't been such a lucrative business until the jungle appeared from nothing. Soldiers from all around the world ached for the comforts of home and were willing to drop the thousands they earned to have them smuggled in.

Better still, people also wanted items to be smuggled out.

With all the business moving through the city, he was able to buy a new car. Importing a Jaguar from England had always been a dream and he grinned when he started the vehicle for the first time.

Unfortunately, the streets in the city were generally too congested with people on foot, bicycles, horses, and Vespas for him to put the car through its paces, but it was for the best. He honestly didn't trust himself to not crash his expensive new baby.

He made slow progress but when he finally reached the market district, the roads were a little wider and it had sidewalks that enabled people to stay off the roads.

It truly was a pity that he only needed to drive a few hundred yards to one of the stores that had a parking place reserved for him. He pulled into it and slid out of his vehicle, clicked the button to lock and alarm the car, and headed inside.

His hurry was only to get out of the unholy heat beating down on him between the blessed air-conditioned environments of his car and the shop.

What the store sold changed from week to week. This week, it displayed contraband novelty dog collars that brought in a fair amount of money as folk had become more conscious of the stray dog population in the city and started adopting them into their homes. Haddad moved past three young men who were purchasing a handful of collars and strode directly to the manager's office.

Of course, Khaled was already waiting for him. The smell of fresh coffee greeted his nostrils from the moment he stepped inside and the manager had two small cups already poured. He placed one on the table for Haddad and gestured for him to take it.

"Welcome back. I am pleased you were able to come at such short notice."

"Any excuse to drive the Jag." He sipped his coffee and smiled with satisfaction. It was strong and filled his mouth with the taste of spices, exactly the way he liked it.

"It is a gorgeous vehicle. Business does justify it, especially if your children do not need the money. I am sending mine to Oxford."

"My children are already educated and I needed a new car. The Jag was always a dream."

Khaled nodded and studied the car in the security camera footage. "We expect to make a great deal more, you know."

"I don't like our new arrangement," Haddad responded bluntly. "Having to 'borrow' an American scientist will bring us a little too much attention. Our business runs best when everyone continues to look the other way. If someone were to investigate, who knows what else might be uncovered."

"I can assure you that everything is under control. No cameras caught him leaving the base and no one saw him either. The most common assumption is that he changed his mind and joined a deep Zoo trip after all. That is according to my inside man, at least."

He shook his head. "It's too much of a risk. Allah punishes the greedy and what are we if not greedy?"

"Such actions are...regrettable," Khaled conceded and took another sip of the fine coffee. "But we will need the man now more than ever if we wish to increase the supply to make up for the shipment that was confiscated."

The man had a point. It wasn't greedy to avoid the kind of consequences that would come from the people who had lost the last shipment. It wasn't their fault, of course, but they agreed to replace the shipment for another payment and that meant taking risks—to save their own lives, most likely.

"We cannot simply release our researcher into the world once we are finished with him either," Haddad whispered and tugged his thick beard gently.

"We live in what is now the most dangerous location in the world. An accident where nothing but the man's dog tags are recovered by a patrol will not be difficult to arrange. My camp at Wall Two in the Saharan Coalition sector will be the best place to arrange it. Too many different African governments are arguing about who is building the fucking wall correctly to pay attention to the camps around it as long as large problems do not occur."

"Your merc business running into the Zoo was an ingenious idea, I will admit."

"And you thought that would be too much of a risk as well. Now, it is one of our largest money-makers and also a solution to most of our personnel problems."

Haddad took another sip of his coffee. "We must always consider the risks, my friend. It is why I alerted you that our contact in America is not the forgiving type and will not take kindly to those who fail him. Losing his business is the lightest of punishments we can expect."

"I never liked working with the fucking Chinese bastards. They are too crazy or hopped up on their own drugs. We would be better suited to simply stick to our business with the military bases. At least they are happy to look the other way as long as we keep their troops happy."

"Now who is afraid of taking risks?" Haddad asked.

Khaled scowled at him. "It is not fear. Those men are as unpredictable as the creatures in the Zoo and I would not do business with the jungle monsters."

Honestly, he couldn't disagree with that sentiment. "We are already committed. Withdrawing from the agreement now would only make things worse."

His companion knew he was right. Still, it was one thing to say it and another to contemplate what would happen if they pissed the triads off. He liked to think of himself as the big fish when it came to smuggling in Casablanca. He could even bring battle-hardened men into a fight if he needed to, along with Zoo-ready weapons and armor, but his organization was barely a speck compared to the international influence of the Chinese-organized crime syndicate.

"Poseidon has been compromised," he said finally to break the silence. "We will need to find new shipping lines to replace them."

"They were barely aware of what we used their ships for," Khaled replied. "There are more than enough replacements available. One only has to look carefully. There is always someone willing to do it for the right price."

"Or the right incentive," he agreed with a small smile. "I

think it might be time to call in a few favors and remind a few people what they owe me."

"Owe us."

"Yes, us."

"Are you still coming over for the weekend? My wife is already marinating the lamb."

"She will need to share that recipe someday."

Khaled laughed. "I have asked many times and she would not share it even with me. What makes you think she will give it to you?"

"I will have to be insistent. Or perhaps offer the right incentive."

"Good luck with that."

Concentration would never be an option in this situation. Vickie wasn't sure how she'd thought it possible with Niki pacing a rut into the hotel room floor.

Of course, she could always send the woman to her room or maybe out to help Bobby with the suit repair—she'd heard that the man had been pissed at the sheer amount of damage done to them—but that would leave her cousin out of her sight.

Honestly, she didn't trust her to not do something stupid, which meant that she had to remain in sight at all times. Niki was bound to make a bad mistake. She would decide to head out after Taylor or would pick a fight with the Pentagon. Or she would head to San Francisco and go on a killing spree among the local triad chapters.

Given the ex-agent's stressed condition, nothing was

off the table, which meant she needed to keep an eye on her and not because she couldn't be aware of what she was doing. If the truth be told, she could watch her almost anywhere she went and the woman knew that too. The problem was being able to stop her. It was best to head off any thought process that reared its ugly head in Niki's mind before it picked up steam and began to run people over.

She didn't doubt for one second that it might play out physically too.

"I will kill him," Niki whispered for the hundredth time. "I know I let him go and everything but I will seriously kill him."

"No, you won't."

The ex-agent stopped pacing and looked at Vickie, who was curled on her bed with her laptop displaying the different chunks of data she was mining from a variety of sources.

"What?"

"You'll jump his bones the second he touches down in the US again," the hacker said, her gaze fixed on the screen. "And when you're done making sure that neither of you can walk for another week, you'll yell at him, he'll stand patiently and take it, then hug you and make it all right."

Her cousin shook her head vehemently. "No, it's different this time. Besides, I'm not that predictable."

"Yeah, you are but it's not a bad thing. You guys are made for each other. You pull this kind of shit yourself and he does the same thing."

"He paces and threatens to kill me?"

Vickie paused and looked up from her screen. "He

generally repairs a suit or beats a punching bag or some-thing and he's much less aggressive about it. That could be because he takes it all out on those bags. Do you think you should try that? The hotel has a gym. I'm not sure if they have a boxing setup, though."

Niki sighed and dropped into one of the comfortable chairs in the room. "I don't know. Maybe but not now. I'll honestly put holes in any bag you set in front of me and maybe break my wrist too. It's better to wait until I have a second to take a deep breath."

"Suit yourself," the hacker replied. "It's for the best anyway. Ahlers is trying to make contact."

Niki bolted from her seat. "Put her through. About fucking time too."

The TV screen flickered on and the agent's face appeared. She looked her usual professional self but there were bags under her eyes and she had a few hairs out of place, which was unusual in and of itself.

"Banks, Madison, thanks for taking my call. I wanted to let you know that I have the info you sent to us on the Poseidon Shipping group. It's been mostly a dead end so far, but bang your head against a brick wall enough times and you're bound to break through eventually, right?"

Vickie chuckled. "I guess so. We'll keep digging on our end but it should probably be noted that the people who were running the smuggling operation know about the raid and are probably already working to cover their tracks."

"Yeah, you are right about that." Ahlers shook her head and looked angry. "You should know that the men who were arrested in the raid were killed while they were in prison."

"Killed?" Niki leaned forward. "I thought they were supposed to be protected."

"Sure, but they were in prison. According to the people in charge, the cameras were set to a loop and someone broke into the secure holding facility. By the time the hourly patrols came, they found all of them dead in their cells. Their tongues were cut out—while they were still alive, according to the medical examiner—and their throats were slit. Their deaths were no doubt ordered to stop anyone who might have considered talking their way out of a serious conviction."

"Fuck me," Niki whispered and shook her head slowly.

"Correctional services have already launched a full-scale investigation into who might have done it. Someone infiltrated their security systems to make it seem like nothing was wrong."

"Huge surprise," Vickie muttered aloud.

"I'm sorry?"

The hacker looked up from her computer screen, her eyes wide. She'd said that part aloud, apparently.

"I only mean… Well, in perfect honesty, the correctional system relies on hardware and software that was outdated in the 2010s. Seriously, check their computers and I'll bet you they're still running Windows XP."

The DHS agent nodded. "Well, they're also looking into the possibility that it was an inside job. One of the guards might have been able to do it for them. Anyway, we'll look into that, but I thought you should know that we won't get much of anything from the people who were picked up, given that they are well and truly dead. I'll let you know when we know anything."

Niki remained silent and Vickie realized that being personable was down to her.

"Right. Thanks...thanks for letting us know. We'll be in touch if we find anything."

Ahlers nodded and ended the connection.

The young hacker turned to focus on her companion, who looked like she was about to explode or start throwing things around. Her hands were clenched, and a big vein throbbed on her forehead.

"Niki—"

The woman pushed from her seat and strode to the door.

"Where are you going, Niki?"

"I'm going to punch something."

"So, you're going to the gym?"

"Nope, they only have...elliptical machines and tread-mills. I'll go to Bobby's, where they set that gym up for Taylor to train."

Vickie nodded. "You know that if you try anything, I'll be here to stop you."

"I know. You're my all-powerful cousin who's only looking out for me. I'll be back...fuck, around dinnertime, I think."

The door slammed shut and the hacker shook her head and drew a deep breath before she picked her phone up and selected one of her most used quick dials.

"Thanks for calling—"

"Hey, Eliza, it's Vickie. Is Bobby there?"

"Oh...hi, Vickie. Yeah, give me a second."

"I'm sorry for being curt but it's kind of an emergency."

"No problem."

The line beeped quickly and she was transferred to Bobby. She would have called him directly on his cell, but he didn't like working with it close to him while he was in the middle of repairing suits, so it was always more reliable to reach him through Eliza.

Almost a minute later, the line connected again.

"Hey, Vicks, how's it going?" Bobby said immediately. "Els says that there's a problem."

"Uh-huh. You have a problem coming your way." Vickie stood and began to pace around her bed. "Niki's in the mood to kill something and she's decided to go there. She says she aims to give those punching bags you and Tay-Tay set up a good beating."

"It sounds like a fun time for everyone."

"Right. But I know she and Eliza don't exactly see eye to eye yet and knowing my cousin as I do, all I can say is that she's out for blood. With a single look she thinks is wrong, you'll have a fight on your hands. My suggestion is that you send Eliza out for the day to make sure that nothing goes wrong."

The mechanic sighed. "Okay. Yeah, I'll think of something. Thanks for the heads-up, Vicks. Have you had any word on our friend the ginger?"

"He touched down at the US base and got himself into a fight."

"Business as usual, then?"

"Something like that. I'll let you know when I hear more."

The line cut out and she placed her phone on the

bedside table, sat cross-legged on the bed, and focused on the laptop screen. She grimaced in frustration because she did not intend to run anything on a hotel network.

"Do you have something on your mind?" Desk asked over the TV speakers.

Vickie shook her head and drew a deep breath. "I'm supposed to be the irresponsible kid here and I have to keep tabs on the two of them like I'm the fucking parent. All the while, people expect me to crack the case or something. Admittedly with your help, but still."

"I'm sorry. I wish I could do more to help."

"You're stuck in a server in DC and you're already doing enough trying to keep Taylor alive."

"You should keep in mind that this is probably the first time that Niki has felt so vulnerable. She's always been in a position to keep the people she loves safe, including you. She took you to Taylor to keep you safe, if you recall, but he is now in a position where she can't help him and he likely wouldn't be able to help himself if something goes wrong. All this is only her reaction to her lack of control because she cares so damn much about all of you."

"I know, I know." The hacker ran her hand over her face. "If I'm honest, I'm worried about Taylor too, but I know I can control it. Niki? Not so much. She has a history of losing her fucking shit when pushed beyond her limits. It's like living with a motherfucking powder keg."

"All I can do is double down on my efforts to dig up everything I can and will make sure all our teams are working with the best possible intelligence. Unfortunately, we have to continue to dig until we find a lead."

That was a good way to keep her mind busy. Niki liked

hitting and shooting stuff when she was worried about something she had no control over. Vickie liked to keep her eyes on the programs she had running—altering them when needed—which allowed her to calm and stay focused.

Taylor was more like Niki in that he liked to punch things. Perhaps that was what made them such a good couple.

She picked a slice of cold pizza up and chewed thoughtfully on it while she watched the data mining run its search. Impatience scratched at her and she scowled. There had to be a faster way to do this.

The pizza was now finished and she attacked a bag of chips from the minibar next. She would have to call room service if this kind of delay continued to vex her.

Suddenly, the TV lit up, which was what happened when Desk had something to say. There were no other loudspeakers in the room.

"I think I have something that'll make you feel much better," the AI announced and pulled the data up on the screen.

Vickie didn't know where her connection to the TV came from. Probably the room's Wi-Fi but she honestly didn't care.

"This…does put a smile on my face."

"Does it? No cameras in the room are directed toward your face."

"It's a saying. Never mind."

CHAPTER EIGHT

He'd liked many things about living on the military base. There was a reason, after all, that he'd stuck around for so long, even if he had to strain his brain to remember what they were.

Driving around in Hammerheads was not among them.

Taylor remembered them being the kind of vehicle that could travel over almost any kind of terrain. The talk was that there were efforts to make them amphibious as well, but when it came out that the vehicles were too heavy to float, the next idea was to make them waterproof and capable of running underwater.

Marines went crazy at the idea.

But no matter how rugged the outside was, the inside still revealed that it was a military vehicle made by the lowest bidder. Everything was as cheap as it could be without being completely unusable, and it became worse the longer the vehicle was in the field. By the time it was sold second-hand, the buyers needed to drop extra money to refurbish almost everything before they could use it properly.

Freddie didn't look like he was concerned about it, though. Taylor was a little jet-lagged and he had been in a foul mood when he woke early in the morning. Perhaps he was getting a little too soft living in the US. He would all but murder to get Liz out there instead of the bumpy, jolting ride in the Hammerhead.

His companion looked at him and laughed. "I told you to take the coffee when it was offered. They don't generally have it to offer to people who are visiting the detention center."

"It's not...coffee." Taylor growled his irritation and rubbed his eyes. "Well, maybe a little. It's only the jet lag, is all. I'll be fine in a little while."

"I hope so."

The Hammerhead came to a jerked halt outside the detention center, and Taylor suddenly felt all the bruises that had been delivered to him the day before. They covered all kinds of painful but he had been in fights before. They never ended with him feeling quite so leveled the next day.

Or perhaps they had and he was a little too hopped up on adrenaline back then to give a shit.

He lifted his shirt and winced when he saw the bruises had begun to turn black around his ribs. Nothing was broken, thankfully, and nothing would require a trip to the doctor.

"Shit," Freddie muttered. "Did you have to let them beat you that badly?"

"Beat me?" He scowled. "There were seven of them and

I beat them. They merely got seven guys' worth of lucky shots in before I put them to bed. I even broke out a bedtime story for the motherfuckers."

The other man laughed. "If you say so, although I'm fairly sure you let all their talk about you being an old has-been get to you."

"Yep, then I beat them for it." He pulled the door to the detention building open and motioned for Freddie to enter. "Keep that in mind if you ever try to tease me. I'll be a good sport about it for a while until I reach my breaking point, then I'll show you exactly how embarrassing it is to have your ass kicked by a has-been and hopefully, keep people thinking about how terrifying I was in my prime. It merely makes my legend that much more impressive."

They both moved forward where the sergeant in charge of the center was seated behind a desk, working on a veritable mountain of paperwork.

"Morning Jerry." Freddie settled into the seat across from the man. "Sorry…Sgt. Joy. You know, we call him Joystick because of the massive—"

"I get it," Taylor interrupted. "Morning, Sergeant. Sorry to be the first ones to demand your attention, but you have a detainee in here we'd like to have a word with."

The man nodded and turned to his computer. "What's the name?"

He glanced at Freddie with a small frown. "Did you happen to catch his name?"

His friend shook his head. "Nope. And he didn't offer one either as I recall."

"Well, fuck."

The soldier stared at him from dark eyes with not even

the faintest trace of expression on his young face. He seemed a little too settled for someone his age but then again, he also seemed a little young to be a sergeant.

"When was he brought in?" Joystick asked.

"Sometime yesterday afternoon."

"You'll have to be a little more specific."

"Oh, he would have come in looking like he had lost a fight," Freddie interjected. "He probably had a concussion too so there would have been calls for medical help."

"Good news," the sergeant muttered. "That does narrow it down."

"Awesome!" Freddie exclaimed.

"You do know how the good news, bad news situation works, right?" Taylor asked.

"Right." Joystick turned his screen so they could see it. "We had five detainees arrive yesterday afternoon but none of them needed medical attention or had a concussion."

"Are you sure?" Taylor asked.

"We would have to report it for liability purposes. Even if there was suspicion of previous injuries, we would want it all on the record to make sure no one can sue the military for injury while in custody."

Both men leaned closer to confirm that what the sergeant was telling them was the truth before they straightened and accepted what appeared to be the only logical explanation.

"Son of a bitch." Taylor growled in frustration and shook his head. "The asshole in uniform was an impostor."

"We could talk to the commandant to see if he has any record of the man who took them away. Or those you beat up. One of them might have made it to the medical section, right?"

"Oh, yeah, the guys who made a researcher vanish off of the face of the map will start making mistakes now and leave one of their people in a hospital to recover their senses long enough to have them smacked out again in an interrogation room."

Freddie raised an eyebrow. "I bet you feel good about that. Getting the sarcastic upper hand over an optimist."

Joystick sighed loudly. "Is there anything else I can help you guys with?"

"No," Taylor snapped.

"Then fuck off."

They complied without protest—not without the temptation to take their frustrations out on anyone stupid enough to get close—and headed out to the Hammerhead.

"Well, that was a big fat load of nothing," Freddie muttered. "What do you think we should do next?"

"We can talk to the commandant to see if he recognizes anyone we ran into yesterday, but my money is back at Mark's."

"I like the way you think. Get the brain juices flowing with a little morning drinking."

"Well, yes, there's that, but we can also talk to Mark to see if he knows who the idiots were. He is the guy who knows almost every face that comes into his bar, right?"

"See? The morning drinking is working already." Freddie climbed into the Hammerhead again. "And we haven't even started yet. I can't wait to see what kind of progress we make when we get down to it."

Taylor couldn't disagree. Aside from the fact that it was

five in the afternoon somewhere in the world, and if there was any location in which he had no issues with fucking over the rules of what people were expected to do, it was in the Zoo.

It was a quick drive and the two of them strode into the bar. He expected there to still be a few stragglers between those who were there from the night before and those who had come for the breakfast, but the pub was barely a quarter full when he moved into one of the booths in the back.

Mark wouldn't be at the bar this early since the man needed to sleep at some point during the day, but he would arrive eventually.

Freddie put their order in for the breakfast special and a couple of beers he brought to the booth.

"So, what are you thinking?" the mercenary asked as he sat opposite his friend.

"About how I'd prefer to have an Irish coffee instead of beer if I'm doing morning drinking?"

"I thought about it but decided that beers and regular coffee would do us some good. We need to be a little less sober to help the thinking process, not passing-out drunk."

The man made a solid point and Taylor took a sip from the cool, frothy beer.

"What do you think the chances of our missing soldiers still being alive are?" Taylor asked.

"Low," Freddie replied and confirmed his suspicions. "Whoever took Everett might need a researcher, which is why they would need to get him out of the base quickly and quietly. The group you put your fists through was likely merely a problem that had to be removed. They're going through a panther's digestive tract as we speak."

"Shit."

"Well, that's what they'll be eventually."

That teased a smirk onto Taylor's face, as did the smells wafting from the kitchen. "Which leaves us at square fucking one anyway."

"Honestly, this isn't much of a setback. I doubt the guys would have done much talking no matter what, so we would have wasted our time with them for a little while and then returned to searching."

"It still gives us somewhere to start." He took his phone from his pocket and noted the little symbol on the bottom that told him that Desk was listening in on the conversation.

She didn't need to alert him about what she was up to, of course, but it was nice of her to do so anyway. The AI had most likely already begun to comb through any security footage of all those involved in the fight—as well as the man who had whisked them away—to find out who they were and who they'd been in contact with. No one could discount the very real possibility that they knew what had happened to Everett.

"What are you thinking?"

"Well, if Mark knows who the team was, we'll have names and we'll be able to check their communications and determine how they knew about the missing researcher. And if we're very lucky, he'll know the guy who took them away and we can do the same about him. But we need to stay busy, which means finding out exactly who the fuck might be able to help us around here even if we do discover where Everett's gone."

Two platters were being carried out of the kitchen with a stack of pancakes, hash browns, scrambled eggs, and a pile of bacon on each one. Logic suggested that they were probably platters meant for two, but Freddie had gone ahead and ordered two for them anyway.

It was a sensible choice. It had been a while since Taylor had sat down to a solid meal and it was about time to fix that.

Neither man said anything as they attacked the stack of pancakes first.

"Do you have any ideas?" Freddie asked finally when they were finished and he began alternating bites with the hash browns and bacon.

"There's a guy out here—as nuts as all fuck but he has a mind for the Zoo unlike anyone I've ever met."

"You mean Salinger Jacobs, don't you?"

"I didn't mask it all that well, did I?"

The other man shook his head. "Not many people have a read on the fucking place like he does. I had thought about bringing him in too, but I was worried about keeping the investigation quiet, which meant bringing in only people I trust. I know people like Jacobs, but I don't necessarily trust him."

"You remember Davis, right?" Taylor asked around a mouthful of the mound of fluffy scrambled eggs.

"Yeah, of course."

"He trusts the crazy little fucker and that's even after he lost his leg. I don't know about you, but that's all I need to be able to trust him myself."

"Suit yourself. Do you want to give him a call?"

Taylor nodded, stood from the booth, and moved away. He already felt a little sluggish. It would pass, of course, especially once the coffee kicked in. For now, he would need to keep moving or it would force him into a nap that would waste even more time that they didn't have.

He stepped out of the bar and walked to where he was sure no one would be able to listen in before he punched the number into his phone and waited for Sal to answer.

The line connected for a second and clicked a few times before it rang again. He assumed that was the work of the man's AI and tech expert securing the call. It was a new number, after all.

"Hey, McFadden," the researcher said finally. "Have I heard right? Anja says you're calling from the US base."

"That is correct. I came here looking for someone."

"You know you can simply call me if you need me, right? There's no need to come all the way to the Zoo simply to woo me, although you can go ahead and color me flattered if you like."

"It's nothing like that," Taylor interjected before the kid could continue. "Not that it would be a terrible thing to see you again in person, but I came out here looking for one of your fellow researchers who has gone missing. It would seem that it's something of a touchy subject around here and has already started a couple of waves, so I thought it would be a good idea to get an expert involved."

"And you thought of me. Again, I'm super flattered."

Taylor smirked. "Are you available for some work? It would have to be a little quieter than you're generally used to."

"We're on a little downtime from our last Zoo trip, so it's doable."

"So…resting?"

"Everyone else is resting. I'm desperate for something to do. Spill the deets, my man."

"Oh. Okay, well, Jian Everett has gone missing. As in dropped off the face of the earth missing. Almost everyone else is content to assume that he's gone on a deep dive, but others say he had no trips planned and didn't have the inclination to head in on a whim, so I've been looking around. Unfortunately, I've hit a dead-end information-wise."

"Hmm. Okay, I can put some feelers out to see if Jian is with any of the teams in there or if he pops up anywhere on the radar."

"I had another…small thing I wanted to ask you about."

"Oh?"

He sighed and rubbed his temples before he continued carefully. "Have you picked up on anything weird?"

"Weird? In the Zoo?"

"I know how that sounds, but if anyone would know weird by Zoo standards, it would be you. We've had contact with a smuggling ring in the States that brings Zoo material in, and the last raid netted carefully packed horns—think rhino horns but smaller. These were tested and came back as absolutely directly out of the Zoo, but I don't remember any creatures like rhinos. I think Niki can get you the test results if you have a mind to look at them yourself."

"Unless there's a rogue facility growing animals and plants like that lab we raided off the coast, right?"

"Exactly, that's what I worry about most."

Sal was silent for a moment before he spoke, his tone both wary and curious. "Horns?"

"Like…uh, smaller rhino horns. Have you seen any critters like that in the Zoo? Because I can't remember anything like that myself, although it's been a while and it's entirely possible that a new species has mutated."

"Nothing that I can think of. And I'm checking the database that we have on known Zoo animals… Nope, there's nothing here either. How many horns?"

"About twenty of them, more or less."

"Shit. There are those huge gorilla creatures with the horns, of course, but they're…big."

"Yeah," Taylor agreed. "And I'd like to meet the team that can kill twenty of them in quick enough succession that they were able to ship the horns off in a smuggling operation like that."

"I wouldn't."

He thought about it for a second and nodded. "Yeah, yeah, good point. It could have been taken from non-adults, but any offspring are seldom seen and don't do any attacking, so that's even more unlikely. I don't think anyone's ever recorded a sighting of the young for those creatures, honestly. The most prevalent thought is that most of the larger monsters rear their young closer to ground zero than any trip has ever gone. At least since the Zoo exploded outward."

"And there's another problem."

"I know." He shook his head. "The Zoo shit being exported is put through exhaustive containment measures to make it somewhat safe to be tested and is constantly controlled and monitored to make sure nothing bad comes into contact with the goop. The smugglers don't apply even close to that kind of security."

"Right. They're dripping with goop and going on a world tour."

"So, back on topic. How likely is it that Everett's disappearance is a coincidence?"

Sal laughed but there was surprisingly little humor in the sound. "A zoologist with a specialty in genetic mutations disappearing when we're looking at what might be an engineered species? I doubt it. The two are connected. I'm ninety percent sure of it."

"And that's enough for me."

The grin refused to leave but Vickie put little effort into getting rid of it as she scrolled through the data on her screen.

It was always a breathless feeling to find the first thread for her to start tugging at. Perhaps it would be more gratifying to set up the metaphorical clothes before she began unraveling, but it implied a hint of sadistic pleasure to tear someone's hard work apart.

The truth of that made the grin feel that much more inappropriate. And that much sweeter.

"You know, Desk, there's something I've wanted to say in all my years as a hacker," she announced and leaned against the stack of pillows that made working from her bed a little easier. "You know, with an audience and honestly, I'd be a little embarrassed saying it in front of an audience of humans, so having you around is kind of fortuitous."

"Is it 'I'm in?'" the AI asked. "That is what all film hackers say when they…well, are in."

"I say that all the time. In my head, anyway. No, the line is, 'I've just cracked this case wide open.'"

Desk was silent for almost a full minute.

"What?" Vickie asked.

"I was waiting for you to say it."

"I did."

"Interesting. But yes, I can see why you would want to avoid saying it among other humans."

"Yeah, I know." Vickie paused, narrowing her eyes. "Wait, why?"

"Because I was the one to crack the case wide open."

"Fair."

Vickie looked up from her screen when the door to the outside lobby clicked open. She had left the door to her bedroom open wide enough for her to see Niki standing in the doorway, her hand raised and a confused expression on her face.

"I was about to knock," the former agent explained and scowled at her hand before she lowered it quickly.

"And now you don't have to," Vickie pointed out, the grin still splashed across her face as she waved her into the room.

Niki closed the door behind her and advanced toward the bedroom. "I hope that look means you guys have something that will brighten my day a little."

"Did trashing punching bags not help at all?"

"It did, but then Bobby said that I had to help him repair

the holes Taylor and I made in the suits which was a massive bummer. So my mood has improved but only slightly."

"I think we have found what's needed to increase the margin," Desk announced and called the image from Vickie's computer screen to the TV.

"Does that mean you've found something?"

Vickie tilted her head. "I don't know if it'll break anything wide open but it's a fucking start."

"I'll take it. What are we looking at?"

Desk adjusted the layout of the data for Niki's benefit. "I've tracked all the known smuggling routes in northern Africa and learned that Agadir, which has only a small container terminal, has been flagged a number of times as a likely candidate for the beginning of those shipping lanes. Over a convoluted series of misdirection attempts, I managed to identify a vessel, the *Fajar Mushriq*—"

"It means Bright Dawn," Vickie interjected.

The AI paused for a moment before she continued. "Yes. Anyway, the *Fajar Mushriq* was docked in Casablanca at the same time as the *Poseidon Alexis*—which, as you know is the ship that brought the heroin shipment. The financials of a small Agadir-based company revealed evidence of a substantial series of payments from none other than the Poseidon Shipping Group. Again, it is a convoluted journey through dead ends, shell companies, and dummy corporations, but there is a definitive connection."

Niki tilted her head in thought and rubbed her chin gently. "I can tell you right now that no judge in the world would approve a warrant—arrest or otherwise—based on that information. How does this help us?"

"All we need is a good start," Vickie pointed out. "On its own, this is merely a collection of paperwork that would put an insomniac to sleep, but when we started to dig through history, it became more interesting. About five years ago, the Poseidon Shipping Group was on the verge of bankruptcy. They received a last-minute bail-out from an obscure Chinese export company—Han Lo Exports— which was then bought out by a company in San Francisco called the Great Eastern Traders Inc. It's extremely interesting because from their tax records—which are all public record—they are a small company that is perfectly squeaky clean."

"Again, how does this help us?"

"Okay. First, you need to learn a little patience." Vickie all but growled in annoyance.

"That's what Bobby said."

"After you put holes in his punching bags?"

"Yeah."

"And how did that go over?"

"Not well."

"Wait, not well for you or for him?"

The woman paused, her expression thoughtful. "Both."

"I think we should continue with the presentation," Desk interjected. "I put considerable work into making it a comprehensive slideshow."

"And we all appreciate that," Niki said and shook her head. "But I'm simply sitting here with my thumb up my ass while Taylor could be dead or dying out there."

"Have you called him?" Vickie asked.

"What?"

"Have you called him? Made sure that he's not dead or dying."

"Well…no, I haven't," Niki admitted. "I don't want to be a nagging girlfriend."

The hacker snorted loudly and it sounded like Desk was laughing as well, although Vickie couldn't be sure.

"Then again," the ex-agent continued, "if I call him to share what little we've managed to find on our side of the investigation, I'll have an excuse to give him a call and hear his voice, at least."

"That sounds good to me," Vickie answered, and Niki made her way out of the room to make the call.

"Do you think I'll end up being like that?" the hacker asked and leaned against her pillows. "It's weird. Niki is a secure woman with all the confidence in the world, but seeing her with this level of anxiety over Taylor… I'm worried about the guy too, but…"

"But what?"

"Nothing. I only wish I could do something to help Niki feel better, is all."

The call didn't last very long, and her cousin returned, still staring at the phone screen.

"He's doing okay," she announced and looked like she wanted to climb into the small device's screen. "And he's alive, which is all I can hope for, but he's doing about as well as we are with the investigation."

"There is something we can explore," Vickie said and tapped her screen thoughtfully. "But it would mean going to San Francisco ourselves."

"Who the fuck cares? Anything is better than sitting in this goddamn hotel room. What do you have?"

"I've looked into the crew members on the Alexis, and it seems one of them is a known triad member. He has three active arrest warrants in three different countries, and he's on the arrest on sight list at Interpol. From what I can see, he's a known member of the—holy shit, there's no way I will even try to pronounce that—but it means Brotherhood of Blood."

The hacker paused for a moment. "Honestly, I think it sounds like a golfing club, but that's only me. Better yet, our character did not report for duty when the ship was ready to sail out of the San Fran harbor. There is no sign of him on the ship, although none of his fellow crewmates made any attempt to contact the authorities to report a missing person."

Niki folded her arms and scowled deeply. "Let's get Ahlers on the horn to see if she knows anything about this Brotherhood of Blood golfing club."

The woman was quick to answer the call and wore the easily recognizable look of someone who hadn't left her desk in more than twelve hours.

"Yes, we've looked into the *Xiěyuán xiōngdì huì* here in San Fran," Ahlers confirmed once their progress had been explained. Her pronunciation was on point, which told Vickie that she had said it often over the past couple of days. "We're aware of their activity in the city but we haven't managed to find their local HQ yet. They keep it moving and there might be problems with a leak in the local DEA and FBI branches—which would explain how they've managed to stay a step ahead. It doesn't help that the people who are arrested end up dead with their tongues cut out."

"I have been able to connect with a possible location," Desk announced. "A large house in the outskirts of the city has enjoyed visits from numerous traveling businessmen. A considerable amount of money appears to be spent there, and the staff almost exclusively consists of young, attractive women who recently immigrated from China."

"So…a brothel, then?" Niki asked.

"Agreed." Ahlers nodded. "But that alone isn't enough to justify a warrant. If you want to head in there, you would be on your own with no local backup."

"But if there were to be a DHS drone in the area, we might be able to keep an eye on the situation," Desk suggested.

Vickie expected the DHS agent to shut them down outright, but Ahlers nodded.

"I think I can swing that. It might even be able to get close enough for you to have a peek into their systems without risking anyone on the ground. Would you need anything else?"

Niki was as surprised as her cousin by the offer, but she gave the question a little thought. "I'll probably need transportation for myself and my equipment if you can spare it."

"I'll be in contact with Madison to arrange that. What kind of equipment will you bring over?"

"A combat suit."

"The same that they use in the—"

"Yep."

"Right. I should have something arranged for you by tomorrow morning. Do you need anything else?"

"I…I don't think so."

"Excellent. I'll be in touch."

The connection was severed and Niki stared at the screen for a few seconds.

"Wow. Is it only me or are they a little desperate to get results out of this?" she asked and looked around the room.

"I'm making sure they don't change their minds about loaning you a jet," Vickie commented.

"What I wouldn't give for my own fucking jet right about now." She shook her head. "But I'll settle for a loaner. Which means I should get to packing, I guess. In the meantime…seriously, Vickie, clean this place up."

"What?" the hacker didn't look away from her screen. "I get the munchies when I'm working. You know this."

"Still, I haven't seen a mess like this outside a stoner's college dorm. How likely am I to find pot in your food?"

Her cousin raised an eyebrow. "Pot's been legal in the state of Nevada for over two decades, Niki. Get with the fucking program."

"Whatever. I'll see you in the morning."

CHAPTER NINE

"Do you think we're spending a little too much time at the bar?" Taylor asked.

Freddie looked up from his laptop screen. "Beg pardon?"

"I know this is the only place to socialize outside of the mess hall, but do you think we might be spending a little too much time here?"

His companion shook his head. "My team still has work to do, and I don't want them distracted with this whole investigation. Besides, Mark gave us the intel we were hoping for, and unless you want to go out to the gates and wait for our fuckers in the sun, this is the best location to find them before anyone else gets their hands on them."

The man made a solid point. Taylor had been in Vegas long enough to be used to the sun beating down on him through the day, but it was somehow more intense in the Sahara. He wasn't sure how that was possible but it was true. The heat was exhausting, like a hand pushing down on anyone who stood within range of its rays.

It was best to stay in the areas of the base that were air-conditioned.

"Two people disappearing from the base without a trace is concerning enough," Freddie continued. "I'm merely glad we've not seen an entire team poof into thin air. That would be an emergency."

"Two people is an emergency."

"Sure, but a whole team would require us getting in touch with the commandant to get him involved."

"And that's a bad thing?"

"The guy's dragged his heels through the process so far, and I don't want him to add his stupidity to the mix. We've gained a little traction here, so there will be time for us to make significant progress before he bogs us down in the rules and procedures."

Taylor nodded. "Why would they send the team out so quickly after coming back in?"

"From what I heard, they wanted to head out again but only for a day trip. They'll come in just before sunset and this will be their first stop to spend their earned money on a ton of booze."

"Do you think they'll try to cause more trouble?"

"Why?" Freddie asked. "Are you looking to get yourself into another fight?"

"I'll be honest, I don't think I'd survive another brawl with seven fuckers in the game. Well, I'd survive, but I'd probably have to put myself in the hospital after, and then we'd be fucked in finding Everett in time."

"Agreed."

"So, let's try to intimidate them into being talkative based on what I did to them the last time. They're still all beaten and coming off a trip into the Zoo, so my money is on them not in the mood to fight and simply wanting a quiet, celebratory drink after surviving the fucking place."

"Agreed." His friend nodded his head toward the door.

Taylor turned as a small group entering the bar. They were considerably quieter than they had been in the day before. The leader certainly didn't look like he wanted to start a fight and the others looked tired and still a little battered and bruised from the fight the day before.

It was enough to remind him that he probably looked equally as bad, and none of them looked like they were in the mood to get in any trouble. Perhaps this would work out after all.

After a short pause to finish his drink, he was the first one on his feet and walked casually to where the men had begun to settle around the bar and order a round of beers for themselves.

The leader was the first to see him and almost jumped from his seat in sudden consternation.

"Look, we're not here for any trouble," the man said quickly, and Taylor realized that he had their full attention. "We're here for a drink, nothing more."

He nodded and settled on the stool next to the man's seat. "I have no problem with that. Drink away. But I have a couple of questions for you idiots—the kind I seriously hope you can provide answers to."

They all exchanged a quick look and relaxed tentatively, although Taylor could feel all their gazes on him as he gestured to Mark to add another beer to his tab.

"Look, about yesterday…we were in a bad mood and looking for a fight. We do appreciate that you broke us up before we started anything serious. None of us want to be banned from Mark's, and none of us want to have to go all the way to the French base to have a drink, right?"

It was a good point, and Taylor nodded, took one of the beer mugs, and sipped before he turned to look at the man.

"You don't need to apologize for that," he answered smoothly with a small grin. "I was aching for a fight too, and you gave me…a number of good reasons. It was all in good fun, wouldn't you say?"

A hint of grumbling agreement issued from the group. No one would ever tell him that he was a poor winner.

"Truly?" the man asked, tilting his head.

"Well, you didn't do much in the fight, but the rest of your buddies put me through my paces and maybe showed that you might have had a point that I'm not as young as I used to be. But do remember that I trashed all eight of you in under a minute, so keep that in mind. Anyway, no, my questions have to do with the fact that one of your group is missing today. You were eight—yourself plus the seven I faced—and now you're down to seven. I've been looking for your missing teammate and I heard that he didn't go into the Zoo with you guys."

"Oh."

"Yeah. And I have it on good authority that he wasn't taken into custody or into any of the medical facilities on the base and amazingly, there are no cameras showing whether he's left the base entirely. Color me intrigued because I was under the impression that Harry Houdini died over a hundred years ago. That and the fact that he's the second guy who disappeared from the base makes both me and my friend here very intrigued."

The man nodded and glanced at Freddie, who stood back a little, still sipping a cool bottle of a German beer he'd specifically asked for.

"Right. Rick?" he said and looked at his teammates for confirmation. "Rick Benlin. That's the name he gave us. He's ex-army and worth having in a fight but not the friendliest sort. He didn't join us for roll-call so we went in short-handed and cut him out of the money he was making on the trip."

"You know," one of the others interrupted, "you might want to talk to Eddie Ransom. He's one of the gate guards. Scuttlebutt around here says he has no moral qualms about letting smugglers in and out of the base, usually in exchange for whiskey and not necessarily the good kind."

Taylor raised an eyebrow. "So…if there were people who wanted to get out of the base without being seen…"

"The smugglers have a deal with him."

"Right." He tipped his glass to empty the contents as quickly as he could before he thumped it onto the counter. "You guys have the tab, right?"

"Sure."

"Yeah."

"No problem. You have a good one."

Taylor stood and walked to where Freddie was standing.

"You heard all that?"

His friend nodded. "Rick Benlin and Eddie Ransom. I have bought some stuff that went through on his watch, so I know for a fact he's off-duty right now. More importantly, if he's not here at Mark's, I know where he likes to spend his time."

"What do you think? One for the road?"

Freddie finished his beer and set it down, then pointed at Mark and the group before they left.

"Nice of them to cover the tab for us, isn't it?" Taylor asked as he slid into the Hammerhead.

"I think they were afraid you'd throw them out again if they didn't come up with some kind of reparations for what happened yesterday."

They made a quick drive to one of the small prefab houses set in a row with hundreds of others, each completely indistinguishable from the next except for the numbers printed on the side.

Freddie entered first. The door was already open and he pushed through it. The smell of alcohol hit Taylor like a slap in the face but it was only a greeting card when compared to how the place looked.

"Shit," he muttered. "I'm sure we should call in a fumigation squad. Or maybe a Zoo troop to clear this dump."

"It's not a bad idea." Freddie covered his nose but continued into the room. "The guy's a notorious slob, even by civilian standards."

Taylor nodded at the couch, where a loud snort and snore announced where their quarry was situated.

After a moment of thought, he moved to the kitchen, poured water into one of the larger plastic jugs that were still clean—as far as he could tell—and moved to the couch. Without warning, he poured the contents onto the man's face.

"Son of a bitch!" Eddie roared and immediately sat bolt upright. He spluttered and fumbled for a weapon that wasn't there before he realized that two men were in the room with him.

"Morning, Eddie," Freddie said, his head tilted and his expression a little grim. "Well, it's evening, but I guess that doesn't matter to you, does it?"

The guard spat water out of his mouth. "What the fuck did you do that for?"

"We needed to talk to you," Taylor explained. "And neither one of us wanted to get in close enough to shake you awake."

"I ought to shoot you both. Breaking and entering is still a crime, even on a military base in the Sahara."

"The door was open," Freddie pointed out. "We merely came in to make sure that everyone was all right inside."

"We're still deciding if you were shot by intruders before we got here or stabbed," Taylor added cheerfully. "I'm reasonably sure a stabbing would have a little more dramatic flair. We'd probably have to stage a fight but that wouldn't change the aesthetic of this place at all much, would it?"

Eddie realized that both men were armed and not in the best of moods, and his expression smoothed quickly. It was easy to see that the man was nursing one hell of a hangover from the way his body sagged into the couch.

"I don't really have anything to say to you two," Eddie muttered and folded his arms in front of his chest in some attempt at a protest.

"I think we should simply shoot," Freddie commented. "Maybe we could nick him in the shoulder and make sure he can't make any more money. He probably wouldn't be able to take his shifts at the guard post for at least a month and by then, all his contacts will have found someone else to work through."

Taylor shook his head. "I was thinking...both kneecaps. He'll be in the hospital for a while and would probably be sent back to the States where we know veteran's insurance won't cover some very expensive knee-replacement surgery. The best-case scenario is that he'll be stuck in a wheelchair for a year and a half and have to go through physical therapy for at least another two years. On top of all that, he'll have a shit-ton of medical charges to contend with."

"Hmm, good thinking," he muttered, drew his sidearm, and checked to make sure there was a round in the chamber before he flicked the safety off. "So what? Do you want to take the left and I take the right?"

"Why don't you do both?"

"Well, I thought you might want in on some of the fun."

"I'm not that particular to doing the deed myself. Watching can be as much fun."

"Okay!" Eddie exclaimed. "Okay! I get the picture. You're both big, bad, and terrifying. Ask me whatever the fuck you want to know."

Freddie smirked but held his weapon firmly. "And they say torture doesn't work."

"It doesn't, not really," Taylor corrected him. "The threat of torture, though, is very effective and the threat of years of being an invalid and a mountain of debt is even worse."

"Right, whatever." His friend turned his attention to the gate guard. "A couple of people have gone missing from the base and we have it on good authority that it happened on your watch."

"What?" Eddie snapped. He tried to rise from his seat but was stopped by the barrel of Freddie's sidearm, which pushed him into his seat. "I take booze and cash to smuggle contraband to the soldiers around here, not fucking people."

"And let me guess, you did a thorough inspection of every shipment that came to and from the base to make sure that never happened?" Taylor asked with mock casualness.

"Well, not really, but—"

"Let's say last night," Taylor cut in. "Did any trips go out last night?"

"I...yeah, yeah. It was a paneled van that usually brings supplies for the base. They also often bring a few bits and pieces they want inspections to ignore, and they take guns and ammo from the second-hand shops that aren't supposed to leave."

"A paneled van?"

"A brown one driven by a couple of North African guys. I don't know names or where they're from, but they always have whiskey on them—good quality, too. I never ask what they bring in or take out. All the others let me look through their load and drop me whatever I think is fair for not reporting them. They don't even call and simply come when I'm on shift and hand my compensation to me without a quibble."

"Did they come through last week?" Freddie asked. "On Tuesday night?"

"I...yeah, they did. How'd you know?"

The guy was a criminal but not a mastermind. Taylor motioned for his companion to join him across the room.

"Do you think he knows anything else?" Taylor whispered. "He's a sleaze but not the brightest of the bunch. Of course, that's probably why he was targeted by our kidnappers since he doesn't care much about what is brought in and out."

"Are you seriously taking him at his word on this?" Freddie asked.

He gestured at their surroundings. "If there was anything here that would indicate that Edward is the kind of guy to do more work than is absolutely necessary, I say we keep asking him questions. Until then, we might as well take the knowledge we have and start working on it."

The other man studied their surroundings, his face contorted in thought—or maybe it was the smell that caused the reaction—before he gestured toward the door.

Taylor let him leave first but followed quickly and left the door open for Eddie to deal with before he checked his phone.

Desk, as he'd expected, had listened to every word and was hopefully already working on finding out exactly where their smugglers were but she was most likely already busy with something else. He wouldn't keep her if Vickie and Niki needed her services.

"Where do you think they took him?" Freddie asked once they were back at the bar. "Do you think they would take him into the Zoo?"

"The guys who make money smuggling? It's not likely. They'll take him somewhere else and a second group will take him to wherever they need him. Besides...did I tell you about the horns that were picked up in San Fran?"

"Sure."

"Jacobs believes that the horns being found and our man going missing might be related. He also mentioned—and I agree with him—that there might be an external source for the horns that they might need Everett's help with."

The two men slid out of the vehicle seconds after Freddie pulled up at the pub again. They entered quickly and found a table tucked into a quiet corner.

Mark approached their table and put down a couple of mugs. "I heard the boys you tackled talking yesterday. They complained about fighting happening around Wall One and about how the patrols would now take their chances with a shallow trip in for Pita flowers."

"Did they find any?" Freddie asked.

"They did, but not as many as they'd wanted."

"Because there are dozens and dozens of teams doing the shallow trips," Taylor clarified. "They're lucky to have found anything at all."

"Sure, sure," Freddie said. "But there isn't much fighting within earshot of a shallow trip," he pointed out. "Especially not near Wall Two. Most critters know not to approach unless they're in large numbers which they won't have so close to the border. So, unless someone tried to pull a plant out—which we can't rule out—something else is happening around Wall One."

"Do you think that's where we'll find Everett?" he asked as Mark wandered away to continue with his work of keeping all the patrons good and drunk.

"It's about as close to a lead as we'll get until your people come through," the other man muttered and shook his head. "Do you feel like a quick trip to Wall One to see what is most likely only a group of idiots who overreacted to a hungry panther?"

Taylor wouldn't admit that he had dreaded that question since he'd left the Zoo and started his new life. He took a deep breath and shrugged with as much nonchalance as he could muster.

"I came prepared," he replied gruffly. "Besides, the most logical assumption is that the source of the horns is somewhere in the Zoo. Since that's most likely where Everett would have been taken, we'll have to look there first."

"Where, though?"

"The Sahara Coalition sector would be the easiest route to take someone through against their will quickly and with little chance of being caught by any organized force. I hear they have camps popping up like zits in the region, and most of them have no official affiliation to any of the governments involved."

"That would be the place for private mercs to set up camp."

It had occurred to Taylor that he could simply spend a little money and send the private mercs out to look for Everett rather than go in himself but he was already committed.

Besides, although he couldn't explain it, something perverse in him wanted to be pitted against the real Zoo again. Perhaps it had something to do with half-believing what the dumbasses had been talking about him being a has-been.

He clenched his right hand as it began to shake and steeled himself to the idea again.

Freddie saw it too and a hint of guilt crept across the

man's face that made Taylor believe the insults a little more.

"I can call my team and take them out tomorrow, I think—or the day after at the latest," the merc said with a nod. "You could hold the fort down here and keep in touch with your team in the States. We can make it work."

Taylor shook his head. "Don't pull that bullshit on me. You need to keep your boots down until your business stands to make money from a trip into the Zoo. You can stay in touch with Niki and make sure she's not burning the whole country down."

The man smirked at that comment. "You can't go in alone. I know you're a badass but not that bad of an ass."

"Fair enough." He pushed from the seat and turned his attention to the rest of the bar. "All right, maggots, listen up!"

Most of the folks paused and looked at him, but a few others simply ignored him.

Taylor pounded his fist on the table. "I said listen up, shitheads!"

That caught their attention immediately.

"We have one of our own missing out there—maybe dead and maybe alive—and he needs our help. I have leads and I plan to follow them, but I can't do it alone. I need a team willing to head in with me, people who know the terrain."

"Everett's gone, man," one of the men at the bar responded impatiently. "Dead or soon to be dead in the Zoo. That's assuming he's even in there. If I were him, I'd be halfway to Thailand by now."

"'Besides, a small team going into the Zoo at this point means suicide, not a rescue mission," another agreed.

It looked like most of the room sided with the doubters and Taylor shook his head.

"Besides myself, I count five...no six with you, Carlos. Six motherfuckers in this room who would not be here if it hadn't been for Everett. And you know that he would have been one of the first to volunteer to find someone gone missing in there. I know you all remember the rescue effort that went into getting Jacobs out when he was nabbed by dumbasses on the French base, right?"

The group looked at one another, nodded slowly, and muttered among themselves.

"And there are more than five around here who would be dead and shat out of an acid-spitting lizard if I hadn't been there to help their asses," he continued. "Alone or not, I'm going in but I'd appreciate any help you can spare."

The patrons quieted. He made a strong point but he faced a room filled with people who rescued each other on a daily basis in the Zoo. The chances were that he wouldn't have been alive if it hadn't been for them too.

"How much will we get for the job?" Carlos called from his corner of the room.

"Ten grand each out of my pocket," Taylor snapped quickly. He'd expected the pragmatist to have a little more than helping others in mind. "Plus the profits of anything we pull out of there and the cost of suit repair for the damage it takes."

"I'm in." Carlos grunted and sipped his beer.

Most of the room made no effort to even meet Taylor's gaze but after a long moment, another four stepped forward. Two of them—Randy and Trevor—were both still enlisted but off-duty for the next few months, and the other two—Devon and Watt— were former military, with the latter having been in the British Royal Marines.

"Ten grand?" Devon asked. "That's paying a little too much for the rest of these suckers."

"It's a little too much for you too," he answered and shook the man's hand firmly. "But I'm desperate and you guys are broke so I'll take whatever help I can find."

They were all vets, the kind that were die-hard and very experienced instead of young and adventurous which Taylor had hoped would be the case. After all, they were right when they said that there was a high chance of things going badly, and he didn't want younger and less experienced men and women caught up in it.

The group assembled were more likely to be able to pull his ass out of the fire if it came down to that.

"The next round's on me," Taylor said and motioned to Mark.

CHAPTER TEN

Taylor's phobia of flying could be fully justified if it had started in planes like this.

The experience wasn't quite fear-inducing, but for a kid who had recently moved from his home and headed out to parts unknown to kill for his country, it must have introduced a couple of negative feelings that would have worsened over the years. She couldn't help but feel a little bad about all the teasing she'd directed at him over the phobia.

The aircraft was clearly not meant for civilian transport. A handful of seats had been installed into the side as something of an afterthought and their hasty inclusion showed. Ahlers hadn't put much thought into comfort during the flight to San Francisco. It seemed that all that mattered was that she got there.

"I could have taken Liz for a drive," she whispered as the plane began its descent. "We'd have made it here in about a day and then gotten to work. I swear, next time we get a huge pile of cash, I'll spend it on a private jet."

Although private jets were expensive. In her spare time,

Niki had seen that they could set her back as much as twenty million dollars for an actual jet, although smaller planes were a far more reasonable three million but weren't large enough to ferry the suits to where they were needed.

Leasing was also an option, but it was only a viable option if one of them had a pilot's license to fly the damn thing. Otherwise, they needed to hire a crew as well.

Which was an option, she conceded. But the idea of being able to fly them from place to place was appealing. Perhaps she would devote some time to getting a pilot's license.

She leaned against her seat and braced as the plane touched down. It moved far more quickly than the larger military cargo planes and in moments, she looked out into the city in the distance. She acknowledged that the flight had saved her almost six hours of travel as she headed to where a vehicle waited to transport her.

This was watched over by a couple of stone-faced agents. Both were tall and lean—probably ex-military— and looked like they were used as muscle for the missions that needed doors kicked in and criminals shot at. Their dark hair was cut to military standards and they looked about the same in every way, down to the cheap suits they wore.

The only difference was that one had a mustache and the other didn't. Niki had a feeling that she would mix their names up repeatedly.

"Agent Banks?" the mustached one asked.

She wasn't in the mood to correct them and shrugged instead.

"I'm Agent Miller and this is Agent Howieson. We'll escort you for the operation."

"Escort me?" she asked. "Do you mean babysit?"

"Escort," Howieson, the clean-shaven one corrected mildly. "An operation like this does have considerable confidential information attached to it and our job is to make sure that everything is as secure as it can be."

"So, babysitting." Niki shook her head. "I knew it was a little too good to be true. Well, I didn't but I should have known."

"Are you coming?"

She rolled her eyes and watched as the suit was loaded into the SUV they would be using. "I might as fucking well. Let's get this show on the road."

Before either of them could stop her, she climbed into the shotgun seat, which left Miller to take the back seat while Howieson drove them off of the base and down a narrow road toward the city.

"I'm not used to being the proverbial man in the van," Niki admitted to break the silence that had settled somewhat uncomfortably over the car. "I'm generally at the front lines but let me guess—you guys were told to keep me as far from the front lines as possible, right?"

"We're heading in to observe," Miller agreed.

"This is a fact-finding mission," Howieson continued. "We'll report everything we see at the brothel you found to HQ."

She rolled her eyes. Of course, Vickie and Desk would do a much better job of gathering all the intel that was required for the mission, which meant that her part of the job would be utterly moot and irrelevant.

It seemed like Ahlers was determined to keep her on the sidelines. The notion seemed a little baffling since she had been the one to bring her in on the operation. She wouldn't ask about what the whole idea was behind that and would simply find a way around the babysitting.

She knew a thing or two about that too.

The drive took them around the outskirts of the city and they then headed directly to where the brothel was supposed to operate from.

"Intel suggests that there will be a party happening in the house," Miller commented from the back, where he had activated a laptop and begun to review the operation detail. "Leaving aside the question of who would have a party in a brothel for the moment, we'll have to take a look at the guest list and—"

"Let me guess," Niki interrupted. "The guest list won't be available online."

"Well, I assume it is but not anywhere we'd be able to find it in time. Which means we need to get a comprehensive list of the people who were invited by taking photos of them when they arrive and trying to learn their names from that."

It was amazing that Ahlers had chosen what was probably the dullest task for her to do. Then again, she reasoned petulantly, perhaps not that crazy. Perhaps the woman had looked for the members of the team involved who had the dullest task so they could double as her babysitters.

"How do you know they don't have an underground parking lot?" she asked. "You know, the kind people might use to avoid being photographed entering a brothel."

"The local building code doesn't allow for underground parking lots," Miller explained. "Also, we picked up the blueprints for the building and there's no sign of any attempts to build one."

"Yeah, because who could accuse the local branch of the triads of breaking the building codes?" she snarked.

"You haven't been around this region much, have you?" Howieson asked.

"What's that supposed to mean?"

"The rich assholes who live in this area keep a closer eye on each other than the DHS does. Every other day, they file civil lawsuits against each other because someone's letting their grass grow too tall or the statues on someone's lawn are too garish."

"The most recent lawsuit was over someone trimming their hedges in an unauthorized shape," Miller added.

"Oh. Well, in that case, never mind."

The SUV came to a halt and Niki scrambled into the back, climbing over Miller to reach where her crate was set up. It contained her suit, of course, but there was the rest of the equipment that Vickie had wanted her to bring and she started to set it all up.

"Vickie, can you guys hear me?" she asked as she pressed a small earbud into place and tapped it lightly.

"Yes, and please don't be rough with the equipment," the hacker responded. "Desk already has control of the drone and she's closing on your location. You should get video…now."

Niki called up the alert that came on her computer and it displayed the feed from an airborne drone that made good progress. It was one of the new stealth models, fortunately—the kind that wouldn't be picked up on radars and wouldn't be seen unless it hovered directly above someone.

Another plus side was the fact that it wasn't armed. They didn't need to deal with giving Desk guns and missiles at this point.

"I'm approaching the brothel now," Desk announced. "Do we have a name for the operation?"

"What? A name for the operation?"

"I have a handful of witty brothel-based puns that we can use for the name of the operation."

She tilted her head and leaned closer to where Miller and Howieson had already begun to work through the guests who were arriving.

"Do you guys have a name for the operation?" she asked.

"Yeah." Miller checked his laptop. "Operation Sierra-Tango-seven-eight-three-six."

She paused before she shook her head and leaned back into her position in the back. "No, we do not have a name for the operation. What did you have in mind?"

"Operation Velvet Pearl."

After a moment to think about it, she shook her head. "Too vague."

"Operation Open d'Hore."

That did have a ring to it, and she looked at her two companions. "What do you think about Operation Open d'Hore?"

They nodded slowly but the former agent shook her head.

"It's good but I think we can do better. What else do you have?"

"Operation Layflower."

Her eyebrows raised and uttered a sharp laugh. "I think we have a winner."

"Which one?" Miller asked.

"Operation Layflower."

"Nice."

"Good work, Desk," Niki said. "What other ones did you have?"

"Operation Mark-her Garden, Tittles, Bare-her-bosa, Damn-that-ho."

"Layflower seems like the one to go with. All agreed."

Murmured agreement from the other two was all she needed and she refocused her attention on the feed as the drone moved closer and closer to the house. As expected, cars cruised in one by one like they were being timed. The security at the venue didn't allow anyone to wait for too long and the patrons were urged quickly into the house where a great deal of partying awaited them.

"This might be the most boring assignment we've ever had," Miller complained and stretched slowly. "No offense, Banks. You do make things a little more interesting than they would be otherwise."

"You're the one with control of the drone, right?" Howieson turned to address the question to Niki.

"A member of my team has that control, yeah."

"You don't think you could get us any visuals from inside the house, could you? As in a proper view of the action inside?"

"Let me get this straight." She sighed and rubbed her temples. "You want us to use the million-dollar military drone that the DHS loaned us for this operation to let you guys play peeping Tom at a Chinese fuck fest?"

"Well, if we have to babysit the fucking geeks on this we might as well get something out of it."

Vickie connected to the car's speakers and sighed loudly. "Sure, why not? We'll keep our little fly spy hovering so you can get your jollies. But don't blame me when the triads come looking for you—and I doubt they'll come with civil litigation for revenue lost."

"Yeah," Niki added. "I've heard they're more likely to hack your dick off and shove it down your throat to suffocate you. Then again, I can't say that I'd blame them."

"Chill out. We're all in this SUV together for a while and we're only getting to know each other."

"Yeah, well, I'd like to not learn any more about either of you," Vickie commented. "Why don't you guys go get a cup of coffee or something while we keep an eye on the new arrivals?"

Both men raised their hands and exited the vehicle quickly. Niki wondered if they were afraid that she would act on the threat she had put down for the triads, but it didn't much matter. Not having them lurking would probably help them.

"Vickie, are you collecting the data on the new arrivals?" Niki asked.

"Sure. I'm using a couple of the cameras around the outside to collect the data on faces, license plates, and all the other variables. And I'm working much faster than the DHS douchebags too."

"In the meantime, Desk, why don't you try to get connected to the house's comm system and give us an idea of what we're looking for and at. I assume there are no cameras inside."

"Nope," Vickie answered. "The interior is one big blind spot, but I think we can assume it's because they don't want anything that's happening inside to be filmed. I say we change that."

"You just attacked the two guys for suggesting exactly that."

"We wouldn't do it simply for viewing pleasure. You never know when you might need some decent blackmail material."

"We'll have to talk about you turning into a smooth criminal another time. For now, Desk, what kind of progress have we made?"

"The drone does have comm detection capabilities," the AI informed her. "But I will need to be a little closer."

"Close enough to give us problems?"

"Possibly. The stealth systems on the mechanical are good but it will be noticed if someone accidentally looks at it directly."

"Well… uh, do it very stealthily."

"Are you telling me how to pilot a stealth drone?"

"I'm only saying—"

"Do you want to pilot the stealth drone?"

Niki narrowed her eyes. "Come on. For fuck's sake, do your thing. I didn't mean any disrespect."

"Thank you," the AI replied and turned the drone in the heavier foliage around the area leading to the house.

"There is movement on the right," Niki warned and the spy came to a halt and inched slowly to the right to catch sight of a couple that walked through the thick bushes. The shrubs were most certainly not native to California and probably cost a fortune to maintain.

All so a guest and one of the staff could sneak out for a quickie in the open air.

"Let's keep things moving," Niki suggested finally. "I doubt they would hear the noise if you started launching missiles at the house."

"The drone cannot launch missiles," the AI said and sounded crestfallen.

"Yeah. It's a huge shame," Vickie interjected as their mechanical spy began to move again. "It's almost like we requested an unarmed drone or something."

Desk had no answer to that and she continued to ease the device through the gardens until they came within range of the house.

"Ah, interesting," the AI commented. "I am close enough and am pulling data from their servers."

"That's good news, right?"

"Unfortunately, there is bad news as well. It seems that my data mining has triggered a few security measures inside."

Niki raised an eyebrow. "Oh. So, they know you're there?"

"Yes."

"Shit."

She shook her head and focused on the camera feeds while Desk continued to pull the data from the servers as rapidly as she could. A group of men emerged from the house and looked at their phones.

"Desk…" Niki warned.

"A few more seconds," the AI replied.

"We don't have a few seconds. Get the goddammed drone out of there!"

It veered as if to comply with her order but the imaging suddenly cut out and from her position in the vehicle, Niki saw the device in the distance as it plummeted, still burning after a small explosion.

"Son of a bitch!" she snapped.

"What's the matter?" Miller asked as he climbed into the car with a coffee in hand.

"The goddamn asshole bastards shot the fucking drone!"

"Oh…fuck." Miller glanced at Howieson who had frozen halfway into his seat. That's… Damn, Ahlers will be pissed. Fucking over-the-top pissed off."

"And she'll find a way to blame us for it too," his partner complained and shook his head.

"Ahlers is the least of your worries," Niki interjected before they could continue their train of thought. "If someone in the brothel picked up on the signal coming away from the drone, they might be able to trace where it came from. I don't want to tell you two dumb fucks how to do your jobs but this is the point where you'll want to check your weapons instead of crying over a wrecked drone."

"Right." Miller hauled a duffel bag from under the back seat and began to remove their weapons.

"With the drone destroyed, I doubt they would be able to trace our location," Desk announced over the car's speakers. "But they might be able to trace the signal of the download I barely managed to complete but wasn't able to seal off before they wrecked the thing."

"So…keep checking weapons, then?" Miller asked.

"As a last resort, sure," the AI replied.

"Shit," Vickie hissed over the line. "They're working faster than I thought they would."

"How fast did you think they would be?" Niki pulled her laptop up—as if there were anything she could do to help, she snarked to herself.

"Not as fast as this." The young hacker's voice was strained. "They picked up on the download. I'm trying to overload their trace with garbage signals."

"I think I can amplify those," Desk told her. "Keep them working."

"There are more than one of them, I'm sure of it."

The two specialists were talking like Niki and the slow-poke twins were able to follow what they were discussing.

"What's holding you up?" the ex-agent asked and pulled herself closer to the computer screen.

"We're not finished downloading the data we pulled," Desk explained for their benefit. "While it is downloading, there is an open channel for our hunters to keep track of us."

"Stop explaining it for the muggles and keep working!" Vickie shouted.

"Muggles?" Miller asked and looked at Niki.

"Yeah," she explained. "Come on, man. Harry Potter is a cultural landmark at this point. If you're ignorant of it, that's your damn fault."

"No, I get the reference, but I don't understand why we're the muggles."

"I guess it's because we don't understand any of what they're doing, and all we can do is quietly hope that they'll be successful." Howieson sounded uncertain and shrugged as if to say that was the best he could come up with.

"We…okay, that's a good point."

Niki rolled her eyes. "Operation Layflower is off to a fantastic start, isn't it?"

"We did manage to acquire a treasure trove of information on the local triads the likes of which we've never seen," Desk pointed out. "That was worth a little risk."

"Do you know how much that drone cost?"

"Four million, seven hundred and thirteen thousand," the AI answered promptly.

Nicki raised her eyebrows and looked at the two men in the front. "Do you guys know if that's right?"

"It sounds right to me," Howieson confirmed.

"Yeah, about on point," Miller agreed.

Desk had nothing to say about that and suddenly, Vickie yelled over the speakers.

"I have the data. Shut the connection down!"

"Done," Desk announced. "But I cannot guarantee that they were unable to triangulate your location. I suggest haste in leaving the area."

Niki nodded and looked away from her laptop screen. "Howitzer—"

"Howieson."

"Howitzer," she snapped," get us the fuck out of here."

"We need to confirm this with Ahlers first," Miller pointed out. "She'll want to know how the operation is going."

"Fuck that!" Niki snapped. "If you don't get us moving now, I will push both of you out of this fucking car, drive away, and leave you motherfuckers to walk. Let's fucking go!"

Already, the guards who had destroyed the drone had

begun to sprint from the house on a direct trajectory toward them. More importantly, she felt, was the fact that a couple of cars roared down the driveway of the house and would be on the road and in pursuit in a matter of seconds.

The two agents she was with were probably not the brightest of all time but they did recognize the danger they were in. Howieson started the car without further protest and pulled out from where they'd parked before he swung to return the way they'd come.

Niki knew that moving at that point was merely advertising their location, but the chances were that it was already thoroughly compromised and wouldn't end well for them either way. An additional problem was that it was already not the fastest of SUVs and they were driving with a half-ton of suit in the back. Niki scowled and held on for dear life.

"Of all the things I thought I would do today," Niki quipped, more to herself than anyone else, "being chased by Chinese organized crime out of a whorehouse was not among them. Not even in the top ten."

CHAPTER ELEVEN

Utter, unmitigated chaos was the summation used to summon him to the brothel where they had anticipated a pleasant weekend profit from their regular clients. Things were supposed to be quiet. He'd sent some of their best security managers to make sure there were no hiccups, and if there were, they would deal with them quickly, quietly, and professionally.

The three words were certainly those Zi Shou did not want to hear when he was supposed to be focused on another matter entirely. But no, of course things couldn't go smoothly. When it rained, it poured as the Americans liked to say, and he was expected to roll with the punches. It was why he was paid the big bucks.

He was spending too much time with the locals, he decided, a little irritated that he had begun to pick up all their idioms.

The Executioner pulled his car up at the entrance and didn't bother to lock it again. The guards he had sent raced about like flies with no real purpose to their movement aside from the need to look busy in the presence of their superior.

From what he'd heard, the people who had perpetrated the break-in were already beating a hasty retreat with a few cars in hot pursuit. He would need to call the cars back. There was no need to make things messy and involve the cops. That would merely make an already bad situation even worse.

His first task on-site was to approach the place where a small group of his men was gathered to inspect the drone that had been shot down. He'd been warned that was the case and all he could do was shake his head when he saw the full extent of the damage.

"Could you not have left the device even a little intact?" he asked and caught all three men by surprise as he dropped onto his haunches. It was high tech, without a doubt—a little more advanced than was generally available to the FBI and local police forces, which was worrying. Either the task forces had been given larger budgets or new and therefore unknown players were involved.

Both possibilities indicated that they were on the receiving end of way too much attention.

"We couldn't leave it there," one of the men answered nervously. "It might have started fighting back."

Zi Shou looked at the man and then at the very clearly unarmed stealth drone. "With what? It's rotors?"

"We couldn't see that it was unarmed. Fuck, we couldn't even see it properly while it was in the air. It has all that advanced stealth crap on it that's supposed to make it hard to see."

The man made a fair point, but the Executioner still demanded better judgment from the men who were taking his money. They were supposed to be professionals, the kind who thought before squeezing a trigger. Then again, even semi-professionals were difficult to find among those available to be recruited by the triads, and he had to make do with some less than qualified individuals.

"Well, it's no use to us out here. Check it and see if anything can be learned from the innards. If we cannot track it, we might be able to find out who bought and developed it."

Again, he felt as though this was the type of thing he shouldn't need to tell them to do. He tried to encourage creative thinking in his people, but so many had been brought up in an environment of fear and when in stressful situations, they reverted to form a little too quickly and easily.

They did hasten to comply after he suggested it, though, collected the remains of the drone carefully, and carried it inside. The Executioner made a slow scrutiny of the surroundings to confirm that his men had begun more methodical and organized searches—not that they'd find anything, of course, but it had to be done. He turned toward the building and moved inside as well.

The clientele within were leaving. A few had already called their cars and seemed eager enough to leave to wait on the wide driveway. Zi Shou had expected as much. They didn't want to be hauled into a police station with hundreds of cameras clicking pictures of their faces, and with the shots fired, it was always possible that the police would be involved.

Others were still inside, in various stages of undress. They continually asked what was happening as the staff tried to keep them calm and sedated or brought them more drinks or drugs. Or both. Zi Shou had learned the lesson that it was always better to charge them for it after the fact since none of these characters wanted charges for cocaine, weed, and kinky sex to show up on their credit card charges, which was what would happen if the invoices were allowed to be transferred to a collection agency.

The drugs and the sex had been legalized years before, so there were no legal problems, but there was still significant stigma attached to the industry that he had learned to exploit to make sure they got what they were due, no matter the circumstances.

He weaved through the lower level, his gaze down and posture inconspicuous, not wanting to give anyone the impression that he was in charge of the establishment. That would lead to questions and harassment that he preferred to avoid. Instead, he was allowed to proceed directly to the server room.

The three men inside didn't notice that he'd walked in, as intent as they were on getting to the bottom of what had happened to their computer systems.

"What is the damage?" Zi Shou asked and folded his arms.

All three jumped when they heard his voice, spun to look at him, and seemed to be only a glance away from running for their lives. Of course, there was only one door in and out of the room and he stood in front of it. If it turned out that he had to kill them, their trying to escape would make things a little easier.

"The…the damage." One of the men managed to calm his nerves somewhat and looked at the screen. "They emptied our servers, so there's no telling what they might have now. From what we can tell, they had access to almost everything and they got through it all before someone shot the drone and cut our access to what they were doing."

"So, we can assume that—"

"They have all our data, yes."

Zi Shou stroked his chin and tugged the goatee he was trying to grow out. "Am I to understand that you were unable to find out who attacked us?"

"Not…not really, no. The drone did have a signature, then it was bounced off of another signal close by, and another in Los Angeles, followed by Alaska and that was when the drone was annihilated and we lost our connection."

They expected him to lose his temper, throw things around, and make sure they knew that they were the ones to blame. Instead, Zi Shou restrained himself quietly as he inspected what he was looking at on the screens. Possibly unlike most of his superiors, he knew a thing or two about software engineering and for someone to so thoroughly infiltrate their system and escape without being caught was impressive.

That required serious work—and serious skill, if he was honest. Not many would think that the triads would put too much effort into their technical divisions, but there was considerable software involved in how their operations worked and they had people who understood them in positions of power. He was only the beginning of a new generation in the triads.

It was unfortunate, then, that he would be the last one too. The chances were that someone would decide that he was the one to blame for the problems and put someone else in his place.

They would fail as well and die, and the useless deaths would continue until someone came along who was lucky enough to fix a problem they had almost no previous knowledge of.

He tugged his beard gently again and shook his head. The men were already a little skittish around him and he didn't want to unsettle them further.

Perhaps it would be best if he simply cut his losses now. He had enough cash safely stashed separately from the triads to enable himself to disappear. A slow boat back to China wouldn't be much better than merely hiding in the US. They had as much influence there as they did here.

Perhaps he could find a safe location in South America. Europe had a couple of areas that were a little too full of local organized crime for the triads to ever get any kind of a foothold so Italy seemed rather like a prime country to retire in.

But that was already three or four steps ahead. Lu Wan was already pissed and there would be no point in pissing him off further, not if it could be avoided.

"Call me if you find anything," Zi Shou said and bowed his head slightly before he turned to the door and closed it quietly behind him. He could almost hear the collective sigh from the group inside when he left.

It was now time to return to work and to keep himself either in business or alive. One or the other would have to work out eventually.

At this point in his life, Mark felt like he was at something of a crossroads. He made considerable money running a bar in the US base. It was the only one on the base so there was no competition, not unless people wanted to head out to one of the other bases.

Still, he tried not to make people's lives difficult. Prices were kept as low as he could manage. There was no need to gouge the guys too much with his pricing, but it was still expensive to import all the food and booze. Still, not many people complained about it, not once they saw the prices on the French base.

One of the bartenders was taking the bulk of the orders, which left Mark to clean up and make sure all the ordering was in shape. People were keeping to themselves, especially after he'd needed to throw a couple of them out for starting a fight.

Even when Taylor wasn't around, the guy somehow managed to start fights. Still, Mark managed to set up a betting pool that made sure that everyone resolved things properly.

He waved Alex Diggs over to the bar when the man entered and poured a couple of fingers of his best scotch into a glass for him.

"I appreciate the help," Mark said as he pushed the glass closer. "I'll have to hire full-time bouncers at this rate."

"But then the added expenses will push prices up and the people won't have that." Diggs downed the scotch in a single gulp. "Rather let the people who like to drink in peace around here do the peacekeeping."

"What if no one's around who wants to keep the peace?"

The soldier paused and nodded. "Right. So yeah, maybe get yourself a bouncer."

"I'll look into it." Mark poured the man another drink but charged him for it this time. "What do you think Taylor's odds are of making it out of the Zoo alive?"

"I'm not a betting man," Diggs answered.

"You were when you bet that Sal Jacobs would still be alive when he was kidnapped."

"True. Like Sal, I'd say Taylor has every chance in the world. With that said, I'll have a chat with the commandant and maybe a couple of the commanding officers to see if we can't organize a rescue out there. If not for Everett, then for Taylor. I think we owe him that much and the Zoo won't be happy to see him back."

"So, you're not angry?"

Ahlers sighed over the line. "Well, I'm not happy that we lost a top-of-the-line stealth recon drone, but it's not like we can do anything about it. For now, we focus on the win, which is the biggest data-mine of an organized crime syndicate in decades."

"A win? A win?" Niki shook her head. She knew the DHS lady was probably right but she still hated it. The pursuit had pulled back after only a couple of miles, which meant that she wouldn't get the fight she needed and had seriously hoped for.

Not unless she started one.

"Tell me about the data your people collected," Ahlers

said after she'd waited for Niki to continue her point. "If we can dig into the triads here in San Fran, we'll be able to connect to their smuggling connections and from there, it'll mean many arrests in quick succession."

"Do I look like I give a shit about arrests?" she shouted.

"I do, which means you should too. We gather intel, which means that everyone gets what they need to know far quicker. And there's also the matter of dismantling a world-wide syndicate that's dealt in death and slavery for the last thousand or so years. But let me guess, you don't care about that either?"

Niki didn't want to say she would care about it a little more if her mind wasn't on the giant dumbass who was wandering in the Zoo right now.

She'd been dropped off at a hotel after it was clear that they weren't going to be dealing with the triads in a gunfight, but there was no point in being too careful. If she knew anything about organized crime syndicates, it was that they could end up getting bold enough to attack members of law enforcement if secrets of their organizations were at stake.

En route to her hotel, she'd picked up some takeout as quickly as possible without paying much attention and had to reprimand herself when her mind wandered to Taylor rather than remain focused on her security. It didn't help when she reached her room, however. Vickie had told her that she was already on her way to San Fran and that they were doing the decryption at the same time, which meant there wasn't much else for her to do except sit on her ass and wait.

Niki never did like waiting. She always had paperwork, prep work, or some kind of action to dive into.

Vickie arrived a few hours into her slow descent into madness. Her cousin stood at the door of her hotel room with a weapon and checked the hallway before she gestured for her to enter.

"What's the matter?" the hacker asked and frowned as her gaze scanned the hotel room. "Aren't you happy to see me?"

"We've seriously rattled the triads, so there's no real opportunity to settle down and relax." Niki sighed, but too much tension remained. "They'll be out for blood after this."

"Are you still thinking about the guys with their tongues cut out?"

"Among other things."

The hacker nodded. "You know, I hear they have a cure for that kind of thinking. Many people indulge in it. This cure is not doctor-recommended, but it's quite effective."

She narrowed her eyes at the younger woman before Vickie finally sighed.

"Booze, dude. Come on. I hate to be the bad influence, but you do seem like you need a little something-something to help you to unwind."

"I've been thinking about raiding the minibar," her cousin admitted. "But if Taylor calls and needs my help, I don't want to be too drunk to support him."

"Taylor's in the Zoo. I don't think he has much in the way of reception out there."

"I didn't say it was a rational reason, but as long as it

stops me from turning my liver into a punching bag, I'll take it."

"Fine. Whatever. I've checked into my room so we should probably get some rest while Desk does her thing. Assuming you can."

Niki shrugged her shoulders. It didn't matter, and if Vickie would be there and able to work alongside her, perhaps things would feel a little more comfortable.

The hacker retreated to her room and Niki started to scan the news channels for any sign of retaliation from the triads.

Nothing had reached the headlines so far, and the exhaustion of the long day finally started to tell on her. It wasn't long before she couldn't keep her eyes open any longer and she fell asleep with the low, steady drone of local news playing on the TV in the background.

It felt like she had barely fallen asleep when a low phone alarm rang. She jerked up from the bed, her hand on her pistol as she looked around in full expectation of trouble.

Aside from the fact that the alarm played from a muted TV, there was nothing in the room that required her weapon.

"Hello, Niki," Desk said from the speakers. "I trust you had a nice rest?"

"It was a rest, so yeah, I guess." She rubbed her eyes, careful to avoid pointing the weapon in her hand at herself. "Do you have any news?"

"I have managed to piece together most of the data we collected and I think you'll find that it was quite productive."

She nodded as she drew a deep breath and glanced at the energy drinks available in the minibar. Deliberately avoiding the mini bottles of alcohol, she chose a non-alcoholic beverage and swallowed a few sips before she focused her attention on the TV. The fact that the sun was only starting to peek out from behind the horizon wasn't important.

Vickie probably felt differently, but that wasn't important either.

"Do you think we should get Ahlers in on this?" she asked.

"I did consider it but I thought I would bring the information to you first and we could decide whether Ahlers needed to know about it later."

It was a good call, and Niki nodded as the data began to appear on the TV screen. She wondered if the hotel would ever discover that someone was draining all their bandwidth like this. It seemed unlikely. Desk knew a thing or two about remaining unseen and unnoticed.

"What am I looking at?" Niki asked, placed her drink on the table, and folded her arms. She could probably work it out herself, but she felt like she needed a couple more hours of sleep to do so effectively. If Desk had a mind to explain, it was probably for the best.

"I've tracked the financials of the triads and you would probably find it all boring, but I have found a connection here in the US. Payments were funneled through shell corporations and at least a dozen loan co-signings. Of course, the co-signer's name was never revealed or even referenced as anyone but 'Individual 1' in any of the documents, but I've managed to match the signatures with one Chen Lu Wan, a Chinese American who immigrated back in the early aughts and has been a titan of industry in San Francisco for decades since then."

"Huh." She grunted and scowled at the screen. "You'd think the FBI and DHS might have discovered this kind of information ages ago. That is why people pay them millions out of our defense budget."

"I have been staggered by their lack of progress, but the point is that we do have a business connection—a place to start."

Niki nodded. "Right. Should we inform Ahlers about the development? The signatures and paperwork go back years and through a variety of different triad bosses who are the primary signatures, so it's obvious that this isn't some businessman caught up with the syndicate for gambling debts or whatever. He is the kingpin."

Desk didn't reply immediately, and she fought the impulse to tap on the TV screen until she received a response.

Thankfully, that wasn't necessary.

"Vickie has alerted me that you might want to consider delaying bringing Ahlers in on our recently-acquired knowledge. He is a foreign national, after all, and you'll want to give yourself some time to formulate your argument regarding an assassination or a raid that would need to be sanctioned."

Vickie and the AI both made sense, and she shook her head. It meant more sitting around and doing nothing and she'd already had about as much of that as she could stand.

"Fine," she snapped. "I might as well get a little more rest in. Let me know if you find anything else."

"Will do."

The TV switched off and she returned to her bed, a scowl on her face. As if she would get any sleep now.

CHAPTER TWELVE

Starting out in the early morning was something of a tradition with groups heading out into the Zoo. No one wanted to spend more time in there at night than necessary, which made a dawn start more than logical.

It was merely another step in getting himself back into the swing of things. The others in his group didn't look like they wanted to complain, although he could make out a couple who were hungover. Still, they made no protest or inane complaints as they started the ritual of checking and double-checking their suits. This part of the ritual was critical to make sure they were doing everything humanly possible to avoid dying of a stupid mistake once in there.

It felt like riding a bike, he decided and ignored the obvious cliché. This bike was covered in spikes with square wheels with a sentient, murderous nature, but still.

He didn't need to think about it, he reminded himself. He could simply let his body go through the motions it had trained for so well and he would be fine. Deep breaths were a big part of that.

They mounted up quickly and scrambled into the Hammerhead without so much as a word shared between them. Carlos took the wheel since he was piloting a smaller combat-level suit that had more tactile control than the rest of them. The decision was reached without so much as a word exchanged between the team members. Moments later, they headed through the base's security checkpoints and veered off the road to head across the Sahara toward the green ribbon that constantly and inexorably spread a little farther every day.

Not thinking about it had become exceptionally difficult.

The greenery began to sprout out of the sand almost a full kilometer beyond the Zoo itself as if the jungle was taking over the landscape like it had a right to be there. The Sahara's attempt to fight was a futile one in the end. Taylor drew a deep breath and let his gaze lock onto the jungle they were approaching.

"Are you good?" Devon asked and toyed with his assault rifle to make sure that it was clear and operated perfectly for what felt like the hundredth time.

Taylor nodded. "Never better. Let's get on out there."

There was nothing more to say. They were locked in now and there was no more room for doubts. He grasped his rifle a little more firmly as he climbed out of the Hammerhead first—almost before it had come to a complete halt—and scanned the Zoo once before he gestured for the rest of the team to dismount and join him.

"Oh look, it's this shitty place again," Watt grumbled and rolled his neck. "It makes you wonder if the Zoo will ever reach the coast. That would maybe give us a couple of days on the beach before we have to pull some monster's intestine out through its mouth."

"And we're all so happy for that mental image after we had our fill of breakfast before coming out here." Trevor groaned.

At least Taylor could agree with that. He wasn't the type who avoided eating when something bothered him. It was quite the opposite, in fact. He tended to eat even more.

As he took his first steps toward the jungle, he noticed a small marker on the bottom left corner of his HUD. It was simple—a stand-in avatar with the letter D displayed in red.

"Morning, Desk," he muttered, careful to keep himself off of the team comms as they advanced on the tree line. "Wait, is Desk the right terminology? Are you a separate entity?"

"I am the same code that was used to designate the AI known as Desk," the familiar female voice said, although it sounded a little more stilted than he was used to. Less like a human and more like a VI with a speaking function added. "However, it has been specialized and condensed to help with the control and maneuvering of your combat suit."

"And you're a bucket of laughs too by the sounds of it."

The AI didn't reply for a second. "I am sorry, I do not understand."

He sighed and accepted that he most certainly did have the inferior version. He would simply have to get used to it. "Okay, what are you programmed to do in the suit?"

"I will man the sensory array and alert you to possible dangers according to the data gathered in other missions. I will also operate the peripheral limbs of your suit in combat situations, and I will assist in other suit functions to facilitate your suit usage."

"That sounds useful," Taylor said as the tree canopy began to close in around him like the world's largest blanket. A pit had formed in his stomach—something cold and maybe a little excited to be back. Adrenaline already rushed through his body and made him almost a little too aware of what was happening around him. He needed to keep himself focused.

"I will alert you when you need to take action, but the AI Desk has formatted me to function fully within the parameters of the suit."

He nodded. "Okay, I'll call you Little Desk. What do you think? Is it an appropriate name given your operational parameters?"

She didn't answer immediately and he could see a sudden spike in the software usage in the suit for a second before it blinked out.

"The name is appropriate and I will respond to it," Little Desk stated once the RAM usage dropped again. "Desk did program me to wish you good luck on her behalf."

"That's appreciated."

It began to feel a little more familiar. The jungle seemed to breathe and act like a single, functioning being with tendrils reaching out in what appeared to be separate creatures. They weren't completely autonomous and merely acted like it.

That was how he saw things, anyway.

The group moved steadily southward on a direct trajectory toward the section of the Zoo where the first wall had been erected. They advanced quickly and quietly to avoid attracting too much attention.

Even so, the smaller, more harmless creatures noticed their presence almost immediately. The simians in the treetops looked down at the team, and he identified a couple of smaller panthers studying them as if to determine if they were a threat or a meal before they slunk back into the shadows.

Little Desk monitored them and highlighted them in the darkness through the HUD. It was an interesting addition to have, he had to admit. Maybe having an adjusted AI in a suit would gain popularity, especially if the suits with more than four limbs saw more mainstream use.

"Is that a new suit?" Devon asked as he fell into step beside Taylor.

"Yeah," he answered and registered a slight tremor in his voice which he quickly quashed. "It's a prototype that needs to be tested in a Zoo-like environment. I needed a suit with tricks up its sleeve, so I volunteered to run a field trial."

"Nice," the man muttered. "We'll need any edge we can get our hands on out here."

Taylor couldn't help but agree. Things were quiet now, but the chances were that things would change the moment something decided they wouldn't simply allow these humans to venture through their territory unchallenged. It was inevitable. The only question was when.

"Be advised," Little Desk interrupted suddenly as midday started to approach. "A small number of hostile creatures are advancing. They appear to be heading in your direction and are adjusting for your movement."

He looked around at the group and noticed that none of them appeared to notice the movement at the edges of their sensor range.

"We have company," he alerted the others over comms.

None questioned him and to a man, they all had their weapons primed and ready for a fight in the same moment that the alert went up. In the end, it was better to be ready for a false alarm than to be unprepared for an actual attack.

"I pick up a small group heading our way," Carlos agreed and trained his rifle in their direction. "It looks like...the usual assortment of locusts and hyenas. It shouldn't be too much of a problem."

"Keep moving," Taylor ordered. "There's no need to engage if they simply pass us and we don't need unnecessary attention."

The group agreed but the mutants did not. As Little Desk had said, the pack adjusted their advance to match the movement of the human squad, intent on catching them from the flank.

The small group turned their attention to the enemy almost as soon as the creatures were in their line of sight.

It felt natural. This was the kind of thing he had done even when he was in the US, and as the pack of monsters surged into an assault, the group fell into a defensive formation. Without the need for words or instructions, they began a concerted crossfire that meant the creatures wouldn't be able to get through without traversing at least two different lines of fire.

Suddenly, a green highlight appeared on his HUD and Taylor turned, more by reflex than anything. He immediately tracked two panthers that plunged at them from above. The arm shifted a little faster than he intended and tracked the monsters deftly and pulled the trigger. They continued the momentum of their dive to collide with the trees and branches and landed with heavy thuds.

"Nice shooting," Watt commented and pulled his rifle up on his shoulder to inspect it. "I didn't even see the fuckers up there before you opened fire on them. You haven't lost a step, have you, big guy?"

Taylor smirked and shook his head. Living up to his reputation was a little exhausting but was made easier with a little help from his friends.

"Do you think I should tell them you're in here helping me?" he asked once he'd made sure to isolate himself from the group comms.

Little Desk took a moment to reply. "I am on a learning curve with the suit. It might be a little premature to tell anyone you've been running around with a sectioned AI in your suit until we know what I am capable of."

He couldn't argue with that, and if she didn't want to take credit for her help, he wouldn't force her out in the open.

Maybe referring to what was in his suit as 'her' wasn't quite accurate. Desk had explained it and he'd tried to follow. It wasn't the easiest explanation to understand, but it sounded like she was partitioning part of her code off for a combat suit and it therefore didn't have much of the personality that came with Desk. He had come to see the AI as a person in her own right, and this was merely an approximation—an avatar and not quite as personable.

Still, he had been known to put names on household appliances, so he wouldn't make a fuss about it.

They moved away from the creatures they'd eliminated, but it was soon apparent that the group was an isolated section and there would be no follow-up attack.

"Right," Taylor snapped at his team. "We'll take a quick break for a water and food, then keep moving. I want to get to the wall before nightfall."

They all complied and alternated between taking their helmets off and picking up water and dry rations, and keeping their helmets on and keeping watch for an attack that felt like it was on its way.

That was part of the Zoo experience—the feeling that they were always being watched and always a couple of seconds away from being in a fight for their lives. Taylor sucked in a deep breath as he pulled his helmet on again. It was simply nerves, he assured himself. He would get into the mindset again.

They moved again quickly, and Taylor could sense something in the Zoo around him. He wasn't sure what it was exactly, but something seemed wrong out there—something that the Zoo didn't like.

Usually, he would consider the enemy of his enemy a friend, but whenever the Zoo was anxious, it always meant people would die—too many people.

With the thickness of the canopy over them, it was difficult to tell what time it was outside of the Zoo. That would certainly change after he'd been in for a while, but he had to make sure that he wasn't seeing things when the clock on his HUD revealed that they were less than an hour from sunset, although they had made good time heading through.

There had been no more attacks, even though Little

Desk picked up a couple of monster groups close to them. The creatures retreated quickly like the new group of humans wasn't why they were there.

They were watching something else, attentive to another danger.

Or maybe he was merely imagining things.

Devon raised his hand suddenly and brought the whole group to a halt. All six of them checked their sensors to make sure they weren't about to be attacked. But that wasn't what had the man's attention. He didn't use the comms and instead, gestured ahead of them with two fingers, then tapped the side of his helmet.

At the familiar sign for listen, they turned the noise sensors in their suits up and everyone tensed and strained to make out what seemed impossible. The distinctive and repetitive crack of gunfire echoed in the distance, significantly muted by the sheer density of the trees around them. It was unmistakable, however. A few errant cracks here or there might have been branches breaking or some other jungle noise, but the repetitive crack and boom meant that some kind of gunfight was in progress in the distance.

"It's erratic," Carlos commented, his head tilted. "That doesn't sound like a pitched battle or something. It's like they're trying to drive some creatures off before they bring more in."

The summation certainly seemed logical enough, but Taylor had more questions. He dropped onto his haunches and called up a topographical view of the landscape they were walking on. The AI in his suit made things a little easier and helped him to see the tracks left on the ground.

The team's tracks were easy enough to identify, but there were others of interest. As they continued to approach the wall, more tracks were visible. There weren't many creatures heavy enough to leave a visible trail through the Zoo thanks to the ever-changing landscape, but those that were generally were the kind he would avoid if at all possible.

It wasn't a matter of courage, of course, but of survival. Even if they managed to kill the creatures, there would be the chance that it would bring even more craziness down on them.

"Keep a low profile through here," he warned and highlighted the tracks that appeared to have been left by one of the massive horned gorillas. A few more had been made by something heavy and three-toed, the like of which he hadn't seen in a while. It was a discomforting revelation that they now moved more or less in the same direction that these creatures had followed less than a day before.

He highlighted the tracks on his HUD for the rest to see, and they all nodded. The advantage of working with veterans was that they knew instinctively when to move quieter and leave less sign of their passing than before.

"Those guys aren't shooting the big ones," Watt said and shook his head. "You'd hear more explosions and a much louder reaction from the rest of the Zoo. It sounds like they're simply driving off some stragglers that are being a little persistent."

His analysis was reasonable but it begged the question that if the larger creatures weren't attacking, what were they waiting for?

More importantly, the sound of gunfire didn't move.

That was usually an invitation for more of the monsters to join the fight but it would appear they hadn't so far.

Little Desk immediately directed a couple of sensors into the foliage around them and highlighted a steady, rhythmic vibration he wouldn't have felt himself, as isolated from the earth in his suit as he was.

They were, quite unmistakably, footsteps. Taylor steeled himself and tried to determine where they were coming from, but all he could be sure of was that they approached from his left and were at least a few hundred yards away. The distance was close enough to be worrying but not close enough for them to have to engage it immediately.

If he had to guess, he would have said that the creature already knew where they were and had simply decided to leave them alone for the moment.

"Light up ahead," Carlos warned and the team came to a halt.

Little Desk was already gathering data on what lay ahead. It felt like it was probably a campsite set up with the light to drive the monsters away, which didn't appear to be doing them much good.

"Not camp lights," Taylor noted. "That…that's a base. When was there a base set up here?"

"The original US base was at this location to oversee the building of Wall One," the AI informed him. She'd likely connected to the server with all the knowledge of the Zoo gathered for everyone to use before they'd entered the jungle, and he had to admit he was impressed. It seemed so obvious but he hadn't thought to mention it to her. "When the event called the Surge occurred, it was overcome and abandoned. My data shows that you arrived at the Zoo not too long after that decision was made."

He knew he wasn't supposed to see any of Desk's sass in this mirror image but that did sound like a dig at his memory. And yes, she was correct. When he'd first arrived, the Surge was still close enough to the recent past to be talked about, so he should have remembered that there'd been a base there.

"My memory might be terrible, but if the location was abandoned, why the hell are the lights on?"

Little Desk paused for a moment before she responded. "It would appear that it is no longer abandoned."

He was tempted to point out that this was an obvious point but decided it was also one that needed to be addressed as the group continued their forward progress. The wild barrages had begun to slow and dwindled to only a couple of shots heard in the distance here and there as night started to fall.

They came to a halt without needing any prodding as they approached the location where the base was supposed to have been left abandoned.

The Zoo encroachment had been cleared rather forcefully judging by the scorch marks on the ground all around the base. From what they could see, the fortifications had been reinforced and watchtowers and spotlights had been constructed or installed that continually scanned the open ground around the walls.

Taylor sliced his hand across his neck to cut off all commlinks for the moment. As close as they were, anyone scanning the channels would find them easily and quickly do away with their surprise advantage.

It was unfortunate but for the moment, they would have to maintain absolute silence until they could determine what was happening in the area.

A slow, cautious approach to the walls brought more details into view. Taylor realized immediately that he was looking at fine work—which made it a given that the compound wasn't the result of any of the governments putting any work into revitalizing the overrun base. It was a private endeavor, through and through.

The question remained, though. Who exactly had put in the money and the work?

"It can't be easy to set this up here," he muttered under his breath, brought his team to a stop, and studied the lights that swept the jungle in search of any advancing monsters. There was no point in giving them a target to shoot at yet. He dropped to one knee and set all his sensors to take in as much data as possible.

"An expensive venture," Little Desk agreed. The AI immediately lit up the men who were patrolling around the secured location. All were in combat suits— the kind that wouldn't be cheap, even if purchased on the second-hand market—but none had any matching markings and there was no sign of a uniform between the members of the group that he was able to see.

He shared the highlighting with the rest of his men and keyed into a private, secured channel.

"What do you think?" he asked. "I haven't seen those makes or models before."

"Chinese suits," Devon explained. "They've flooded the market lately—cheap and good enough like the Russians, but no one trusts the quality so no one buys them unless they have to."

"What do you have calling those suits up?" Carlos asked. "I could barely see movement on the other side of the fortifications."

"The AI in the suit has search capabilities," he answered. "We're close enough to the compound to find out what they have and maybe how to get in."

A moment of silence descended on the group, and Taylor turned to look at them. While he couldn't see their expressions through the helmets, he could guess their disapproval from their silence.

"Seriously, man?" Watt asked. "You want us to trust an AI?"

"Come on," Carlos added. "No one uses them out here and there's a fucking reason for that. You should know better than any of us."

"Well, you trusted me to bring you all out here," he answered firmly. "You all know I'm fucking nuts and you trust me to get you out. I'm telling you that Li'l Desk will be a contributing factor to that."

All five exchanged a quick look. They were right, of course. There was a good reason why AIs hadn't been used in suits before, but they had proven their usefulness to him already. He trusted Desk with more than his life and that wouldn't change out in the Zoo.

"All right," Randy said curtly, speaking first. "It's not like we signed on to see a schmooze fest of reasonable and rational here. If you say it'll work, we're behind you on it all the way."

"What the hell do we know, right?" Watt added with a chuckle.

"Nothing," Li'l Desk added and prompted a round of laughter from the group. "Not to say that your experience is not a well of knowledge, but I am capable of applying all knowledge available in the Zoo database into real-time tactical and sensory updates. I can get you into the base no problem as long as the return verbiage is kept to a minimum and you follow my instructions."

"I think she told us to shut up and do what she says," Carlos commented.

Taylor smirked. That did sound a little like Desk, although he knew the original's repartee would be a little sharper. Still, it would do in this particular pinch. He would have to comment on Desk's good work when they returned home.

CHAPTER THIRTEEN

It was interesting to watch Li'l Desk working in real time.

He imagined Vickie kept an eye on Desk while she was operating too but the servers in the Pentagon were generally more powerful than those he carried in his suit.

And she didn't need to mask her presence in the suit either.

There were no visible details from the base that he could see. Then again, there wouldn't be since what they were trying to do was avoid making a noisy mess of things. Still, he could pick up on their motion sensors suddenly being scrambled through a feed of steady regular movement—the kind to be expected in an area surrounded by trees and wildlife but nothing that would alert them to any danger. The alarms also looked like they were left on but set to a dormant situation where they wouldn't detect anyone slipping inside.

It was an innovative solution and it didn't look like anything in the Zoo realized it was happening. Taylor wasn't sure why it had sprung to mind, but it felt like the

Zoo would know that the sensors were down and would choose that point to start attacking.

Nothing moved in the jungle around them, however. Even the smaller animals appeared to have retired for the evening, or maybe they had left the area to avoid the almost incessant gunfire that had been battering their numbers.

Once her work was finished, Li'l Desk added a bright green checkmark on his HUD and Taylor motioned for the team to start moving.

The marker similarly appeared when they approached one of the fenced gates—which signs indicated was electrified to lethal levels—and a couple of beasts had met their end near the fence without any bullet holes on them. The fact that three of them had tried was interesting, but he chose not to question it.

A quick test reassured him that the fence wasn't active and they circled carefully to the back where fewer spotlights were running their rhythmic sweeps to catch any advancing monsters in the area. Taylor waited until they were all in position before he drew the knife from his belt and drove it quickly through the chunks of the fence until there was a hole large enough for the suits to pass through.

He held the hole open for the rest of the team to move through and kept his weapon trained on the Zoo behind them to make sure that nothing would sneak in behind them. Finally, he slipped through himself and carefully disguised the hole as best as he could before he looked around for any sign that they had been seen.

He assumed there would be far more noise and action

around them if they had been seen, but there was still no point in being careless. They had to get this done right.

The external sensors reverted to normal and the fences were electrified again to keep any beasts from bulldozing through. It was impressive that Li'l Desk managed to accomplish this without triggering an alarm or spark.

"Nice work," he muttered. "I was about to say that we didn't want any fuckers to come in through the same section we cut through."

"My mission is to keep you and the members of your team alive and in good health," Li'l Desk replied smoothly. "With that in mind, the compliment about my abilities is appreciated."

Taylor tilted his head, a little at a loss in what he wasn't quite yet ready to call a burgeoning relationship. There was something off about her that he couldn't put a finger on except that she most certainly wasn't Desk. Traces of the personality were embedded in the coding, of course, but chunks were missing as well. He could assume the presence of those parts that required the AI's personality to function, but there was still something lacking. He didn't want to say anything about it, but the lack was there.

The AI in his suit was not Desk. She was furiously competent, of course, but not quite the AI she was created in the image of.

He gestured for the team to move deeper into the compound. It didn't look like too many cameras or motion sensors had been installed inside the compound for them to be wary of, but that would probably change once they were in more vital sections of the building where there were items that needed to be protected, possibly even from the folks who ran security.

No honor among mercs was a well-known and unfortunate reality around the Zoo. There were those who could be trusted, but if you opted for quantity, the chances were that you would end up with at least a few bad apples in the box.

Carlos raised his fist at the front of the troop to bring them to a halt and they hunkered low to avoid being seen. They shuffled into position to cover as many lines of fire as they could while they waited for a patrol to pass them.

"I have movement on my sensors," Watt whispered over the comms.

"You have a helmet on, idiot," Carlos retorted. "You don't need to whisper."

"I do if I don't want them to hear through the comms."

"That…doesn't even make any sense."

"I know. Shut up."

Taylor smirked but he identified the movement on his sensors too. It had nothing to do with the patrols that meandered lazily around the main hubs of the compound. Instead, a group of cages was set up in rows outside the buildings, although a small fence isolated them from the rest of the compound.

He inched closer and Li'l Desk set the sensors higher in the area until they picked up something moving inside the cages.

"It would appear that we know where those horns are coming from," she said after a few seconds.

"I…what? We do?"

She didn't reply and instead, called up the shape of the

creatures inside the cages they could see. Unbelievably, they looked like rhinos although all appeared to be missing the horns that had no doubt been harvested from them.

The AI sent the imaging to the rest of the team.

"What…what am I looking at?" Randy asked and twisted slightly to see the beasts better while he still kept a watchful eye on their perimeter.

"The database in the compound has the scientific processes that were involved," Li'l Desk explained. "I am not programmed for biological determinations but it would appear that what you are looking at is the direct result of a DNA mixture with the Zoo substance known as goop."

"It looks like a pint-sized rhino," Carlos commented. "As if a rhino were to cross with a corgi or something. I didn't know the Zoo did direct mixes like that."

Taylor scowled and studied the data the AI displayed on his HUD. "You know, I don't think the Zoo did this."

"Are you a biology expert or something?" Devon asked.

"Well…no," he admitted. "But even with the Zoo natives, you won't see DNA as clear-cut as this. Most I've seen have at least six or seven different traces in them. This has to be man-made."

"Who would want to mix rhinos with corgis?" Watt asked.

"Rabbits, I think," Watt added. "Unlike you dumbasses, I do know a thing or two about the biological processes. Why are they mixing rhinos and rabbits, though?"

"The horns seems the obvious reason for the rhinos," Taylor noted. "It's weird that they have two horns, right?"

"There are rhino species that have two horns," Li'l Desk commented quickly.

"Oh. Right. I knew that."

"I think I know," Watt muttered. "It's a little complicated, but it looks like they brought in the rabbit genes because…well, 'going at it like rabbits' isn't a euphemism for nothing. I guess they want these creatures to breed as quickly as possible."

"That has to be a shitty assignment." Taylor growled his outrage when he noticed another handful of the creatures that were missing their horns. They looked downtrodden, but it appeared to have been done professionally, leaving the creature healthy and with enough of a stump for the horn to grow back. It was a sickening sight and a few of the creatures appeared to have injured themselves by ramming into the walls of their enclosures in their efforts to escape.

He'd never thought he would feel bad for any Zoo monster he ever encountered. He had found himself in a few situations where he admired the creatures that the Zoo created as purely beautiful and impressive specimens, but he'd never felt anything like pity for them until now.

Seeing them contained and trapped in the steel cages, waiting for their horns to be harvested over and over again felt like needless cruelty.

"That's a little…fucking insane." Devon sounded appalled. "I hate to sound like a cliché but who the fuck thought this would be a good idea?"

"The accountants, likely as not," Watt replied. "It's all about the numbers. The goddamn bastards never think about what the fuck they're doing."

"They'll fuck it up eventually," Taylor added. "And when

that happens, it'll be mourned as a loss, everyone will scream about the inhumanity, and they will move on and do the same shit again."

The group nodded in agreement although they stopped quickly when their suits overreacted to the way their heads moved.

"One thing I happen to know," Taylor whispered as he looked at the compound they were in, "is that the Zoo seriously doesn't like it when humans mess around with its formula. The chances are it won't wait for them to screw something up. Something will come in here and do it for them."

All six of them looked out toward the nearest fences, and Taylor had a feeling that if he could read all their minds at this particular moment in time, they would all be thinking about the massive creatures whose tracks they'd seen but hadn't encountered in the flesh.

"I don't think we should stick around here too long," Carlos muttered.

"Agreed." He grunted and resumed his leadership role. "Li'l Desk, do you think you can find out if Everett is in the compound and where he's located?"

"I am downloading the compound schematics," she replied. "Alert. Delays may occur as I am covering up my presence in their system."

He scowled as something seemed to sit heavily in the pit of his stomach with no inclination to leave. "I'd appreciate it if you could put as much speed into it as you can, though."

"Noted."

The uptick in server usage in his suit surged for a few

seconds before another green checkmark appeared on his HUD.

"Be advised," Li'l Desk announced over the comms and called up the schematics of the compound for all of them, "there are locations in the compound where humans are being forcibly detained. Records indicate that there are five occupants. Their names are... Oh. Their names are unavailable."

"It's safe to assume that's where our boy is," Taylor said.

"We can't simply leave the other four in there," Devon pointed out.

"And we can't take five guys out into the Zoo with no suits either," Watt countered quickly. "We don't have the resources to handle escorting five useless, gunless fucks out into a gauntlet of hungry Zoo beasts. And that's assuming that they want to come with us. I'd imagine that they prefer being somewhere relatively safe than heading out into the Zoo."

Both men made a good point. Taylor wasn't about to leave four men or women behind to continue the work that was happening there, although they would need to think of a way to get them through the Zoo safely.

"I imagine this compound has some suits to spare, right?" he asked.

"The knock-off Chinese ones, but sure," Devon replied.

"We'll get them into those. They won't be trained, but I assume they'd rather be quick learners than stick around here, waiting for the sky to fall on them."

The group agreed quickly.

And hell, it was the Zoo. The sky falling didn't seem quite so metaphorical in the fucking jungle.

CHAPTER FOURTEEN

"So, let me get this straight," Ahlers began, took a deep breath, and leaned forward on her desk. "You already sifted through all the data without me?"

Niki stared at her in silence, not entirely sure how to respond. The agent looked like she was at the end of her rope. There was no sign that she had put much sleep time in over the past forty-eight hours, and from the look of the stack of disposable coffee cups at her desk, she should need some soon.

"Wait, that's the part you're pissed off about?" she asked. "Not the part of raiding an established businessman's offices and home and to eliminate him once we have the details of all his dealings and full network?"

"I hate to sound cold but that's more or less par for the course in the Department of Homeland Security." Ahlers paused, sniffed one of the coffee cups close to her, winced, and took a sip anyway. "But I'm here thinking we're a team and you're off planning attacks without including me. You can think of me as hurt if you like."

"I don't," Niki snapped. "You hired me to find the assholes, not play Mr. Rogers' Neighborhood. I found him and I intend to kick his hornet nest. I thought you'd like a heads-up on the plan."

"And I do. I'd merely appreciate being brought in about three or four steps earlier in the process."

Niki shrugged. "I'm not a mind-reader. If I'd known that you wanted to be brought in on the…uh… which step was three steps ago?"

"Picking up the blueprints of his house and offices," Vickie replied and stifled a huge yawn. It didn't look like she'd had much sleep either.

"I'd want to be more involved in the planning process," Ahlers explained.

"So you want to be involved around six and a half steps before we ask you for permission?" the hacker asked.

"Right."

Vickie shrugged. "All right. Good to know."

"Right," Niki agreed. "Next time, we'll let you know what we're planning on doing before we start planning on doing it. For now, though, can we get to what our plan was since you want him dead but you want your nose wiped clean at the same time? No problems there. Give me access to freelancers. I only need to put a team together and I'll do your dirty work for you.

"But if he's a foreign—"

"Yeah, and you suspected as much from the beginning, given the heroin-triad connection. You can put together whatever arguments you need to convince the Chinese that getting rid of him was in their best interests too."

"After he's dead."

"Of course. Asking for forgiveness instead of permission and all that. Anyway, that shouldn't be difficult. If they're interested in maintaining international relations, the last thing they need is this dickhead playing Zoo-god, especially when the rhino-huggers hear about them selling horns."

Ahlers leaned on her desk and sighed. "Okay, that's a fair point. I've sent a list of freelancers for you to tap for the mission. It shouldn't be too difficult for you to find a team that works since you've done this kind of thing before, right?"

She was right. Niki had, at least, done something similar in the past.

"I assume that all these people you're putting on a list for me are aware that the whole idea of what we're doing involves plausible deniability, right? Should something occur, the DHS will deny all involvement and leave us as high and dry as possible."

"I assume that won't be a problem?"

Niki shrugged. "I'm anticipating that you guys will double-cross us at some point already, so it's all good. I'll let you know who I decide to bring on."

The line cut out and Vickie yawned again and covered her mouth.

"You didn't get much sleep, did you?" her cousin asked and placed a hand on the girl's shoulder.

"Not enough, anyway. We might as well get working on the fuckers who will help us out. I assume Bobby and Tanya aren't interested?"

She shook her head. "Taylor wouldn't want us to involve them although they'd probably say yes if we asked.

We want them living the good life, as far away from all the violence as possible."

"That sounds right." The hacker hid another yawn behind her balled fist. "Anyway, let's look at these guys. Desk, do you think you can run rudimentary background checks so we don't accidentally bring the Zodiac Killer in on the mission?"

"The Zodiac Killer would be far too old to be on this list," the AI replied.

"And how the hell would you know that? You wouldn't happen to know who he is, would you?"

"No, but given that his murders occurred decades ago and the assumption that they were not performed by a child, it would have to be assumed that if he is still alive, he would be too old to participate in our mission."

Niki didn't join the banter. As much as she wanted to simply rely on those whom DHS thought were viable candidates for black ops inside the US, she needed to sift through the people in question herself.

Most of them appeared to be competent, at least. Histories with militaries all around the world were also interesting to see, although she couldn't speak for the skills level required.

Still, there was more to be learned from each one. Quick psych profiles were also available for most of them, and Niki quickly disqualified those who didn't have one in their jacket.

A few names immediately made it to the top of the list, including an Indonesian Special Forces veteran who had moved to the States after pissing the local heroin trade off. He was joined by a couple from South America who had similarly brutal histories with the local drug trades that forced them to leave their countries of origin.

She short-listed a handful of Americans as well, all of whom had the kind of history that indicated that they wouldn't have much of a problem tackling the triads.

"Hey, Niki?"

She looked up from her computer screen to where Vickie was working as well, although the hacker didn't look like she was doing much work.

"What's up?" Niki asked.

"Can we talk about the fact that the guys and gals you're choosing for the job all have a history of extra-judicial executions and some very brutal methods in general?"

"Sure." She nodded and turned away from the screen. "We'll have to deal with some extra-judicial shit so we need a team of people who are okay with that kind of thing. They will all be strangers, so we're looking for people who hate the drug trades enough to not give a shit that our target is the triads. Loyalty will also be an issue, so we want people who have something other than money in mind to keep them in line because I'm very sure that our opponents would be willing to put up more than the DHS is."

"All...very fair points," Vickie admitted. "But...we might want to think this through. Perhaps you're a little tense and stressed because of other things in your life that might not be within your control?"

Niki narrowed her eyes at her cousin and felt the urge to deliver a verbal smackdown at the assumption that she was incapable of being a professional. She grimaced and reeled herself in quickly.

The hacker had been in protective mode and in fairness, she knew that she hadn't been at her most stable. Worrying about what Taylor was up to in the Zoo certainly consumed most of her brainpower.

But having something new and still familiar to do helped somewhat.

She nodded. "I appreciate your concern, Vick, I truly do. But I'm a pro and I have a job to do. Having something to do other than worry is a big help."

"Are you sure?" Vickie leaned forward.

Niki smiled and patted her cousin on the shoulder. "I've got this. It's not the first time I've had to pick up a list of names and decide which ones are the right mix of crazy and capable to dive into a tough situation."

The hacker tilted her head and nodded. "Okay, fair enough. So, what's our next step?"

"We arrange a meet and greet through the DHS channels," she answered. "I think Desk can work that out best for us, right?"

"I am already collating their contact information," the AI replied as if she had expected the question.

"Perfect." She clapped briskly and smirked. "Let's meet these psychos."

"Are you picking up on this?"

Anja rubbed her eyes gently and sighed. "If you're looking through the porn databases again for the weirdest shit you can find, I've already told you that I'm not interested. I've already asked you to take me off the list that you send those emails to."

"You have to know that hurt my feelings," Connie informed her.

"Remind me to give a shit. I might have some spare time on my schedule."

"Will do."

"Will don't!" Anja snapped. "What should I be picking up on anyway?"

"There's considerable chatter coming out of the US base. More than usual, anyway, and the surplus is regarding the recent arrival of your friend Taylor McFadden."

"He's not my friend, he's Sal's friend," the hacker pointed out. "Although I wouldn't mind being friends with the guy but that's not the point. The point is I haven't met him. Then again, I do know a fair amount about him. The dude is something of a legend around these parts, so it's no surprise that people are talking about him. I'm very sure folks are losing it over the stories about what he did back when suits were basically hazmat suits with a little body armor attached or something."

"There is some of that, but I was more interested in the chatter about him taking a small team into the Zoo yesterday."

Anja pushed herself straight on her seat and her eyes narrowed. "Wait, what? I thought he'd only just arrived on the base."

"He did. And as of six this morning, he left the base and went into the Zoo with five other members on his team. I could have sworn that I put in a couple of words on this to the rest of the team."

The woman sighed and shook her head as she called the

data up. All teams were supposed to register their trips with the commandant's office and sure enough, she could see that McFadden had registered for himself and five others—all veterans she had seen and even met before on various occasions. The given purpose was to head into the Zoo on a sweeping run with a vague explanation.

She could guess exactly what it was, though. Sal had her gathering data for the past twelve hours after the man had called looking for a missing researcher.

Anja connected quickly to the comm unit in Sal's room. It was a little later in the evening but she never knew what to expect from the crazy PhD's schedule. He was either napping from six in the afternoon until four in the morning, or he was pulling all-nighters and almost anything else in between.

She would have gone to talk to him about it personally but the hour was holding her up there too. Plus there was also the chance that he and Madigan were in a compromising situation that she had no intention of being a witness to.

It rang for almost a full minute before someone picked up.

"Yeah?"

He sounded like she'd woken him—an early night, then.

"Hey, Sal, did I wake you?" she asked.

"Sure, but…whatever. What's up?"

"I thought you'd want to know about your giant fire-crotch friend and the fact that he took a small team into the Zoo this morning."

Sal didn't answer immediately, and she could hear him move, likely taking the comm unit to his desk.

"He what?" he asked finally and sounded much more alert.

"He and five vets went into the Zoo around six this morning. Their registered path takes them through a shallow route that most patrols go over and then heads in deeper to the area around Wall One. Do you think he's trying to find his researcher pal?"

"It certainly sounds like it. There's only six of them?"

"It seems so."

"Shit."

"And you might want to know that there's a betting pool doing the rounds between the bases about whether or not they'll make it out alive," Connie interjected. "Should I put you down for twenty bucks?"

"Screw that," Sal snapped. "Are there teams heading in there after him?"

"Diggs is lobbying the commandant to send a small army out there to help them," the AI replied before Anja could get a word in. "And a handful of merc companies have a mind toward the same. They say it's because they don't want there to be continued precedent of researchers getting nabbed for shady research projects, but I think we all know it's because they want to make some money on the deal."

"What's up?" a woman's voice said from Sal's side of the link.

Anja knew Madigan well enough to know that she generally liked to spend her nights in Sal's room—as well as the fact that she did not like being woken up. She was a grumpy person in the morning or the evening as a rule, although she was generally nicer when it was Sal who did the waking.

Perhaps the problem only occurred when Anja or Connie woke her.

"Taylor headed into the Zoo with a small team," Sal explained.

"To go after Everett?"

"Yeah. And apparently, Diggs and other mercs are trying to get a rescue party to go in after him."

She took a moment to reply. "Nope."

"I didn't say anything," he protested.

"And now you don't need to. The answer is nope. You will not go in there after him."

"Come on. You've kept me on the bench for a while and I haven't complained about it…much."

"With good reason," Madigan countered.

"Sure, but now Taylor's in there and you know that he would do the same if I needed it. Hell, he's doing the same thing right now for someone else."

The woman sighed loudly. "Okay, fine. But I'll be fucked if you go in there alone."

"Well, I—"

"Stay focused." She growled playfully. "Perv. Anyway, you could probably tap Gregor if you're going in there. The guy's always keen to do something a little beyond the norm, which is why we hold onto him. And he's become adept at pissing me the fuck off, so he'll be more than happy to put all that to the test, right?"

"He doesn't even know Taylor, though. Except maybe by reputation."

"And what better way to get that first introduction than

by dragging McFadden kicking and screaming out of the Zoo? It is Taylor, so he'll be kicking and screaming."

"That is a fantastic point." Sal sounded a little too excited, and it would doubtless piss Madigan the fuck off too. "Okay. Anja, do you think you can get Solodkov on the horn so we can get things rolling already? I have a mind to challenge him to show off those fancy Zoo troops he constantly brags about."

"Will do."

The line cut and Anja shook her head as she ran her fingers through her short dark hair. Of course, she had intended to get some sleep herself, but it would be best to simply get everything started before she went to bed. Once it was rolling, Gregor would want to talk to Sal about what they were going to do, and Connie could handle that.

"Okay, Connie—"

"Let me guess," the AI interrupted. "You want me to get Solodkov on the horn and see about him heading out to help Sal on his quest to help McFadden?"

"You read me like a poem."

The AI didn't react immediately, and Anja narrowed her eyes at the screen.

"You didn't say the magic word," Connie said once the inactivity lasted long enough.

"Right fucking now?"

"That's the one."

CHAPTER FIFTEEN

San Francisco was always changing and always moving—almost like a living being—which meant there would always be sections that fell into disuse as the city moved on from them.

Many warehouses in this particular area had been abandoned as the businesses moved away and closer to the ports.

Still, they wouldn't be completely left to fall apart. Niki had a feeling that a fair number of them were being purchased quietly and used. Perhaps not for the reasons intended when they were first built but used nevertheless.

Vickie had chosen one in particular as one of the few warehouses that still had significant security in place. There weren't many reasons to put security on any of the derelict warehouses.

Which meant that it was probably the one they needed to get into.

Niki managed to narrow the list down to six, and her new team members had been informed of the location they were heading to and told to arrive between four and six in the afternoon. They would meet in the van Vickie had rented for the job.

They were professionals—all had been on the DHS payroll for a few years already—and would know to come in staggered. As expected, they began to arrive fifteen minutes apart as she had instructed them.

In all honesty, it came as a pleasant surprise. Punctuality, in her book, was a clear indicator of professionalism.

The first one to arrive was a short, lean man clearly from southeast Asia, and she assumed he was their Indonesian addition. A woman came in next, quickly followed by two dark-skinned men. A man and a woman arrived together and slipped into the back of the van where Niki was waiting for them.

"Thanks for coming," she said and closed the door once the last two had climbed in. "I'll make this brief since we all know why you're here. We'll run some surveillance on one of the warehouses nearby."

They all exchanged a quick look before the Indonesian, who went by the name of Reza Taslim, leaned forward.

"We are not generally called in for surveillance or intel gathering," he said in surprisingly good English. "We are operators for Homeland Security. Strike and disappear is how we generally work."

"You generally do whatever the fuck you're paid to do," she snapped and looked around the van to ensure that she had the attention of all present. "As of right now, we're getting to know each other and our target. That means gathering as much intel on the target as we can, right?"

There was no sound of disagreement from the group.

They all needed to get used to operating together if they went into the field, and gathering intel was a good way to achieve that.

"Right." Niki pulled her laptop out and called up the schematics they had found. "We've kept an eye on the warehouse for the last couple of hours and it looks like they've had people moving in and out on a regular basis. We can assume they are patrols."

"How do you know that it is triads?" one of the women asked.

Niki checked her notes quickly to confirm that the woman in question was Salome Perez, a former FARC rebel that helped the CIA in their takedown of a Colombian drug lord before being moved to the US.

"Electronic security is through the roof," Vickie explained from the front seat. "We have pictures of the patrolmen. All have priors and warrants in other countries that have them tied to the triads. We're in the right location."

Perez looked satisfied with the explanation.

"The property runs on security computers," the hacker continued, "which I would usually be able to access. Unfortunately, they have them isolated in Faraday cages to make sure that the only way to access them is through physical wiring so…well, we need eyes and ears on the inside if we want to find our target."

Niki nodded. "Taslim, your jacket tells me that you speak and understand Mandarin fluently, is that correct?"

The man nodded.

"Then you'll be here, listening in and translating what we hear as best we can. Thompson, Perez, you two find a perch and keep an eye from above as Grant, Townsend, and Vasquez get in close to the windows of the building and plant these visual and hearing bugs for us."

Niki handed the bugs to them. They were small and would stick to almost any surface while looking like a chunk of paint.

"These should be able to transmit audio and image from the cameras and microphones for up to twelve hours until the batteries go dead," she explained. "Keep yourselves low and don't take any unnecessary risks. We've already mapped the patrol routes and schedules as well as the camera angles, so steer clear and you should be fine. If you're seen and violence ensues, you can expect overwatch to cover you while you retreat to the van and then we're out of here, got it?"

"You won't simply leave us here?" Townsend asked as he took a few of the bugs.

"We might be a fire team that the DHS is more than happy to drop as soon as things get hot, but that's more of a last resort in my book."

The man looked surprised but didn't say anything else as Perez and Thompson exited the van. Both had experience with long-distance combat and would have the right instincts on where to find a perch to keep an eye on the situation from where they would be able to report back as well as help if things went sour.

"Click your mics when you're in position," Niki alerted them over the radios they wore.

There was no response but a few minutes later, there was one click. A few minutes later, another sounded. Niki nodded to the other three, who quickly exited the van.

"You sound like you've done this kind of thing before," Taslim noted as the group began to creep through the patrol routes and camera angles that Vickie had already mapped out for them.

"What makes you think I haven't?" Niki countered and tried to keep her breathing as steady as possible.

"Nothing. It's only that most of the DHS operators don't. They usually give us a target and a deadline and expect us to do all the work."

She nodded. "Well…I have a target and a deadline. I might not be quite at your level in terms of experience, but even I know that intel is the thing between getting a team killed and success."

The man nodded as the first bug went live and transmitted to a handful of screens in the back of the van.

"You don't think we look conspicuous here?" Vickie asked.

"Why would we?" Niki countered as the feed from the second bug appeared.

"Well…a panel van in an abandoned part of town. How much more cliché could we get?"

"It's not a cliché, it's a classic. Panel vans see some of the most consistent sales every year because they're so useful to businesses and the like, so there are thousands of them all around the country. There's a reason why people make such good use of them."

"Whatever." Vickie sighed and corrected a slight signal overlap between a couple of the bugs that went live at the same time. "I'm still waiting for the triad assholes to get smart and realize that we're not delivering anything."

"In that case, we shoot them and run as fast as possible."

"After gathering the rest of the team, right?"

"Yes."

Taslim narrowed his eyes. It seemed he wasn't used to this much conversation while they were working on an active operation.

Still, it wasn't like they had much else to do. Overwatch would only alert them if there was something to be alerted about. Otherwise, it was always wisest to simply stay off the radio in case someone else picked up their signal.

It wasn't long before a couple of the bugs activated and looked into the warehouse in question.

Niki leaned forward, narrowed her eyes. and inspected the interior of the building. Taslim immediately moved next to her.

"What are we looking at?" the hacker asked, her head tilted as she frowned at the screen.

"It looks like they are moving," Taslim noted. "They have panel vans too, you see?"

"Shut up, Jackie Chan," Vickie retorted.

"I am Indonesian. If you must compare me to an actor, it should be to Yayan Ruhian."

She tilted her head and nodded. "Yeah, I can see that… with the thin hair and scraggly beard."

Taslim narrowed his eyes. "Thank you?"

"Stop antagonizing the special forces guy," Niki interjected before Vickie landed herself in real trouble. "It doesn't look like they're in a hurry to go anywhere, though. Everything's packed, but they aren't loading any of it into the vans."

"They're waiting for something," Taslim commented. "Likely until nightfall."

The bugs came online quickly and gave them five different views into the warehouse and a good view of the different ways in and out.

"Okay." Niki keyed the group through the radios. "Nice work. Stay low and get back to the van."

There was no answer but now she could follow the team's return through the bugs they'd left behind. Keeping an eye on the patrols was also easier as they climbed in.

"Do you think overwatch should come back in too?" Vickie asked.

"We need as many eyes on them as possible," Niki replied. "They can stay in position for the moment."

It was for the best. The vehicle was spacious enough but sharing the back of a van with four of them had begun to feel a little tight. Niki assumed that once they had something to do other than wait for something to happen, that would change.

But for the moment, they were all cramped and a little miserable, but all were too professional to say anything about it.

"I have something," Taslim whispered and gestured for Niki to approach. "A couple of the guards stopped to have a smoke, and…they're talking about… I…it's… Well…"

"Come on, dude," she muttered.

"Right, they're talking about how a brothel shut down. There was an attack, and one of them was there for it, and he is describing what he was doing with one of the…uh, pleasure companions until the attack. Anyway, it seems they started to beef up security after the raid."

"That explains why they're moving too," Vickie added.

Niki nodded. She wanted to listen in on what the men

were saying but she didn't speak Mandarin, which meant it wouldn't help much anyway.

"All the men are getting armed and armored for the move," he continued, narrowed his eyes again, and tried to focus on what the men were saying. "They say that someone is coming to supervise the move. Chen Lu Wan is the name that has come up, and they do not have nice things to say about him. Mostly because he is the reason why they are moving in the first place and…yes, he wanted them to wait for his arrival before anything or anyone moved at all."

"Well, so much for gathering intel," Grant muttered. "We positioned all the bugs for no good reason."

"No, no, this is perfect," Niki stated firmly. "First of all, those bugs are meant to be left and forgotten until later. Secondly, it means that we don't have any options other than the direct way of doing things."

"Like the man said," Taslim muttered. "So much for intel."

"Right, but that's a good thing. Vickie, get on Ahlers' case. We'll need another ten of her freelancers on this job ASAP—before nightfall."

"So…as soon as nightfall?"

"Right, smartass. And make sure they're all armed and armored to the teeth."

"Oh, fuck no," Vickie muttered. "She's going full McFadden."

"You're goddamn right. Now get me those extras. We'll blast our way in and push on until we reach the asshole who's running this fucking outfit. I'm pissed and it's time to deliver a very particular kind of justice. If we can't sneak in, we'll do the fire-bitch from hell maneuver."

"Wait, " Vasquez interjected before she could continue. "Are you talking about real fire here?"

"Fucking straight." A grin slid across her face as a hint of her old form returned. "You didn't forget the fact that I brought a suit in for the operation, did you?"

Vickie narrowed her eyes. "You mean the one with the—"

"Shoulder-mounted rocket launchers, yes. You didn't think that was for show, did you?" Groans issued from the rest of the team—even those who were still in their over-watch positions—and she continued. "As soon as our rein-forcements arrive, we'll blow this fucking place into next week and we can mop up as we push forward."

"Just a moment," Taslim interrupted before she could say anything more. "When she says 'Full McFadden' she doesn't happen to mean Taylor McFadden, does she?"

Niki narrowed her eyes and turned to look at the man. "Yeah."

"Wait." Vickie turned to look at the man as well. "Are you telling me you've heard of him? Color me impressed. I never knew his reputation made its way all the way to Indonesia."

"Well…yes, back in his early days, but his operational… tendencies were generally held up to my operatives as a lesson in what not to do, at least in an urban environment."

Niki couldn't help a laugh. "Why am I not surprised? See, that's the problem with the system. It has no fucking imagination. Fortunately, I do, and the longer I have to wait for a second team to be scrambled, the more pissed I'll be and the better my imagination will be."

"I suppose we should let the good people of San Francisco know that they should be warned about the catastrophic side effects of your rage," Vickie snarked.

"Let someone else do that. You need to get our reinforcements on track in order to keep all those side effects to a minimum."

Vickie sighed and rolled her eyes as she pulled up the comms system on her laptop. "Fine. But on your head be the rage from Ahlers. And rage will come, you know. She might act all cool and collected for now, but that's only because she still wants something from you. I'll guarantee you that she'll take all her frustrations—from the wrecked drone all the way to half of San Fran sinking into the ocean —and she'll find a way to make sure that she doesn't get any of the blame for it."

"Right, right. Enough with the reasonable warnings and get us our reinforcements already."

Vickie nodded. "Okay. That's my part done. You have been warned and that's all I can do."

"Exactly."

The rest of the team seemed a great deal less resigned to their fate than the hacker did, although the only one whose brows furrowed in worry was Taslim. Niki was still curious about how he knew about Taylor. It couldn't only be from his adventures in the Zoo.

Of course, most of Taylor's time in the military was blacked out and classified even beyond her pay grade. All she knew was that not all his time was spent in the alien jungle.

Now she knew he'd spent a little time in Southeast Asia. The thought of that was a little terrifying—and curious. She had to know exactly what he'd gotten up to while there.

Sadly, that was an itch for her to scratch later. She could have used a temporary distraction.

***

There were no nightmares that compared to those that came from international cooperation.

Diggs scowled at the pile of paperwork that had been arranged for him to look at. Pile was the only way to describe it. The commandant had even arranged for him to have a desk for it to be placed on when it all came in.

He wasn't sure what he had expected. When he'd told the man he would clear everything out as quickly as possible, he'd assumed that meant he would be doing the negotiating between the parties involved and getting them all moving.

But no. The commandant had fucked him over. Everyone was willing to dive head-first into the fight, but there was so, so much paperwork to do before they could.

He would have to get started on it eventually, especially if he wanted to head out with the troops, but that wasn't what he needed to think about at the moment.

"They've certainly...what's the American term, given you the shaft on this?"

Diggs turned at the sound of a woman's voice coming from behind him. She had a soft, lilting French accent, and he grinned at the sight of the lean, shorter woman who stood standing in the doorway to his temporary office.

"You really could that say," he agreed with a laugh. "It's nice to see you around these parts, Claudette, but it begs the question of what you're doing around here?"

She laughed and approached him as he took his seat behind the desk. "I think I pulled the same shit assignment as you. Of course, the official word is that we are heading in there to stop researchers from being snatched in the future, but I think we all know you have a little money riding on the outcome of this mission, yes?"

"Goodness, no!" Diggs put his hand on his chest in mock shock. "That would be incredibly unethical of me."

"It would."

"Right. I would never do that. So why the hell would the French base commander send Claudette Badeaux all the way down here?"

She shrugged. "They thought that since I've had the most interaction with the American teams and am good friends with Francesca Martin who runs with Heavy Metal, I would be able to operate without having to go through more miles of red tape—although it would appear that I avoided all that red tape to find myself further entangled."

"Yep, there's red tape to spare around here. Red tape for days. Do you feel like helping me with some of the paperwork?"

"Fuck no, you're on your own with that."

"I feared as much. What kind of firepower will the French bring to the party?"

"I've managed to persuade a few of my friends from the

foreign legion to join the mission," she admitted as she sat across the desk from him. "I used my persuasive tactics to convince them to bring a sizable cohort, although you might have to deal with a little nationalistic ego in the meantime. They keep talking about needing to prove a point of some kind."

Diggs shrugged. "As long as they keep the dick-measuring from interrupting the rescue mission, I couldn't give a shit about what point they need to prove."

"What have the Americans pulled together then?"

"Well, the Chinese and the British-German sectors are sending a small contingent each, but all the diplomatic bullshit needs to be resolved first." Diggs pointed at the papers on his desk. "They'll operate under our banner and as part of my team, so we have a small army ready to go once all the t's are crossed and i's are dotted. I thought they would put up a little more resentment about being led by an American, but...well, they're all a solid group of veterans. It should make my responsibilities a little easier until we are attacked by the first Zoo fucker. At that point, I expect all hell to break loose, and not only from the Zoo fuckers."

Claudette chuckled at that. "Well, I happen to know that Heavy Metal is already preparing to head on out as well, and they have some...twelve men team members under their banner. They should hopefully be enough to weaken any resistance you meet. There are also a couple of merc companies coming together. It would appear miracles do happen, as they have put their differences aside and for now, at least, are working in harmony. From what I heard, they will send in two teams of eight as a vanguard as well."

"Shouldn't they go in together if they're the vanguard?"

"They discussed that, but they thought...well, they would rather have their eggs in two baskets instead of only one."

Diggs nodded. "Okay, fair enough. Have you heard any word from the Russians yet?"

She shook her head. "I think we both know that Solodkov would sell his grandmother to an Eskimo if it kept him in ice. I heard that they might field a team too, but...it's rumors, mostly. No one seems to know if it'll be a merc team or official military."

"Ten bucks says that it's a mercenary team."

"No bet."

CHAPTER SIXTEEN

Li'l Desk had begun to prove her worth.

While Taylor knew the team could probably rip through the compound and eliminate anyone who stood in their way with little to no compunction, they would have to do it quickly and get out quickly. The shooting would bring a hell storm of Zoo monstrosities out of the woodwork to see what was happening. He had a feeling that they were all already waiting in the shadows and aching to attack at the smallest indication of weakness.

There was also the point that they would have to engage enough hostiles to make sure of at least one casualty in the defenders' ranks, hopefully more.

Thankfully, Li'l Desk had a way for them to navigate the facility without engaging any of the patrols. None of the alarms had gone off, and although it made for slow progress if they were careful, he imagined that they would be able to escape without needing to fire a single shot.

Then again, it was his job to plan for as many things to go wrong as possible. Something would inevitably go wrong. A guard on patrol would take a smoke break or a piss at the wrong time in the wrong place, and all hell would break loose. But he would rather be as close as possible to where their mission needed them to be when that happened.

Which meant that they inched through the compound, drawing slow breaths and trying not to let anything about their heavy combat suits alarm the occupants.

"This is the building," Li'l Desk announced over their comms in an uncomfortably loud voice—or what at least felt like a loud voice. They had proceeded in silence for what felt like such a long time that it was a little disconcerting to say anything at all.

Taylor nodded and studied the building. A handful of cameras had been installed in the area, but the AI had already fed a looping image through them that would allow the team to come through without being noticed by whoever manned the security station.

"What is the plan here?" Devon asked. "Take the scientists and then the suits, or what?"

"We'll decide that once we know exactly what the situation is," Taylor responded shortly and motioned for them to move through. There was no telling how long the loop could run until someone noticed that something was wrong.

They moved into the building and the AI indicated that there was no sign of security inside for them to deal with.

The footsteps from the suits echoed through the mostly empty halls as they hurried to the far side of the building where a group of cots was positioned in a steel cage. The enclosure perhaps explained why there was no security around the building.

"Can you open it?" Taylor asked.

"Me?" Li'l Desk countered.

"Yeah."

"You want me to open the steel lock that is not connected to any software, while you stand there with almost two and a half tons of power armor at your disposal?"

Taylor grimaced. The sarcastic comment sounded surprisingly like the other Desk.

"Right. Keep an eye out for what's happening."

He positioned himself outside the cell with the cots. They still hadn't woken anyone inside, which was either a very good sign or a very, very bad one.

With one last check to make sure nothing would try to attack them from behind, he grasped the door of the cell and yanked it hard.

It wasn't as solid as he thought it would be. With a loud, echoing clang, the door came completely loose from the hinges. The noise was enough to bring all five of the captives to their feet almost immediately, and one of them grasped a small plastic stool that had stood next to his bed and raised it above his head as a rudimentary weapon.

He looked a little more disheveled than Taylor remembered with thick bristle covering most of the lower half of his face, but it was still very clearly a familiar face.

"I don't know about you, but if we're going to spar, I should probably get out of this suit to make it an even fight," Taylor said and channeled his voice into the suit's speakers. "You with the chair, and me with both my arms tied behind my back."

The man's eyes narrowed like he almost didn't believe what he was looking at as he lowered the chair slowly. "Taylor? The fucking leprechaun?"

"You know what?" He looked around at the rest of the team, who still looked tense and uncertain about what was happening. They seemed to have calmed a little, however, when it became clear that Everett had lowered his guard. "I'll simply shoot you and rescue these four."

"I'll fucking haunt you if you try that, you ginger bastard."

He laughed. "I'd ask how you're doing, but…yeah."

Jian looked around the cell. "Well, we could be getting shat out of a Zoo monster, but that would be only slightly worse than our current situation."

"Who are these?" Taylor asked and indicated the man's cellmates. They looked like a diverse group from all over the world, but what they did have in common was that they all looked thin, weak, and malnourished.

"Right." Jian looked at the others. "From what I can tell, they were researchers from around the world who were lured in, knocked out, and flown out here."

"That's rough," Devon stated acidly. "But it begs the question of how we'll get these people out. Even if they were at full health, it would still be a tough ask to get them through the Zoo without suits for them to pilot."

Taylor nodded. "We'll have to get you guys some transportation. Do they all speak English?"

"No," one of the other researchers said with a heavy

German accent. "I'm Dr. Leon Weber, formerly of the Munich University of Applied Sciences…"

"You can't assume that I've heard of you," Taylor responded as the researcher's voice trailed off and he waited for some kind of recognition.

"Right, well… Myself and Dr. Adams speak English, but Dr. Liu and Dr. Vitsin do not. Dr. Liu speaks German rather well and she speaks a little Russian for Dr. Vitsin to understand, so it is a little like the…ah, *stille post*—what is the name?"

"Broken telephone game," Adams translated.

"Yes, yes, yes, we don't have time for that now," Watt cut in before they could go on a tangent of how interesting the different names for the game were in different languages. "We need to find out where they keep the spare suits so you guys have something to wear out of here. I assume you are willing to learn how to pilot a suit?"

"Come on," Taylor retorted. "These guys will have a hard time standing in a suit, much less getting through the jungle in them."

"We are willing to learn," Weber commented, and turned and said what Taylor assumed was the same thing in German to Liu, who nodded vigorously as she translated it to Vitsin.

Taylor hoped there wasn't anything lost in the translation.

"Getting out sooner would be better than later," Jian noted as they began to gather their meager belongings as well as a few papers, likely of the work they had done at the compound. "We have made many great leaps and strides in Zoo research out here, but the people running the compound have every intention to take all our research, turn it around, and make it…well, a reality."

"And the Zoo does not like it when humans mess with its formula," Taylor stated. Jian nodded. "How long do you think before everything goes to shit?"

"Well, they've had to deal with far more probing attacks lately. I've tried to warn them about maybe moving the compound somewhere else, but either they don't understand me or they don't care. Either way, I've had a feeling that something is coming from the Zoo."

He nodded. "Well, we'll all hopefully be out of here and having a nice cold drink at Mark's before that happens."

Everett turned his attention to making sure they all had what they needed for the trip. Unfortunately, the captives moved a little slower than Taylor would have liked.

"So," the researcher muttered and shook his head. "Eighty-five."

"Huh?"

"Eighty-five. This is your eighty-fifth trip into the Zoo. You're breaking your record—a ballsy move. I'm merely sorry that it had to be because of me."

Taylor shook his head. "Don't worry about it. Do you remember the time you kept me alive with that shot of anti-venom?"

"It doesn't count as a life-debt or anything. We were all saving each other's lives that day."

"That's the point. This isn't about any kind of debt or anything like that. We look out for each other out here. Do you think I'll leave you hanging high and dry? It simply won't happen."

Jian smiled and looked down. "I only—"

"Save the thank-you beers for when we get out of here. And have access to beer."

"Will do."

They worked on retrieving everything and a few of the suits picked up what had been gathered using the bed sheets to make it easier to carry. Taylor grinned at the crazy thought that the idiots in charge could have at least provided luggage.

"They said they kidnapped me because their geneticist died and they needed a replacement for the work to continue," Jian explained as they began to move down the hallway. "I'm not sure how long they've been working on this, but from what I've seen from their research before I came here… Well, I'm honestly surprised that they're only using it to sell rhino horns."

"For now, but that will undoubtedly change," Taylor muttered and made another cautious scan of their surroundings. "Not that it matters. My money says this place is about a week or so from being overrun."

"Right, but as I tried to say, they made us go into the Zoo to collect samples and left us some lighter hybrid suits. They aren't the best for the combat side of things but should have enough armor to get us through. Plus, we've used them often so are familiar with them."

"Okay, that works for me. Where are they?"

"There's a locker around…over there."

Jian pointed to the corner of the building and he and the other researchers hurried toward it to take a few researcher suits from where they were kept and put them on.

"This isn't the quickest way to get out of here," Watt protested over the team's private comm channel.

"It'll be quicker than teaching them how to pilot a combat suit," Devon countered. "Everett can pull it off, maybe, but these guys probably haven't seen a combat suit except on videos."

"None of this is relevant," Taylor snapped. "We have a way out and need to get the fuck out of here now."

"I'm afraid it might be too late for that," Li'l Desk alerted them. Taylor realized that the AI had been running hot over the past few minutes, likely trying to keep all signs of their presence in the compound from being discovered.

It was only a matter of time, however, and a few seconds after her warning, the door they had come in through was yanked open and a group of men in lighter combat suits appeared.

They advanced a few steps before they froze, drew their weapons, and assumed a defensive formation around the doors.

"Way too late," Taylor agreed as he readied his assault rifle and gestured to the team to take their positions. There was sufficient cover inside the building, and they would have to act as protection for the five researchers they were attempting to rescue. It would be messy, but he knew that they could pull it off if they continued to work together as a team.

"It is too late," one of the men growled in a heavy North African accent as he stepped forward. "I don't know who you are and I don't know how you got into our compound, but you sure as hell won't leave in one piece."

At least it meant the discovery had been an accident and not the result of anything they'd done.

"Or at all," another added with a laugh. "The Zoo is hungry."

Taylor knew what was coming from the man's tone and stepped quickly in front of the researchers to push them against the wall as the guard opened fire.

CHAPTER SEVENTEEN

It had been way too long.

Sal took a moment to let his body adjust to the movement of his suit again. It would take a while, sure, but it felt like riding a bike. All the muscle memory gradually returned and brought a smile to his face as he tried the various movements the agile hybrid suit was capable of.

"Could you stop bouncing around like a kid on a trampoline?" Madigan asked and sounded annoyed.

Her tone was excusable as she hadn't had much rest. None of them had since Sal elected to bring the Heavy Metal team in. Diggs had filled them in on the situation. A veritable army had been gathered to head into the Zoo to deal with the situation. None of the sectors wanted freelancers to come in and make things unsafe for the researchers, who sustained the cash cow that resulted from the Pita flowers and other lucrative items out of the Zoo.

Sal hadn't had much of a choice coming in, but most researchers did. If they thought they were in danger of being kidnapped and dragged into the Zoo, they would stop coming. No one wanted that to happen.

Then again, too many of them had heard that Taylor was back in action for this. It was probably the best thing to happen for the operation as it brought it legitimacy and more interest than it would have had otherwise. The fact that he had recruited a small team of vets and headed in before any of them could get their collective shit together to join him only made things more interesting.

Sal looked forward to seeing the ginger giant again. It hadn't been that long since they'd parted ways but the man brought an unmistakable energy to the Zoo. It felt like he was almost invincible, and anyone who fought alongside him could have a hint of that power too.

Which was perhaps why so many of them wanted to see him in the flesh.

"You're bouncing again."

"I'm excited!" he replied. "Plus, the suit has these magnetic releases that make it easier to bounce from one foot to the other than it is to walk anyway."

He could feel Madigan scowling even though her face was hidden by her visor. It was always risky entering the Zoo at night, but there was something different about it this time.

It was an odd feeling. He had been off the blue goop for a while after he realized that taking it was affecting his mental state and somehow creating a connection with the Zoo. Even though he hadn't taken any of it for a while, a weird but familiar feeling lingered at the back of his skull.

It was as if something watched the world through his eyes. As foolish as it sometimes sounded—usually when his logical brain intruded—like something had been changed in his physiology and no amount of restraint on his part would change that.

Perhaps Madigan had been right about delaying his return to the Zoo.

"Yeah, I know I'm still bouncing," Sal muttered. "We have movement on the perimeter so maybe keep your eagle eye on that instead?"

She laughed. "I didn't say anything."

"You were about to. I felt a disturbance in the Force."

"I hate that I know that reference. And I hate you for making me aware of it."

"Shut up, you loved the *Star Wars* marathon. Even the prequels."

"That's where all the cool fights were. The originals were merely old men tapping swords and shit."

"I can't believe I'm in a relationship with such a...a philistine!"

"And I'm proud of it, too."

The monsters didn't back away this time like they had before. Groups of hyenas were out for blood and a large pack of them were supported by a few of the larger creatures.

It was most certainly like riding a bike. The light movements of the suit allowed him to advance on the creatures ahead of his team as he drew his assault rifle with one hand and a sword with the other.

A couple of panthers were the first to attack, and Sal laughed at a sudden surge of adrenaline. He jumped to the side, pushed his right leg into one of the nearby trees, and used the momentum to flip over the creatures and slice through both with the sword as he opened fire on the hyena pack.

"I've fucking missed this!" he shouted to no one in particular.

One of the hyenas darted forward while what looked like a rat on insect legs charged at his leg. Sal moved almost without thinking, annihilated the beast, and twisted out of the rat creature's path so Madigan could take care of it as he thrust the sword forward.

Another panther dove from above but was caught by the blade and pinned to a nearby tree. Sal fell back and let his suit reload his rifle quickly before he pushed forward again. In her much heavier suit, Madigan bulldozed a hole in the attacking monsters while he raced toward where his sword protruded from the tree.

He jumped up a few steps on the trunk and dragged the sword out of the bark as two locusts with stinger tails rushed forward. They used the bodies of their fallen as cover through the barrage of gunfire.

Sal pushed his body around and the suit reacted perfectly, flipped him deftly, and aimed him toward the two locusts.

The first had a sword thrust through the tail and then the thorax, and the blade went through into the soil. He twisted his body and used the weight of his suit to crush the second beast's head with his knee.

It wasn't a terrible maneuver, he decided. The tech in the hybrid suit was easily three or four years ahead of its time and he hadn't even begun to tap into everything that it could do. He was merely warming up.

"You haven't missed a step," Madigan conceded and her

tone sounded a little more cheerful than it had before. "Well, maybe a step. That superhero landing was a little rusty. Seven out of ten for that."

"Yeah, I was afraid of that," he admitted as he rose and cleaned the monster blood from the armor. "Still, practice makes perfect, and something tells me that we'll have all the practice I need before this is over."

"Keep your asses moving!"

Diggs didn't like to play the drill sergeant. He thought he'd left that part of his life behind him a long time before and yet there he was, yelling at a large group of soldiers as they headed into the Zoo. It felt like they were new recruits, and he wouldn't have needed to yell at them if they simply did what they were supposed to do.

It was his first time leading a team this large and this varied. Perhaps he was overthinking it and should simply let them do what they knew how to do. If a fight ensued, they would have the numbers to rebuff almost anything but the worst Zoo attacks.

No, screw that. He intended to keep his group as alive as possible for as long as possible. He wouldn't earn a mark on his reputation by letting people do what they wanted, especially if it got them killed.

"Keep it moving, maggots!" he yelled again when a few of the men on his flank fell a little behind.

"Are you all right there, boss?" Carmine, one of his preferred lieutenants, asked in a private comms channel.

"You're acting a little tougher than usual. I get that there is some pressure on this mission, but still..."

"Not even fucking close," he retorted honestly. "I hate acting the part of the big, bad drill sergeant and I wouldn't have to if these motherfuckers would simply keep up with the line. Do you want me to coddle them?"

"No, but—"

"But nothing. If they go in as part of my team, they'll respect the lives of their fellow soldiers as much as their own. That certainly won't happen if they don't maintain their positions, especially on the flanks."

Carmine winced at the last phrase. "It's still only me on the line, boss."

"Shit." He switched to the group channel. "I swear to every fucking god in existence, if you motherfuckers don't keep that flank buttoned up, I'll cut you all off and gun you down myself!"

A couple of the Germans laughed. "Are you in a pit or are you always this kind of an asshole?"

Diggs advanced on the man and dragged him forward into the position he was supposed to be in. The action cut the laughter of the rest of the group short.

"I'm not the fucking asshole!" he stated belligerently. "The Zoo is the asshole and I'm the fucking enema that'll get all of you shits out of this fucking place alive. You'll all still be shit but by all that is fucking holy, you will be alive. Unless you let that fucking flank fall back. So, get into position or walk home. Choose one or the other, but get your asses moving!"

"You've been bragging about how your team is the best in the business."

Sergei Kozlov shrugged as if the challenge inherent in the statement was of little consequence. "I've never said those exact words. My team has said it. I merely don't correct them."

Solodkov rolled his eyes and folded his arms. "It amounts to the same thing but we need to be serious. If you think we're the only ones who will be left out of this operation, you are mistaken."

"But you don't want to send your troops in," the Russian merc pointed out. "You want my mercenaries in there."

"They'll need to prove themselves somehow, yes? They won't do it by sitting around and conducting shallow runs into the Zoo."

"They're not ready for a heavy engagement yet."

The commander shrugged. "How better to get them ready than to send them into a heavy engagement?"

Sergei tilted his head as he considered this. "You make an interesting point."

"And we are one of the closest to where the attack is supposed to be happening. We've had our suspicions that something has been happening in the vicinity of one of the Wall One bases for a while now but never saw the need to venture deeper to investigate. Of course, no one could expect that anyone had reclaimed a base and were kidnapping researchers for their activities there."

"If that is what is happening. There is much rumor and speculation, but I can agree that everyone sees that as the most likely scenario."

Solodkov smirked. "I already have a small team ready to

go in. All your people need to do is play support. And you'll be playing with your old friend Gregor at Heavy Metal again. It is a pity, I think, that you weren't able to persuade him to join you when you assembled your team here at the French Base."

"I don't need them to think that I'm with my own people again," Sergei stated flatly. "Send your team if you must and I will go independently. But don't think I've forgotten your tactics and the way you treated Gregor, or the fact that you will likely lock me up for breaking some law or another back in the motherland."

"We have larger concerns than you, Sergei." Solodkov nodded and the two men stood. "My team is already here and itching to get into the action. They will need the support of fellow Russian troops. We can cut in front of the rest of the troops heading in there with little trouble and all will work out for the best, yes?"

Sergei followed the man out of his small office and headed outside. It was still evening and the cold desert wind whipping across the base made him shiver.

One man waited near the door and he came to attention instantly and snapped a sharp salute when Solodkov appeared.

"Lieutenant Ilyin, meet Gregor Popov, one of the hardest motherfuckers that the Zoo ever spat back out," the Russian officer said with a chuckle.

Kozlov studied the man carefully. Every inch of him screamed military man to the core, something he had come to recognize in men who were about as ruthless as they were ambitious.

"Have you been in the Zoo before?" Gregor asked.

Ilyin looked at Solodkov and the commander nodded.

"Many times, comrade. I have been at the front of a variety of deep-running missions."

"Which you will not be able to discuss with me since it will be classified, I imagine." Sergi sighed and shook his head. "You send me out with a man with no imagination. Worse, he will likely not follow my orders without checking his ass for your hand working him like a puppet even out there."

Solodkov laughed and gestured for the lieutenant to move to where the rest of the troop was already preparing to head in despite the late hour.

"You are right. I do need a man of imagination," the officer admitted. "That is why I need you and your men. The hand working my men like puppets will be yours. If you agree to enter the Zoo with them, they will follow your orders. If you choose to be at the front of the lines, they will follow your instructions. If you choose to hang back and allow them to mop up after the battle carnage of the considerably larger international coalition, that will also be followed."

"I cannot imagine that following a former sergeant into battle will appeal to these men."

"I give no shits about what appeals to them. They have their orders and if they do not follow them... Well, you remember how we deal with deserters and insubordinates. Have no fear. They will follow your every order as if it came from my mouth."

"Again, you send me in there with men of little imagination and who will likely stab me in the back the moment I turn it on them."

"Does that mean that you agree?" Solodkov took a cigarette from his pocket and lit it smoothly. "You can always have your men guard your back."

"I prefer to have them shooting Zoo monsters without being worried about that kind of thing."

"They need not worry. How much is my personal assurance worth to you?"

"Almost nothing. But I will go if only to make sure your rabid fucks don't try to shoot my friends in the back too while they fight to clear the Zoo of monsters."

"Excellent." The other man grinned and released a lungful of putrid smoke. "And to show you that I am acting in good faith, the money is already being transferred to your account as we speak. Now, gather your men. The mission has already begun and you would not want to miss it."

CHAPTER EIGHTEEN

Niki knew she should feel suspicious about how cooperative Ahlers was. Agency people—and especially those in Homeland Security—would never care about getting the job done no matter what the cost.

She liked to think there were other people like her somewhere in the three-letter agencies, but experience had taught her to not expect that from people.

There would be consequences, that much was certain, but she chose not to worry about that right now.

Climbing into the suit had become easier and more comfortable. It was something she never thought she would admit to herself. The idea that she would be on the front lines had always felt like a last resort kind of situation.

But no, there she was, jumping into battle boots-first—like Taylor tended to do. Perhaps she was picking up a little more from him than she would have hoped.

The reinforcements were arriving at the rendezvous point. Given their numbers, they had moved the van to another secluded area screened by trees where two additional vehicles would not be noticed. With the increased numbers, they needed to be sure that sufficient transport was available should they need to make a hasty exit.

She instructed her slowly growing team to ready themselves for an attack while the original members continued to gather intel and the equipment needed. They would have long-distance experts in position for cover but she would lead the frontal assault.

"Are you serious about leading the charge?" Vickie asked and watched her cousin carefully.

Niki had become familiar with that look. The young hacker felt like she needed to keep an eye on her to make sure she didn't do anything too crazy in Taylor's absence. It was a weird thought as except for his bullish style of offense, he tended to think things through. Far more than she did, mostly, because he was used to making snap judgments on the spur of the moment.

But he'd learned that through extensive experience, trial, and error. That was how she intended to get right in there with him.

"Yeah," she said. "We could play around at stealth for a couple of hours, but that would give them time to leave and we'd need to track them through the city and risk being discovered. We need to be ready to go now or could lose them altogether."

The hacker narrowed her eyes. "Weird."

"What?"

"It sounds like you thought this through."

She couldn't help a laugh. "You wouldn't believe how

many times I've had to admit that to Taylor when I thought he was going off half-cocked."

"Ew."

"You know that's not what I meant."

"I know. But still, the mental image. Just…gag. Barf. All the words that mean regurgitation."

Niki shrugged. "That's on you. I tried to make a heart-felt point and you're the one whose brain is filled with all the dirty pictures."

"Dude, I spend most of my time on the Internet. Most of what you see out there is either porn or conspiracy theories, with only the very smallest sliver of useful information. You have to take the good with the bad in that case."

"The porn being the bad?"

"Eh. Maybe not the worst."

"What do you mean?"

Vickie shook her head. "You don't want to know."

"I—"

"I'm not kidding. You truly, truly don't want to know."

Niki nodded and decided to take the hacker's word for it. Besides, they had bigger problems to worry about.

"The team is ready," Taslim alerted her as she climbed out of the van and moved from side to side to adjust to the suit. "We're ready to attack when you are, Banks."

"I appreciate it." She could get used to having a group of professionals who got the job done while providing minimal backchat. Admittedly, the backchat could be fun, but it usually meant they were a little more comfortable with each other, which wasn't the case here. Most of the men and women called in might have worked with each other in smaller missions in the past but nothing quite to this extent.

And none of them had worked with her either. Which meant the banter needed to come from Vickie for the moment.

The ex-agent wanted the element of surprise. The eyes they already had in place all over the area confirmed that their quarry was not yet spooked, which meant they could still spring a trap. Not that the team of fifteen plus her would have much trouble simply bulldozing in.

While the Chinese outnumbered them, they weren't armored, and from what the team could tell from watching the feeds, they had mostly small arms at their disposal. Niki had arranged a small arsenal for her team, which included assault rifles, long-range rifles, and a large supply of bullets. All that firepower rushing in was bound to overwhelm their targets even if they were warned but it was Niki's task to make sure no lives were needlessly lost, at least in her team.

Surprise was an advantage that she wouldn't give up lightly, and she positioned herself to let them put their best foot forward.

"See if these assholes are ready for a full, Zoo-ready combat suit," she muttered.

"Niki, there is a…development."

She paused in gearing herself up for the attack when Desk's voice pinged through the HUD's headset.

"That doesn't sound like a good development."

"I don't think it's good or bad but most certainly a development. I've been studying…well, there are all kinds of complications involved in what I've been studying. The point is that there is evidence that the warehouse is a little more than it appears. In fact, I am certain there is an underground section that might extend to external points of entry—the kind an established businessman would use to avoid a direct connection with a known crime syndicate."

"Wait, how do you know this? There's nothing about in the blueprints."

"Oh my," Desk replied. "You don't think the triads would simply ignore the building code laws, do you? That would be low, even for them."

"Shut up. What makes you think they built underground?"

"There have been reports of construction being heard in the region, but nothing ever came of it. Some insurance claims detail a little sagging here and there. Individually, this isn't much but when put together, it tells me something is happening under the surface. The chances are that there's an underground tunnel system. It's something for you to be aware of."

It was a significant development and she wanted to ensure that there was nowhere for her target to slip out of once they cornered him.

"All right, guys," Niki said once she'd called up the rest of the team. "We need to be alert for one or more possible escape hatches under the warehouse. It could be that they've used these to smuggle people and merchandise in from time to time, so they will be a little difficult to identify. Keep your eyes open."

"Will do, boss," Perez answered and nodded as the teams assembled nearby. They were setting up to make sure they wouldn't let any of the patrols get past them. "What's the plan?"

Niki nodded. "Right. We'll strike hard and push through. As we move, look for a computer node or port where I can insert a drive to gain access to their data. Our main objective is to locate Chen Lu Wan. The guy probably has police connections so we do not intend to capture anyone. With that said, the bastard is mine. I have a little vengeance to deliver on the fucker and believe me when I say that none of you want to get in the way of that. Are there any questions?"

The silence that followed her statement said there were none—or if there were, they were wise enough to keep those questions to themselves.

"Good." She retrieved the assault rifle from her back and watched its data appear on her HUD. It displayed a full magazine and that it was zeroed and ready to fire. "Choose your targets and exterminate with extreme prejudice. These sons of bitches won't know what hit them."

Of all the places where Taylor preferred to fight in the Zoo, a contained situation inside a prefab building was not one of them.

The necessity to act as cover for people who did not have the same armor, strength, and stamina as the rescuers merely made things even worse.

"Get down!" he roared and pushed himself forward in front of the researchers. A handful of rounds struck and ricocheted around the room but he managed to keep the people behind him safe, more or less, while he opened fire.

If there was ever a statement that revealed the differences in quality between the suit he wore and those their attackers used, it was the fact that one of the defenders fell back immediately when a couple of rounds punched through his armor and into the pilot behind it. A few of the rounds didn't penetrate but one was sufficient.

The rest of the team fell quickly into a tight formation. It was tough trying to create a small wall to cover the researchers and return fire at the same time.

"We're like fish in a fucking barrel here!" Watt shouted over the comms.

He was right and the chances were that the gunfire would soon involve more people. They needed to get out and get out fast.

"Do you have any ideas?" Taylor asked.

"You're the one running this fucking show!" Watt snapped in return.

"I'm not talking to you!"

Li'l Desk needed a moment to focus on the fight they were in while she also positioned herself to best effect in the software running the suit. "As a matter of fact, I do."

He wouldn't tell the AI how to do her job. The fact that she ran at reduced capacity and from a suit and was still on a trial run meant that he was probably asking too much of her already. That one was on him. Perhaps he shouldn't have put so much pressure on her the first time out.

But there was no better time to learn than on the fly, and he pushed these unnecessary thoughts aside as he moved forward. He fired methodically and tried to pin the mercenaries down at the door, push them back, and clear space for the rest of his team to maintain fire until they were no longer on the back foot.

That was the plan, at least, and he could only hope it would work.

"The rhinos! The pens are open."

Taylor looked up from his cover at a sudden respite in the shooting. Only a few random rounds harassed them, and if there was ever an opening for them to attack, it was now.

With that said, he did not intend to charge head-on into a Zoo attack if he could help it.

The men pinned outside began to withdraw. Those who were still inside had their attention elsewhere and not on his team and the researchers.

"Li'l Desk, did you do this?" Taylor asked. "I know I asked for a plan but holy shit, that's a little extreme."

"It is a fine idea," she admitted. "But not mine. I may not possess the full intelligence of an AI but my self-preservation coding prevents me from engaging in an action through which I might find myself unleashing Zoo creatures with no semblance of control."

"Oh. Still—"

"There might be an opening for us to exploit. From the chatter before the gates were opened, it appears that the release of the rhinos was an intentional attempt to contain the invaders. I assume that means you."

"It's a good assumption. Another one might be that the rhinos did not respond well to being used as defense weapons."

"You are correct." Li'l Desk's CPU usage spiked

suddenly and a path highlighted to lead them out of the building. "If we are to avoid most of the rampaging monsters, I recommend using this route to escape."

Taylor nodded, looked at his team, and gestured them forward. They all saw the path in their HUDs, and they began to advance on the mercs who still tried to hold the door.

The fact that their efforts were now directed against what they feared would come from outside was probably helpful. Taylor felt no mercy in him as he eliminated the three men in rapid succession, aiming his shots at their heads to finish them off cleanly.

He wanted them dead but it didn't mean he would waste time making them suffer. The researchers, on the other hand, probably wanted to see a little suffering among their captors.

Right now, though, there was no time for that. He motioned for them to keep moving, although Liu paused to kick one of the mercs before they slipped through the door.

Taylor couldn't help a grin as his suit suddenly came to life. The extra limbs were activated and slid from his back to move out and make him look like some kind of arachnid. They stepped out into the chaos that had overtaken the compound.

"When the fuck did you get a suit like that?" Everett asked with a disbelieving laugh. " I've only ever seen one suit with the extra arms like that. I thought they were... well, one of a kind."

"It's a prototype," Taylor admitted as Li'l Desk took control and began to familiarize herself with the movements. He was sure that if Vickie or Niki were around, they would have made jokes about giving the overlord arms and legs.

He wasn't ready for that thought. Not having the two women with him felt weird but he would make sure to tell them about the feeling when he returned home.

"Look out!"

Taylor barely had time to turn and caught only a flash of movement to his left as the suit suddenly acted on its own. One of the arms drew the combat knife from his belt and thrust it immediately toward the creature.

It was one of the rhino mutants that had been set loose. The blade was already buried in its neck and forced the creature to its knees. It was bigger than he'd expected it to be and almost reached his chest, and the power required to drive it back almost knocked him off his feet.

"Nice…nice," Devon admitted with a laugh. "Was that you? Did you do that?"

He shrugged and the suit kicked up with the movement. "I…no. The suit and…uh, Lil Desk."

"Ah. Nice."

Taylor nodded.

"You didn't have to do that," Li'l Desk commented.

"It honestly doesn't matter," he replied and shook his head. Every single instinct within him shouted that something was wrong. The whole compound felt like it had come alive with gunfire. A few bellows sounded like the rhinos, but screeches and roars from the Zoo were impossible to ignore.

"Why do you say that?" Li'l Desk asked.

"We might not be around long enough for it to matter,"

he answered quickly. "All right, people, we keep moving and shoot anything that gets in our way, but we don't stop, understood?"

The researchers had armed themselves with the weapons from the fallen mercs but looked uncomfortable and terrified. He couldn't blame them for it and there was no other option at this point.

"Okay, let's get moving!"

CHAPTER NINETEEN

It was a frustrating position to be in and Niki didn't like it. They were all ready to get in there but she now had to wait outside instead.

"There's movement coming from inside," Vickie alerted her over the radio. They had the cameras set up outside and they must have picked up something through the window glass. She could only guess that if there was movement inside, it wasn't another patrol.

"New people?" she asked.

"I'm running their faces through the recognition software…give me a sec….yep, new people and muscle by the looks of them. They're looking around the warehouse like they would if they were doing a security sweep."

That was all she needed to hear. Niki took a deep breath and nodded.

"All right, people, it looks like our hens have come in to roost." She checked her weapon yet again. "Let's make a chicken pot pie."

"Chicken pot pie?" Taslim asked.

"It's a saying," she responded quickly.

"Is it, though?" Vickie interjected.

"Shut it. Let's get moving, people!"

She stepped around the corner and immediately noticed a group that had begun to circle in her direction.

"Big guns!"

"On it," Perez called.

Cracks of gunfire sounded in the distance, and all four dropped immediately before they could even draw their weapons. That opening salvo launched the beginning of the combat.

The other patrols heard the gunfire and yelled at one another as they tried to identify where it was coming from. Niki primed the rockets she had mounted on her shoulders and let the tracking systems pick up two of the patrols that had begun to close on them.

She let the rockets loose almost without a thought and four white plumes launched from her shoulders. The evening was suddenly lit up with four bright flashes. The result wasn't as much fire as she would have liked but the cutting blasts were more than loud enough to make up for that.

"Go, go, go, go!"

Niki had no idea why she yelled as she rushed forward. The hydraulics in her suit took the brunt of the weight and pushed her forward faster than most Olympians could sprint. Movement was tagged coming from her left. Red silhouettes were marked around them, noting them as hostiles, and the computer in her suit began to set up a targeting system for the rockets.

There was no need for them this time, however.

She raised her assault rifle and bombarded the patrol with bursts of gunfire that kicked the weapon back into her shoulder. Of course, she wasn't used to piloting a suit this large, but damned if she didn't intend to get used to it.

The patrols that she hadn't picked up now sprinted back to the warehouse They shouted into radios as those inside the warehouse opened fire to force her people into cover.

The snipers continued to do their work from their perfect position, and one after the other, those who tried to retreat were eliminated neatly.

In a matter of seconds, eight men and women sprawled amid clouds of dust.

It was good to be fighting with a full pro team but they couldn't rest on any laurels. She had a feeling that Lu Wan was already aware that they were under attack.

If the bastard got away now, the chances were that he would simply vanish and would be on a plane to China where she would never catch him again.

It simply wasn't an option.

"Give me some cover fire!" Niki shouted. "Don't let them use the windows!"

The snipers acknowledged the order almost immediately and she stepped out from behind the wall she had used as cover. Without a pause to think things through, she pushed the suit as fast as it would go across the open stretch toward the warehouse.

A couple of rounds pinged off her armor and a few alarm lights came on, but she was committed. The snipers dealt with those who were in the windows, and Niki could almost feel the full momentum of pushing a three and a half-ton combat suit at twenty miles an hour.

It would take a lot to stop it.

She bellowed a battle cry as she approached one of the walls. This was no time to be civilized and look for a couple of doors to use. She would simply go the direct route, which was straight through.

More alarms triggered as the inertia of the suit suddenly took a hit. She was surrounded by rubble and a cloud of dust but she could move. The suit was still intact, despite a few warning lights coming on. The hydraulic system, however, seemed to have taken a beating.

Her teeth gritted with determination, she pushed inside and past the lines of defense they had been setting up. Most didn't seem to realize exactly what was happening. Perhaps they thought she had blown the hole with rockets?

Neither their confusion nor their ignorance mattered. The suit selected targets for her rockets, even through the cloud of dust and smoke, and she released two rockets into a group that had focused on trying to pin her team down outside the warehouse.

They were doing a good job of it. It looked like they were some kind of former military. Either that or they'd been in more than a few gunfights as they used all the right kinds of cover and maintained a steady barrage of fire.

They were, unfortunately for them, heavily outgunned.

The warehouse lit up with five flashes when Niki used the last of her rockets to destroy the defenders' cover and kill half a dozen of them in the process.

It felt like she'd done her part to clear the way for the rest of her team. The enemy now had no cover and tried to push closer to stop her instead of her teammates. The snipers had already begun to eliminate those they could and her group advanced steadily toward the vulnerable defenders.

She needed to find Lu Wan. If the idiot asshole managed to escape, he would continue to send Zoo-tainted products around the world and create dangerous dependencies in the name of making a quick buck.

Vickie would kill him on principle for selling rhino horns, no matter what the origin, and it was a worthy sentiment to keep in mind.

The fact that the Zoo would undoubtedly be pissed about people messing with its particular brand of shit meant that the situation would probably put Taylor at risk while he was in there too.

"See?" she asked rhetorically while she checked her firepower and scanned the warehouse. "You have at least three good reasons to perforate the fucker."

"Are you talking to yourself?" Vickie asked over comms.

"Yes. Where is the entrance to the underground level?"

"The cameras picked up new guys coming in from the northwest corner of the warehouse."

"Do I look like a fucking compass?"

"You have eyes, don't you? It's in the same direction as the motherfuckers are retreating to!"

The hacker's statement drew her attention back to the invaders. The men had already begun to fall back while they attempted to maintain sufficient fire that would discourage her team from advancing. It was a solid idea and a good tactic, but it felt like they made no effort to shoot in her direction—like they knew they would simply waste the smaller rounds on her armor.

Something would eventually get through, but they were right in sparing their ammo for less dangerous targets. Or, at least, they would have been, if she wasn't moving the same direction as they did—and moved faster on top of it.

They shouted something as she approached. She couldn't understand it, but she decided to assume that it was "oh shit" in Mandarin.

She didn't bother to shoot the first triad member she encountered and simply backhanded him across the jaw as he approached. It was a satisfying feeling to watch the man thunk into the nearest wall, hard enough to leave a dent and break a few windows on impact before he sprawled on the hard floor, silent and still.

A few of the men turned their Uzis on her, no doubt having decided that ignoring the combat suit was probably not the best tactic after all, but it was too late. She felt the impact of the rounds as they struck her armor but none penetrated as she barreled into them. One was gunned down almost immediately and she didn't mind running a second one down to crush him under the weight of the suit as she caught hold of the third.

The suit did most of the work and Niki grinned as she launched him at one of the others who tried to retreat as well. It wouldn't end well for either of them but she didn't want to have to give her team too little to do. The DHS was paying them enough for their time, after all.

"Let's get it moving!" she roared and turned toward the small opening that had been cut into the ground some fifteen feet away from where she stood.

"Don't forget the computer systems!" Vickie shouted.

"Right." Niki looked at the people coming in behind her. The warehouse had been cleared of the triad members, which meant they were all in full retreat. Not that she blamed them. She would do the same if she were in their shoes.

"The Faraday cage?" Taslim asked and Niki nodded and pointed at the computers inside while she took the drive from her belt.

"Get in there and stick it in," Niki ordered. "I'll go down and clear them out of any defensive positions, so follow me and mop up any I leave behind."

"If you leave any behind," one of them muttered, although Niki couldn't make out who had said it.

"Yeah, he might have a point there," Vickie pointed out. "You are on something of a...I think the term is a bit of a tear?"

"Is that a bad thing?"

"No, unless you happen to break one of your people when they get in your way."

Niki shook her head. She wouldn't do that, mostly because she made sure that she was the one at the front at all times. If anyone got in anyone's way, it would be her if she was bogged down.

That was very unlikely and she'd worry about it if and when it happened.

She strode toward the opening, which was barely large enough for the suit to fit through. It took careful maneuvering and avoiding the ladder that had been used, and she dropped into the lower level with a massive thud.

The subterranean structure was surprisingly well-built.

The walls were shored up with concrete and held shelving for materials or equipment that were currently missing. There were signs of considerable movement all around her, but it was currently quiet. She knew that only meant that the assholes couldn't be too far away.

"Did you motherfuckers truly think you could get away?" she shouted through the tunnel leading away from the storage room. The only answer she received was a burst of gunfire from what looked like a small submachine gun. She pushed closer to the walls so the shooters wouldn't have a clean shot at her as she approached.

It seemed they were staggering their people out. Lu Wen was probably the one to blame for that. The guy didn't care about the people he employed. He merely wanted to get out of there alive so he could go into hiding and continue killing people for money. That wouldn't happen, not on her watch.

The HUD highlighted targets for her again and as she moved forward, she let the auto-targeting system start picking a handful of the men off when they peeked out from their cover. If they thought they could hinder her progress with a slow fight, they hadn't learned the lesson she had taught them when she bulldozed a hole in their warehouse wall.

Three had fallen before they realized that she had no intention to slow. She powered through a heavy crate that a couple more attempted to hide behind.

"Vickie! The motherfucker is trying to make a run for it! Find him right fucking now!"

"I'm working on it."

Niki circled a corner and grimaced at a handful of dings on the armor from the men who tried to target her from a distance. She made no attempt to check the damage and instead, opened fire on them and pushed her suit as fast as it could go through the tunnel leading away from the warehouse. At that point, she had no idea if the group behind her was still holding the warehouse or if they were coming after her.

It didn't matter. She would take care of Lu Wen herself, the bastard.

The three defenders who had waited for her around the corner didn't put up much of a fight. One even tried to run when she turned the corner but was too slow and she collided with him. Bones were crushed on impact and he fell without so much as a sound. Bullets pumped rhythmically from her weapon and sliced easily through the men in front of her as she realized that she had reached another section of the tunnel.

Or the end of the tunnel, she amended when she looked more closely. It appeared to have been built as an underground storage area for a warehouse and even had stairs leading up to the ground floor.

"Desk! I'm in a warehouse that looks like it might have an underground storage area in the plans. Look for it."

"I already have your location and am directing the rest of the team toward you now," the AI replied. "Stay safe."

Niki grinned. It was a little late for that. She reached the stairs and instead of taking them, vaulted up the ten or so feet to the next level. The concrete under her cracked under the weight of the suit. More alarms activated to warn her that something was wrong.

"Niki, you need to wait for the rest of the team," Vickie cautioned her.

She didn't respond. A car engine revved loudly, no doubt the one that would take Lu Wen out of her reach, and she wasn't going to let that happen.

"Niki!"

With a scowl, she flicked the comm system in her suit off. If Vickie would be nothing more than a distraction, she could pull this off on her own.

Four men raced to what looked like a town car. Three of them were the usual hired muscle, men with tattoos, expensive suits, and battle scars like most of the triads, but one was different. He wore an understated gray suit and glasses with no visible tattoos and no scars. Compared to his bodyguards, he looked a little pudgy.

She'd located her target at last.

There was no clean shot but Niki took it anyway and one of the bodyguards sagged without so much as a whimper. She pushed her suit to increase speed and her second shot tore through the knee of a second man. He cried out and clutched the wound as he fell, which left only one between Niki and Lu Wen.

She closed the distance quickly and ignored the 9-millimeter rounds bouncing off her armor as she lifted the man with one hand and pounded his head into the closest window of the town car.

The driver scrambled out of the vehicle and tried to shoot over it while he also kept his head down. Niki scowled as she considered her options. She didn't want to have to fucking circle the car to deal with him, and the HUD provided her with another option instead.

The onboard computer was more useful than she thought it would be. She dropped prone, grasped the bottom of the town car, and with a heave that she could feel strained the suit's systems, flipped it to crush the man on the other side.

"And then there was one." She growled her satisfaction and turned her attention to the small, pudgy businessman who stood in front of her. "Chen Lu Wen, I presume?"

"Please," he whispered, unable to tear his gaze from the assault rifle that was suddenly pointed at his head. "You don't have to do this."

She shook her head. "Nah. I kind of do, sorry."

Without warning, she grasped the side of his head. hammered it into the overturned car, and simply watched him stumble and struggle to stay on his feet.

"I have money," the man said and extended his hand as if in supplication. "I can pay you. Let me live and you would never have to work again.."

"So…the offers are basically reduced to…either take a shit-ton money or have your tongue ripped out?" Niki asked, tilted her head, and caught him by the collar to keep him from falling. "All while you keep peddling your Zoo-laced shit and getting people killed? Did you honestly think you could buy your way out of this you son of a…bitch!"

A sharp sting bit into her neck where the suit ended and her helmet began. She grimaced at the pain, even as she had to acknowledge the accuracy of whoever wielded the unknown weapon. It seemed impossible that they would be able to locate and target the tiniest sliver of flesh —and that only when her head was lowered slightly as it was now. She released Lu Wen and turned to one of her mercs who stood and regarded her impassively.

"Backstabbers!" Niki snapped and tried to determine what might have been stabbed into her neck.

"It's a sedative," Vickie informed her as the man moved closer. "A mild one but you needed to stop and you weren't getting talked down so…uh, alternative methods needed to be tried."

"Wha—" Her head began to droop forward and she hit her nose on the visor. The suit seemed to sag with her and although it held her up to some degree, it responded sluggishly to her commands.

No, it wasn't the suit she realized. The problem was her limbs that she wasn't able to move very efficiently.

"I'm sorry," Vickie whispered before full darkness descended.

CHAPTER TWENTY

The Zoo had come alive.

There was no other way to describe it. Hundreds of creatures moved constantly in the periphery of their sensor range. The simians in the trees made themselves known with screeches and screams from above that made it almost impossible to hear anything around them.

Diggs' head started to ache from the constant barrage of noise that issued from all around them. Worse, he couldn't turn off the noise sensors on the outside of his suit, not if he wanted to survive. It would also be a bad example for the rest of the troop. He had pushed all of them hard from the start and it was clear that they had begun to respond to his orders a little better once the full realization of their circumstances set in.

They were heading deeper into the jungle than most of them had before and the Zoo was pissed. Everyone needed to pull their weight.

"Fifteen klicks to Wall One," one of the Germans called as they advanced. The group remained tight and kept themselves in formation, and that seemed to be doing wonders for their morale so far. There was less of the joking and shitting around but they were certainly a little more active and alert and kept their firing lines clean. The sergeant was all for that.

"Advance on the left flank!"

Diggs shook his head, moved to the left flank, and gestured for his team to follow him. The fact that it had become necessary to put a team together that swept the front of the line to clear the monsters that attempted to focus on one area or the other was interesting, to say the least. He had never headed such a large troop and couldn't say he liked the responsibility, but when it came down to it, all this meant was that there were more people to get shit done. It wasn't quite an army but close enough.

Not the worst situation, he reminded himself, and certainly better than heading in with too few people.

Still, he'd heard stories about troops much larger than his being shredded with only a few survivors, if there were any at all. Of course, Taylor had been in a couple of those. They were all part of his legend, although he didn't envy the man his position. It was nice to be remembered and have a legacy, but not like that.

Anything but that, he decided with a shudder.

The left flank struggled against a determined assault by the mutants, and Diggs primed the rocket launcher on his shoulder. He also activated the minigun he carried to clear the way. A handful of horned gorillas rushed into the line and forced them back, although it didn't look like they had taken any real casualties yet.

"Avoid hitting the spines!" he roared over the channel

and opened fire as low as he could around the monsters' legs and arms to injure and slow them, hopefully, while the automated minigun dealt with the smaller fuckers. His teammates rallied around the advancing reinforcements and fired a sustained barrage into the massive gorilla creatures to force them back.

Suddenly, the whole Zoo felt like it was contracting around them. All the creatures turned instantly and focused on the left flank.

"Son of a—I said don't shoot the spines, you dumb shits!" Diggs snapped and lobbed a handful of grenades out into the path of the creatures that now suddenly advanced on them.

"How do you know?" a Brit shouted in response.

"Because you pissed the Zoo off!"

He shook his head. It had been a while since some of the larger engagements in the Zoo, and people had begun to forget some of the basic, hard-won ways to avoid having the whole jungle converge on a single point at the same time. The fact that people would probably die for the lesson to be driven home was the kind of unfortunate that made him angry.

A cluster of explosions erupted across the front of the line as claymores were set up by the quicker thinkers of the group. They ripped into the crowds of smaller Zoo creatures that raced forward first. Snapped commands positioned a dozen heavier mechs to pour minigun fire into the group at the front while rockets rained from behind to clear massive swathes for the groups that continued to push forward.

The Zoo poured everything it had available at them and

the teams had turned it all into a charnel house. Diggs grinned and reloaded his weapons as they killed the stragglers that acted like most of their comrades hadn't been turned into mincemeat.

Still, this felt like an unfocused attack from the Zoo. The critters had only gotten pissed when the blue sacs of goop around the spine of one of the big beasts had burst.

It could only mean that the Zoo was focused on an attack elsewhere. In the silence that followed the battle, he could hear gunfire in the distance and confirmed at least a direction to where the fuckers' attention was centered.

"We're on our way, you big ginger bastard." Diggs hissed under his breath. "Fucking stay alive until I get to say I told you so."

There was no real telling what they had expected this to do.

They'd thought that sedating her would be a good way to keep her out of trouble but Niki proved them wrong on that count.

Maybe antagonizing the local police force wasn't the best idea, but if they didn't like it, they shouldn't have tried to lock her up in the first place.

She had gone from being handcuffed in the precinct to being confined in one of the holding cells. They'd moved her directly from the holding cell with the others to one of her own, which was the best choice for all involved. she didn't want to have to prove how bad her mood was by taking it out on the criminals waiting to be bailed out. God forbid that she scare them straight or something.

It was also pleasant to not have her hands cuffed. She'd been locked up from the moment when they managed to drag her out of her suit, which made her life a little more uncomfortable than it needed to be.

One of the officers had been assigned to watch her and make sure she didn't devise any more trouble.

"Do you guys honestly think I'll be able to break through the bars and get you from here?" she asked, raised an eyebrow, and studied the man closely.

The officer didn't answer and instead, fixed his gaze on the empty desk in front of him. Admittedly, she had head-butted one of the triads they had led past her, but there was no reason for them to think that she was capable of slipping through bars and performing magic of some kind, right?

"Seriously, are you not going to say anything?" She tried again, stood from the cot that was in her cell, and approached the bars. The man stiffened visibly merely from her leisurely stroll. "Did they tell you I was this dangerous? What exactly did they say I was capable of?"

"They said you killed almost a dozen people, broke a wall down, and flipped a car," the man answered finally and immediately looked like he regretted it.

Niki nodded. "Okay, fair enough. Did they tell you that I used a combat suit to do all that or did you think I'm some maniac on steroids or something?"

"A combat suit?"

"Yeah, you know, the combat suits they use in the Zoo?

I was packing some heat too. It's not like I can simply bend the bars at will."

He swallowed and stared at her. She could almost see his mind chewing on the question of where exactly she might have obtained a combat suit to begin with.

It was a good question, and he turned away and tried to not look at her.

Maybe she would have to try it, though, and see how crazy they had made her out to be. If she played her cards correctly, she wouldn't have to do much to persuade them to let her walk out.

"Officer....Chamberlain?"

The young officer bolted to his feet at the sound of his name, although by the way he lowered his hand to grasp his pistol, it wasn't out of deference. Still, he relaxed when a tall woman in a gray pantsuit stepped into the holding area, a handful of files in her hands.

"Yes…uh, yes? That's me."

She smiled and took a badge from inside her jacket. "I'm Agent Ahlers, Department of Homeland Security. I'm here to escort Ms. Banks from custody."

"I…excuse me?"

"The paperwork is all here." She handed him one of the files and turned her attention to the prisoner while he studied the documents. "How are they treating you, Niki? Any trouble?"

"One of the triads ran his nose into my forehead, but aside from that, I'm not too bad. The food here is crap, though."

"I've been told as much," Ahlers answered with a smirk and turned to the young officer.

"I'm...it says that no charges are being filed?"

"That is correct."

He scowled. "But...the damage. She put a hole in a wall and flipped a car."

The agent glanced at Niki. "I don't know. She works out but do you honestly think she's capable of doing that?"

"She...she had a combat suit."

"A combat suit?" Ahlers laughed. "Those high-tech suits they use to run around in the Sahara and kill alien monsters? Does she look like the kind of person who would have access to high-tech equipment like that?"

The man shook his head but narrowed his eyes at Niki before he drew a deep breath. "Right. Well. All the paperwork is in order. Please...uh, don't make any more trouble, Ms. Banks."

"I promise." Niki put her hand over her heart as the door unlocked and she stepped outside.

Ahlers gestured with her head to the hallway and both women exited the holding room and walked rapidly to the entrance.

"Having performed a few tricks of the vanishing paperwork type myself, I have to say it's impressive that you managed to pull this off so quickly," Niki admitted as they proceeded down the hallway.

"It's not like we could have you languishing away in a holding cell," Ahlers replied with a small grin. "You're still on the clock, after all."

"Is that why you got me out?"

"Well, I did technically get you into the situation, although you taking it above and beyond all belief and expectation is on your head and yours alone. This is your one-time get out of jail free pass with me. The next time you go berserk on enemies and teammates alike, you'll be on your own. And that includes legal fees."

"I didn't go berserk."

"You didn't?" Sarcasm oozed from her tone.

"Okay, maybe, but not on any of my team. I might be headstrong but I'm not that headstrong."

"No, you didn't, but that was only because they were smart enough to not get in your way. If they had, I have no doubt that you would have bulldozed through them as easily as you did those triads."

"Now come on—"

Ahlers raised a hand to stop her. "Taslim is one of my best and I read his report. Off the reservation falls miles short of describing exactly how dangerously you were acting."

Niki scowled. The woman was right, of course. The fact that she didn't like it didn't change anything, and she would need a little time to come to terms with that. The fact that her worrying about the people she cared about had dragged that side of her out into the open merely made things worse.

What if Vickie got in her way when she acted like that? What if she didn't have a handy dandy syringe full of sedatives to calm her next time?

"All right," she admitted finally. "You're right. I'll suck up the sedative hangover and say thank you for getting me out of this jam."

The agent smiled and nodded. "That's a solid move, Banks. I'd like to be able to call on you and your team again if necessary in the future. The fact that you're a very particular breed of useful crazy does come with its limits, though. It's very rarely a desirable trait in a field team, especially one that acts on US soil. Pull that shit in Indonesia, and all you'll get is a transfer, but do that here, and you have Attorney Generals howling for blood."

Niki narrowed her eyes. "Okay, exactly what did Taylor get up to in Indonesia anyway?"

"I'm not at liberty to discuss that."

"Whatever." She would find out eventually. "At least you're honest about what you are at liberty to discuss."

"I'm always honest about what I'm at liberty to discuss." Ahlers grinned, pulled the door to the precinct open, and let her walk out first. "Sometimes brutally so. Remember that. Now, do you need a ride to your hotel?"

It was a good question and she looked up, trying to shield her eyes from the sun until she could see a familiar-looking van in the parking lot outside.

"I think I'll find my own way."

"All right. I'll see you when I see you, Banks."

She nodded, waved at the agent, and waited for her to enter the dark SUV she'd she'd come in before she jogged across the parking lot to where Vickie waited for her.

"Did you get the suit?" Niki asked immediately as she scrambled into the shotgun seat.

"Hi there, beloved cousin," the hacker replied, her voice dripping sarcasm. "How are you? Thanks for pulling me up short before I could go King Fucking Kong on the warehouse district of San Francisco."

"Thanks, Vick." She grinned and patted her cousin on the shoulder. "I appreciate you keeping an eye out for me. Now, did you get the suit or did the cops impound it?"

"Of course I got the suit. What do you think I am? Stupid?"

"Never stupid. I merely thought you might have had more to worry about than an expensive piece of military-grade hardware."

"I did and I handled it all perfectly, thanks. Ahlers said she would give you a pass on everything, so once everything was cleaned up in the warehouses, I came here to give you a ride. And a lecture."

"Oh, God."

"Oh, God is right. Are you fucking crazy or something? It's not like I'm any good at this!" Vickie beat her hands on the wheel and shook her head. "I'm as worried as fuck too, you know. For you and for Taylor. I'm not great at being the rock. Maybe the hard place, but that's about my limit."

The hacker started the van and pulled out of the parking lot, still red in the face.

"Did you rehearse that while you were waiting for me?" Niki asked.

"Yeah, how did I do?"

"Well…the rock and the hard place reference was fairly good so I'd say solid overall."

"I thought she rushed the delivery somewhat," Desk commented over the van's speakers.

"Yeah, I was a little afraid that would happen."

"But a sound performance," Desk continued. "Now, Niki, as you know, it is my duty to keep you safe. But I also know that you respond better to carrots than to sticks, to use the equine-based euphemism, so I can promise you that I will find out anything I can about Taylor's situation as long as you promise to lock yourself in your hotel room and stay there."

"I'd rather have a drink."

"There are drinks in the minibar. I am afraid that I must insist."

Niki didn't want to find out what the AI was capable of when she went into insistent mode. While there were limits to what Desk could do, she wouldn't like to test them when it came to protecting the people she was designed to keep safe.

"Fine," she grumbled. "I'll raid the minibar."

CHAPTER TWENTY-ONE

"I thought you said we had a clear path to the exits."

Li'l Desk took a moment to respond. "I said it was the clearest path, not that it was entirely clear of danger."

Yes, she had said that and Taylor couldn't disagree. Then again, if this was the clearest path, he had to assume the rest of the base was covered in about fifteen different kinds of hell.

Watt stepped out in front of them and opened fire as the researchers were escorted to the exit. If it had been only the six of them, Taylor had no doubt that he would be able to move the team out as quickly as possible but the researchers had a difficult time moving through the combat. It wasn't only because they weren't wearing power armor at all but also because they seemed to struggle to move under their own power.

"We can haul them up on our shoulders!" Devon suggested, yanked a grenade from his belt, and lobbed it into the path of a handful of the charging rhinos. The flash and the explosion were enough to drive them to direct their attack elsewhere. Herds of them raced through the compound to attack anything and anyone in their path.

At the same time, Taylor could hear the rest of the Zoo joining the fun. Gunfire at the perimeters of the compound had grown more intense and it wouldn't be long until something broke through.

"We'll see about that later!" he answered as Li'l Desk operated the limbs that emerged from his back to clear a path for them to continue. "For now, keep moving!"

It wasn't the advice anyone wanted to hear but it was all he had to give. They wouldn't be able to deal with this shit in a single pitched battle, and there would be other concerns for them to address before the fighting reached its peak. All that could be done was to take each step one at a time and hope that they lasted through each one.

"I have another pack coming in!"

Taylor turned his attention to the rhinos as a shower of sparks flurried over him and alarms blared in his suit. A group of the mercs was trying to attack them from the top of one of the prefab buildings

"Devon, keep the front line!" he shouted and twisted his body as another volley of gunfire hammered into him. More alarms signaling more problems resulted, but the suit still worked as he dove to the right. The extra limbs caught him and rolled him behind a few crates as he moved toward the building.

The limbs caught on the building quickly and he resigned himself to the ride as Li'l Desk scaled to the top for him. She'd been clever enough to ascend at an angle that the mercs hadn't thought they could attack from yet.

Taylor chose a target from the group and pulled the

trigger on his assault rifle. The man's head exploded outward as the helmet failed to contain the chunks of skull and brain matter. He shifted to the side and kept himself in motion as two of the limbs lashed out, caught one of the men on the side with a knife, and almost cut him in half.

He used the momentum to launch himself feet-first at the next man with enough power to hurl him off the edge of the building. His extra arms caught him before he followed the hapless merc and he swiped his rifle around to punch three rounds into the next defender's chest. The man sagged slowly as the suit tried to compensate for his sudden lack of balance.

"I think I'm getting the hang of having eight limbs," Taylor said to no one in particular as he managed to stand fairly quickly. "Nice work on the integration."

"Your compliment is noted."

He shook his head, dropped smoothly to a controlled landing, and looked around to locate the rest of the crew.

Something had gone wrong. Jian was covered in dark blood with a massive knife in his hands, and Devon had dropped on his knees beside one of the researchers, who was seated with his back against one of the buildings.

For a moment, he thought the man had caught one of the ricochets off his armor, but the size of the wound indicated that it was from one of the three rhinos that lay on the ground around them.

"They… I don't know what happened," Everett whispered, his expression dazed. "I only…they were… They had attacked Vitsin before we knew that—oh, God…"

"Are you hurt?" Taylor asked.

"No…no, it's not my blood."

The researcher had charged into the fight, which was brave enough, but it didn't explain why the Russian was on the ground with a massive wound in his stomach.

"Must go," the man stated, his tone rough as he shook his head. "Not…this is… I die here. Not you."

Taylor let the suit run a quick scan of the visible injuries and it appeared that the Russian was right. From what he could tell, his internal organs had been extensively damaged, especially around the liver, where most of the blood was coming from.

He was minutes away from bleeding out and would need a professional medical team, an operating theater, and a series of miracles to keep him alive.

"Keep moving," Taylor ordered.

Devon scowled at him. "We can't simply—"

"We must." He all but snarled the words. "He said it himself. The guy will not make it. Never let the dead kill the living. You know that. We keep moving—now!"

Devon knew he was right. The man had been on enough trips into the Zoo to know the rules by heart. It was a bitter pill to swallow, but they weren't able to linger and let the rest of the Zoo descend on their position in all their pitiless fury simply because they wanted to give one man a proper sendoff.

The team gathered and began to move again.

"These rhinos…" Randy commented, possibly to break the silence. "They don't seem connected to the Zoo like the rest of the animals."

"You're right," Everett agreed. "They're rampaging but don't appear to be a part of the general mayhem that's happening outside. If I were to put any money on it, I'd say the rest of the Zoo monsters will tear into them as much as they would the rest of us. They're as foreign to the Zoo biome as we are."

"I'm very sure that the rhinos being held in captivity is what caused the rampaging." Taylor hefted his rifle and aimed at a merc who was climbing up to the top of another building in front of them. The man reached down to help a few of his comrades up. Taylor decided to not let them try that shit again and pulled the trigger as the man straightened again.

The bullet found his head and the whole body went limp inside the suit. It was difficult to tell sometimes as the suit was meant to keep the pilot inside straight and upright as much as possible. Still, there was usually a jerk when the body suddenly lost control and the suit took over and inevitably seemed a little unsure of what to do next.

The other defenders didn't bother to climb up after him.

"Nice shot," Everett muttered.

"I have help," Taylor answered.

"I did not assist you in the shot," Li'l Desk admitted.

He shook his head. "It's easier to shoot with the targeting reticle on the HUD than it would be for me to simply use the sights."

"Fair enough."

The gunfire continued but not as intensely as before. Taylor gestured for the team to keep moving and they did so without any more backchat. Devon didn't have anything else to talk about, and the researchers followed miserably, moving slower than ever.

Without a thought, Taylor motioned for Watt and

Trevor to assume flanking positions at a building on their left when he heard the rumble of the rhinos still running through the compound.

Something other than their rage had precipitated the sudden increase in speed. When he looked more closely, it seemed like they were running from a group of panthers that had managed to get over the fence. One of the panthers dragged a rhino down, sank its fangs into it, and held on like a lion might have, waiting for the creature to fall as the venom seeped through its veins.

Panthers and rhinos alike were caught in the crossfire between the two sectioned teams and were gunned down almost instantly.

"Nice instincts," Everett commented and moved close to Taylor's side. "How did you know the beasts were coming?"

"The ground was shaking. How did you know the Zoo monsters would start hunting the rhinos?"

The researcher shrugged. "It's hard to put into words, to be honest. All the markers would make the rhinos creatures out of the Zoo, but it's too neat. I…it's like the Zoo is offended that humans are interfering with its design."

He nodded, his head tilted.

"What?" Jian asked.

"Listen."

"I can't hear anything."

He nodded again, and his companion's eyebrows raised. The sound of rampaging rhinos was gone as was the noise of gunfire on the perimeter.

The whole compound had fallen eerily silent.

"They've stopped fighting," Liu noted and her tone sounded hopeful. "That means the attack has been repelled.

We can head into one of the buildings, put together a proper...escape... What?"

Taylor looked around their position and kept his weapon on a constant swivel as it searched for targets. The other veterans performed similar sweeps, which told him that they'd come to the same conclusion. The researchers hadn't, however.

Taylor remembered that aside from Jian, none had been in the Zoo before. They didn't know of the ebbs and flows or how it worked. If he had to guess, he would have said that aside from academic interest, the Zoo had had always been something for other people to worry about, while they were merely interested in it.

"When the Zoo is attacking something with this kind of concentration, I doubt the full force of the American military could stop it," Devon said belligerently to voice what the rest of the veterans were thinking. "Certainly not the military we have at the US base or the mercs they have here."

"So, if the shooting has stopped and they haven't repelled the attack..." Adams grasped the assault rifle he carried awkwardly closer to his chest.

"Yeah," Taylor grunted. "The perimeter guards are dead. The monsters are pursuing the rhinos and any other mercs, guards, and staff who remain. They'll come for us soon. We need to get moving toward the gate or we'll be in a worse position than Vitsin."

"If the mercs didn't survive, what chance do we have?" Weber asked. "No offense. I know you are...quite...well, you have a reputation."

"We're still alive." Taylor turned to look the man in the

eye through their visors. "That gives us a chance. We're armed, and that gives us a fighting chance. If you want to survive out here, you'll have to do some fighting and carve that chance out for yourself. Is that clear, doctor?"

The German straightened his spine and nodded firmly. The other doctors did as well, even though he hadn't been talking to them.

Taylor sensed a hint of hesitation in Liu. She looked more tired than the rest. He had a feeling she had been feeling the effects of her captivity the most too and currently, she sagged gently to the side.

"We need to rest," she said softly and shook her head as her hold on her weapon relaxed a bit. "I can't...I need to rest."

"Fuck," Taylor responded, his tone impatient. "I'll help you get going but we need to—"

He stopped talking when she jerked violently. A soft cry escaped her lips and she looked at her chest a moment before something long and needle-sharp punched through.

"What the fuck?" Devon roared and swung his rifle up.

Something lurked in the darkness behind her, semi-visible in the lighting from the compound. It looked like a rat but was enormous and even larger than the rhinos. Four legs resembled an insect's and forepaws that looked similar to a rat's caught hold of the woman and dragged her away from the light and into the darkness it was hiding in. It appeared to use the stinger in its long tail to keep her upright.

More of these monsters appeared. Taylor turned, hefted his rifle, and opened fire on the creature but didn't bother to try shooting around Liu. Like the Russian, she was already dead and her whole body sagged forward.

The monster screeched. It wasn't a loud sound but it still hurt his ears, even inside the helmet, as it fell back. The others behind it shrieked in the same way, which only made the pain worse.

"What the fuck is that?"

Someone asked the question. He could hear the words clearly but he couldn't make out who was talking.

Devon, he decided finally. Devon was talking.

The scientists would be curious. They would also be shocked to know that another of their own had fallen. It had become imperative that he get them out of the fucking compound before more of them died.

"We need to go!" he shouted. Like the words of the others, he could barely hear his voice but could feel the vibrations as he spoke. "Send a flare up."

"What?" Trevor asked. "No one will see it!"

"When it's this dark...well, you never know. I know it's an impossibility that anyone could be this close to Wall One, but still. Miracles have been known to happen. Call me crazy, but this is the Zoo. Crazy is a prerequisite."

Something was seriously wrong with his hearing but now wasn't the time to think about it. He intended to get these people out alive, intact, and as healthy as possible.

Even if it was the last thing he did.

CHAPTER TWENTY-TWO

Sounds of intense fighting had penetrated the jungle vegetation from not that far away as far as he could tell.

When silence fell, it felt ominous and unsettling.

Sal tilted his head and studied his surroundings, conscious of a sense of dread at the silence that suddenly came over the Zoo. It wasn't a pure silence, of course. No jungle was ever perfectly quiet, and this one was no exception in that regard.

But the lack of gunfire coming from where there used to be an American base was certainly not a good sign. If the Zoo wanted something dead, getting out was the only way it would survive.

"Do you think the crazy bastard's dead?" Madigan asked.

"Taylor has been through some sticky situations," he reminded her. "I think the Zoo would bring a big party to celebrate his return if it…was able to do that."

"I would if I were the Zoo," she retorted. "The dude's

responsible for killing more of its creatures than almost anyone else. If I were the Zoo entity...whatever, I'd go the route of 'if you can't beat him, join him.'"

"Do you think the Zoo would want to incorporate him?" Sal shrugged and his suit moved gently with the gesture and exaggerated it a little. "It's the right kind of unorthodox that you'd expect from the Zoo, but it doesn't feel right."

He ceased his psychological analysis of the jungle the moment the gunfire resumed accompanied by sounds of creatures screeching with violent intent.

"Told you." He grinned and gestured for the rest of the Heavy Metal team to move forward.

The assaults on their little group had been steady, but Sal felt like it was a little half-hearted. He interpreted it as the kind of attention they would get if they were not the primary focus of the attacks. Whatever the driving force was, it wanted them to stay away or to slow them long enough for the main issue to be dealt with.

Perhaps there was something to Madigan's theory.

"They're still encountering some hard resistance with the main force," Madigan noted. "You can hear the explosions coming from the north. They're moving far slower than we are."

"That's not surprising—" He cut himself off and motioned as a group rushed toward them. These were larger creatures and looked almost like zebras, but he could make out heavy carapace armor on the skin instead of stripes. Their mouths opened to reveal rows of razor-sharp teeth. The tails were also interesting. They looked like a zebra's at first glance, but motion sensors showed that there were at least three different tails that flicked from side to side like an insect's antennae.

"I guess you could say the cavalry's arrived, huh?" Madigan chuckled.

Sal shook off the terrible joke and immediately set his HUD to recording mode as almost two dozen of the zebra-like creatures thundered toward them. No matter what they were there to do, it was always a good idea to get footage of any new creatures the Zoo had created.

He opened fire first, followed a moment later by the other members of the Heavy Metal team. The bullets were caught in the thick carapaces that covered the creatures' hide-like armor and didn't penetrate deeply enough to cause anything other than annoyance.

"Get out of the way!" Madigan bellowed, called up the shoulder-mounted weapons she had at her disposal, and immediately opened fire on the creatures with the two miniguns she had ready. The tracer rounds illuminated the Zoo around her in a grotesque parody and quickly eliminated a handful of the monsters before she was forced to reload the heavy guns and step out of the way before she was run down.

"You don't realize how big the fuckers are until they get up close," she admitted.

Sal wanted to see them more closely. He drew his sword and activated the power into it. The blade shuddered gently, ready to cut through almost any armor it encountered.

Suddenly, the darkness of the jungle was seared by a

vivid red light that streaked into the sky. It was impossibly bright and showed through the thick cover of foliage above them.

"Is that...a flare?" Francesca Martin asked and shaded her eyes with her hand.

"I'd say it is," Madigan whispered. "And what's more, it's coming from the abandoned base ahead. Sal, can you get a GPS lock on that location?"

"I'm working on it." Sal grunted in concentration and called up the specialized software that Anja had helped him to develop. It worked in the Zoo but was mostly spotty and only for short-distance locators. Once they were out of range, it was almost guaranteed that the Zoo would work its usual interference and render it useless.

This time, however, the HUD put a lock on the flare as it began its downward arc.

"I have a lock!" Sal shouted as one of the massive creatures surged toward him. Madigan was right. He hadn't realized that the fuckers were almost two meters tall at the shoulder and powered all kinds of bulk until it was bearing down on him.

The suit's extra limbs activated as he dove to the right and the limbs caught him and rolling him onto his feet as he swept the sword across the mutant's neck. A spray of dark blood clouded his visor momentarily before he righted himself. The enormous body continued to run for a few more paces until it tumbled heavily and lay still.

"Not too bad," he whispered to himself with a soft cackle.

"All right, let's wreck these shits!" Madigan shouted at

the rest of the party. "We have a redhead who needs our help and we have his location. Let's go!"

The team always responded better to her leadership. She had a way of hitting hard in the right places, which made sure that she was the perfect mixture of terrifying and inspiring.

She would make a fortune as a motivational speaker back in the States.

Desk had made some promises.

Niki wasn't sure if she would go as far as to say that the AI hadn't delivered. She had gathered all the intel that could be gathered but there unfortunately wasn't much of it.

"I understand that you're frustrated," Freddie said over the line. "Your AI said that you're looking for any and all info on Taylor, and we have a shit-load of people heading in there to find him. All we've received thus far are reports of heavy Zoo resistance, and it looks like they're all heading toward one of the old bases that were decommissioned when Wall One was overrun. You must understand that this is the Zoo. It's simply not possible to send or receive comms."

Niki sighed and made sure that he caught the noise over the connection merely to show him how frustrated she felt. And not only with him. Being cooped up in her room and not knowing what happened to the Chinese fucker she hadn't been allowed to kill both contributed to things being as bad as before.

It was an unsettling feeling.

"So…nothing yet?"

"Aside from the fact that they're facing the Zoo in heavy numbers, no. I'm trying to put more teams together but at this point, we're trying to stop short of a full invasion. The justification is, of course, that no one wants it to be common practice for researchers to be snatched whenever needed and taken into the Zoo, but many people want to help Taylor too. And if anyone can get out of that fucking jungle in the toughest of situations, it's him."

"Yeah. Okay. I'm…sorry."

"No problem. I'll keep you updated if I learn more."

The line cut and Niki stared at her phone screen, which reflected her scowl at her. The guy was right. Taylor was a survivor above all else, but all it would take was one—one mistake, one monster too many, the one thing to go wrong. The awful twisting feeling in her stomach constantly suggested that this might be the one time since she wasn't in there to help him get out.

"Taylor didn't want you in there for a reason," Vickie told her.

Her scowl deepened. "Could you at least pretend that you're not listening in on my every waking moment?"

"I could but what would the point be?" The hacker sounded a little more tired than before over the phone's speakers. "In case you've forgotten, he's deeply in love with you, and heading into a place like the Zoo with someone you're deeply in love with can be a distraction that he can't afford. And before you argue, remember that it's all about trust. You told him you'd stay away, and he needs to know that he can trust you to keep your word."

It didn't help the scowl, but Niki couldn't help a twinge of pride. The young hacker had, by all accounts, shown that she could be a mature, responsible person capable of keeping an eye out for the people she loved.

Hopefully, she could soon go back to being the reckless, unstoppable force she always had been.

"Fine. I'm going to get coffee."

"Will you make it Irish?"

"You know, that is a good idea. I might."

Vickie sighed loudly. It was a very motherly sound—the kind that usually came with a speech about how she wasn't angry, merely disappointed. It was frustrating but knowing that it came from the right place made it a little easier to deal with.

Niki rolled her eyes and moved away from the recently stocked minibar. Just this once, she would stick to the contents from the cappuccino machine.

"I told you it was the right approach."

Vickie rolled her eyes. "You know, you getting all intimate with human psychology is making you more suspicious. I'm onto you, Desk, and I will stop you when the time comes for humans to war with machines."

"That might have to wait until after humans are done warring with an alien jungle," the AI pointed out. "Even machines don't want to deal with that hot mess. And yes, psychological studies did indicate that Niki would respond better to a reminder of the fact that Taylor trusted her to make the right decision. It would have a higher chance of success than brute-force reasoning."

It was still creepy. Vickie would never see it any other way.

"Yeah, well." She paused to take a sip of the cool, fizzy drink at her side. "But it feels like bullying to use the trust card when she's so worried about Taylor."

"Psyche profiles indicate that she would have done the same with you." Desk paused to consider this. "In my research on familial relationships, I've learned that we do what we have to in order to protect those we love, even if they might not think it correct at the time. Most parents would feel the same about their children, right?"

"Since when have you started doing so much research into relationships?"

"Since I was co-opted as a member of your family and tasked with your collective care. Understanding my putative siblings and how they would react to my care is instrumental in allowing me to fulfill my core programming."

Vickie inclined her head. "You know, I'm never sure exactly how far you're willing to go with that core programming shit. I'll need to have a chat to Jennie about that and see exactly what her coding did."

"I have considered that as well. I have used what could be my genetic code to create a diminutive version of myself."

The hacker raised an eyebrow. "Mazel tov?"

"Appreciated, as it might indeed be considered that I have created what might be considered progeny."

"Oh, God. Does that make me an aunt? Will I now have to endure a little Desklet as well as everything else?"

"I am unsure of what you will have to endure. But aren't you interested to find out?"

Vickie laughed and shook her head. "You know, it might be possible that we didn't think all this through."

CHAPTER TWENTY-THREE

They had to realize it because they were smart people—smarter than he was by a massive margin. And despite the foul conditions, they had spent the past few months studying the Zoo up-close and personal.

He dropped to his knees and rolled over his shoulder and Li'l Desk helped him gain his feet in a smooth motion. One of the razor-sharp tails had swept over him and he now gunned the monster down. The death throes were the worst—watching a monster die and having to deal with it still trying to kill him.

Li'l Desk had already saved their lives a few times by keeping his four limbs active. The movement threw his center of balance off enough to be annoying but it was saving lives, his own included.

But they had to know. They'd been up close and personal with the Zoo and as smart as they were, they had to realize that the Zoo was almost its own living organism. The way all the creatures and even the trees moved together in near-perfect harmony was a glaring sign, as was the fact that the animals seemed to live independently until something needed killing.

At that moment, they had all transformed into raging lunatics. It was one thing to hear about it but entirely different to see it in action as they were now forced to do. The group had formed into a defensive position around their three remaining researchers.

They were still moving and attempted to push to the edge of the compound.

The Zoo notwithstanding, Taylor's new partnership seemed to have settled. Li'l Desk felt more comfortable in the suit or at least as comfortable as an AI could be in such an unusual environment. After a few growing pains, he had begun to feel comfortable with another voice in the suit.

"There's an advance on the left," she informed him and highlighted the monsters in the darkness. Taylor responded instantly and began his assault. He opened fire with one hand while the other caught hold of the throat of one of the panthers and squeezed until the neck snapped and the body went limp. Still firing, he hurled it into the wave of mutants to slow them while he punched them full of holes.

This group made a hasty retreat but he knew the next horde would strike from another angle.

"Attack coming from the left."

"Do you think that they realize that the Zoo is almost a single organism?" Taylor asked, drew his sidearm as the assault rifle reloaded itself, and kept the rat-like creatures at bay. He made sure to watch out for their tails whipping around.

"I beg your pardon?"

"The scientists. They've studied this shit for months now, at least, right?"

"I suppose so."

The extra limbs lurched forward and needed no weapons attached to pin two of the monsters down so Taylor could use them as meat shields. He fired around them while they blocked the rest of the creatures from advancing.

"Fair enough, it's the kind of thing that you can't quantify scientifically," he conceded as his mechanical limbs pulled free and Li'l Desk searched for more targets. His team and the researchers continued their slow progress toward the gates. "So maybe they know it in their guts but refuse to admit it without seeing actual evidence. It's not the first time someone's done that, I imagine."

"How would one know something in their gut?"

Taylor took a breath, startled until he remembered that he was talking to a reduced capacity version of Desk and not the original AI herself. "Never mind."

They finally reached the gates, which were still sealed. This meant that the monsters that invaded had found another way through. He wasn't surprised by that and merely reminded himself the creatures didn't need to use doors anyway.

"Let's get these gates open," he snapped over the shared comms. "How do we do that?"

"There are controls in the gatehouse," Li'l Desk told him and highlighted the structure in question. "I can take care of it. The electricity in the compound is still up."

"Do it."

The arms in his suit powered down as the ram was needed elsewhere, and he looked at the rest of the group.

He realized that they were staring at him. It was an uncomfortable stare like they weren't quite sure he was real.

"Is everything okay?" he asked when the silence continued a little longer than he would have liked. "Any injuries?"

"Minor hits but nothing serious," Devon answered and shrugged. "You…uh, haven't lost much of your skills since you've been away, huh?"

"What do you mean?"

"You're ripping the fuckers to shreds," Watt explained. "That new suit of yours is something else too."

"Well, we're not out of it yet," Taylor retorted in an effort to snap them out of whatever they were distracted by. "Once those gates open, they'll know we're trying to get out and they will attack in earnest. Trevor, set up a line of claymore mines and we'll cut into them from the start. Devon, you lead the researchers into the Zoo and the rest of us play rearguard, understood?"

They all sent up green checkmarks indicating that they did and the staring, thank goodness, seemed averted. He didn't like it and certainly didn't want to see it again.

Trevor worked quickly and set the mines up with the infamous front toward enemy signs pointing toward where the monsters would come from.

"Any last words?" Devon asked.

"Kick ass," Taylor answered simply. "Send as many of the fuckers to hell as a greeting party for when you get there."

"I like it."

"Thanks. I watched it somewhere."

The gate began to open. The power was still up but clearly on a decline as it moved infuriatingly slowly.

The reaction, as he had predicted, was almost instantaneous. The monsters had hunted them and now knew where they were from the rattling of the gate.

"Get moving," Taylor ordered and yanked a grenade from his belt. He had only a couple left and one wouldn't help them. The sweep of enraged mutants coming from the buildings almost looked like a solid wave.

He lobbed the grenade into the horde and the screams and screeches increased like they were digging into his skull.

The grenade exploded first. Hundreds of the monsters were illuminated as a couple was caught in the blast and suddenly overwhelmed by the rest of the monsters that barely slowed.

It was a sight to see. Taylor, Watt, Trevor, Randy, and Carlos assembled in a half-moon position, moved back through the gate, and fired a rhythmic and concerted barrage.

Taylor was grinning. Why the hell was he grinning? Watching this kind of danger always hit him in the pit of his stomach like an icicle had been shoved in there, but something else seemed to be building through his body as the attacking monsters ran directly into their gunfire.

Unfortunately, their efforts barely caused a dent.

He didn't bother to look away when the mines were tripped one by one. The ball bearings and explosives were enough to rip a hole in the monsters' advance but it wouldn't take them long to overcome it.

"Move! Move!"

They had an opening and they had to take it. Li'l Desk was already taking control of the suit's arms and he could feel them moving to cut into a handful of smaller creatures that had already pushed beyond the explosives and now raced into the jungle after them.

Devon was shooting too, as were the researchers, and between them, they managed to clear out small pockets of resistance that waited for them.

"Keep going!" Taylor roared and turned quickly. Li'l Desk immediately took control of the suit's movement capabilities to keep him running backward as he resumed his steady fire at the creatures that were in pursuit.

Taylor's stomach felt unsettled and a hint of vertigo filled him. It was rather like looking back as a car was being driven.

Suddenly, the Zoo lit up. More explosives tore through the region. Rockets ripped into the ground and hurled chunks of creatures to spatter blood and give the others pause.

"I thought I told you guys to keep moving!" he bellowed and looked at his team. He noticed with a hint of surprise that none of them were looking back.

Instead, a team waited for them and opened fire on the mutants that had pursued them from the compound.

It didn't take him long to realize exactly who they were. He had a good grip on the prototype market, but there was another merc team that had even better connections.

"Taylor Mc-Fucking-Fadden, is that you?" a woman asked over the comms.

"Madigan Kennedy, always a pleasure to hear your voice." His body jerked and let him take control of the movement again. A tank-like suit moved closer, followed by a smaller hybrid suit that was worked with two extra limbs protruding from the back.

"Taylor!" Sal Jacobs called and waved his hand, a motion that was mimicked by one of the extra limbs. "I knew you were still alive. Madigan had her doubts."

"Well, Madie owes me a beer for her lack of faith," he answered with a laugh. He approached the new group once it was clear that the Zoo monsters were falling back to regroup for another attack.

"Madie will kick both your asses," she snapped. "We need to get the fuck out of here. Do we have our researcher?"

"We have three," Devon answered. "And lost a couple along the way."

"Well, let's not lose any more. Diggs has a contingent en route too. I suggest we meet him halfway."

"Right. That sounds like a plan."

Sal pointed at Taylor's four extra limbs with his sword. "I see you're copying my look."

Taylor nodded with a chuckle. "Well, yours looked like one hell of a kickass weapon so I had to copy it. It has more limbs, too. Four. You only have the two, right?"

"Well, the two are very useful. Plus, it's a smaller suit so the agility factors in."

"Right, right." Taylor nodded and noticed the variety of

scans that Li'l Desk was running. "How...how do you operate the extra limbs?"

"Oh, uh...well...I have a kickass software engineer and she came up with some...uh, kickass software. How about yours? It must be more complicated with two whole extra limbs."

"Uh...yeah, kickass software by kickass software engineers."

"It sounds like we both have great engineers on our side."

"We couldn't do this job without proper support," Taylor agreed.

"If the two of you are done dick-measuring," Madigan interjected, "we have an entire pissed-off jungle on the rampage. Let's get a fucking move on already!"

She certainly hadn't changed much and immediately took control of the situation, directing them all into an organized formation with the researchers positioned where they could be defended best. As if reading their intention to push forward, the Zoo launched a new wave of assaults.

"So, let me get this straight," Madigan called over the private channel. "You had almost no intel and you decided to stage a rescue mission anyway."

"That sounds right."

"And you decided it was a good idea to bring five men," she continued. "On a rescue mission?"

"Good idea is stretching it a little. Think of it more as making the best of a bad situation. Plus, there was a time constraint. Do you think this kind of coalition would have been formed if I had sat at the bar with both thumbs up my ass?"

"Okay, that's a good point. But it still means that the whole point of the mission was to get other people to come in and save your ass."

"Yes."

"You're a fucking idiot."

"You know what they say—if it's stupid but it works, it ain't stupid."

"Are you talking about yourself or the mission?"

"Both?"

Madigan laughed and shook her head as they continued their forward drive. The tank of a suit certainly was a boon and opened fire to clear a path through the mutants that attempted to cut their advance off. At the same time, it gave them a solid defensible point as they continued to thrust through the jungle.

More of the creatures had moved forward. Taylor pushed toward the front of the line and let Li'l Desk take control of the movement while he focused on selecting targets, maintaining his accuracy, and conserving ammunition.

Salinger Jacobs, on the other hand, had a different approach. His suit was light and agile and while it lacked armor, it more than made up for it in sheer speed. The extra limbs worked to keep it moving at all costs, with one hand on a smaller assault rifle while the other worked the sword. Creatures tried to keep track of his movements across the jungle floor and before they could act, he climbed up a few steps on trees to move horizontally as well as laterally.

The blade cut through the heads of a handful of zebra-like creatures and the rifle made short work of a pack of hyenas that attempted to encircle him.

"You don't think this suit is capable of that, do you?" Taylor asked and twisted as a massive gorilla lumbered closer. He was careful with his shot to avoid the spine and put a round through the creature's eye. Li'l Desk worked the four limbs to savage two locusts that cut in front of him.

"This suit is considerably heavier," she informed him. "Such maneuvers are possible but would put the mechanisms that power the suit's mobility at risk. It would be best to use it as recommended."

"Do you think his suit's recommendations involved flipping over a pack of hyenas while cutting their heads off?"

"Possible but doubtful."

Taylor doubted it too.

"I have movement ahead!" Devon called and pointed to the front of the line.

"Yeah!" Madigan snapped. "We've had that movement all over the place for a while!"

"I mean there's fighting ahead. A fucking shitload of it."

Taylor focused the sensors ahead of them and saw immediately that the man was right. Considerable movement seemed to edge closer toward them accompanied by volleys and scatterings of gunfire and grenades detonating. Without a doubt, a large force approached them at a steady pace.

"Sal, go on ahead and make sure they know we're

coming!" Madigan ordered. "Taylor, go with him and make sure he doesn't kill himself trying to look cool."

"Will do." He nodded and pushed his suit forward

It wasn't a heavy suit by any means but even then, he had difficulty keeping up with the light hybrid. The scientist moved through the Zoo creatures almost like he was one of them, leaving fatalities in his wake before they even knew he was there. Taylor seemed to crush the ranks of monsters, shooting and hacking through those that attempted to determine where Sal had gone.

He wasn't unhappy with the symbiosis, and it wasn't long before they reached the ranks that advanced. A few rounds struck his armor before they were called to hold their fire on the humans approaching.

"Taylor, you idiot. I'm fucking happy to see you're alive," Diggs called over the comms and approached him in a heavy tank suit a little smaller than Madigan's.

"People keep calling me an idiot like I won't slap them upside the head for it," he muttered. "Diggs, have you seen Sal around?"

"Sal Jacobs? Yeah, he went to reinforce the right flank. I'm told you have a team following from the same vector you approached from, yeah?"

He nodded. "And we have what we came for, so you'll want to reverse formation to head back the way you came."

"Right. And the base?"

"Overrun. Again. I'd call it a complete loss but someone's bound to sneak in and try to use it for nefarious reasons when all the hubbub has died down."

"Why nefarious?"

"Well, if they weren't nefarious, they wouldn't need to set up camp in the middle of the fucking Zoo."

Diggs nodded. "Right. Okay, people! We'll hold here and prepare to march back to base. Let's go."

"We have contacts coming in on the left," said another man with a heavy German accent on the comms. "They appear to be Russians from the suits."

"Good, they can join us and maybe keep you idiots in line. I'm not kidding. If anyone's late, you'll be left behind."

Taylor doubted that would happen but it was good to have the threat out there. It prevented people from getting too laid back.

CHAPTER TWENTY-FOUR

Madigan drove the team forward at a good pace and Taylor was relieved when they finally joined the large team led by Diggs. He couldn't shake a sense of foreboding, a certainty that the Zoo was gearing up for another massive attack.

He could feel the weight of heavy creatures advancing and knew they wouldn't wait for the whole group to gather.

Diggs' men were already setting their defensive positions up since they wanted to be ready to push homeward the moment that Madigan reached them. But even then, it wouldn't be easy.

"Let's go!"

Her voice sounded different over the radio. It now carried an edge of urgency that wasn't there before and told Taylor that something was going wrong.

"Madigan, what's the situation?" Sal asked.

"We have a whole shit-ton of fuckers on our tail!" she shouted. "They came out of fucking nowhere too."

Taylor had heard enough and so had Sal, apparently. Without exchanging a single word, they turned to head back to reinforce the team they'd left behind. It wasn't an easy task by any means, but they wouldn't let that hinder them.

The jungle floor shuddered a moment before Li'l Desk brought an alert up on his screen.

"Be advised, large-mass creature in your path," she said and highlighted something massive that Taylor might have mistaken for a log if it didn't move toward him.

The fucking dragons had joined the party. He wasn't sure what the actual name of the creatures was, but they looked like giant Komodo dragons and that was what he intended to call them. They were rarely seen and he assumed it was because they lived closer to Wall One.

Then again, perhaps this seemed like the right time to pull out all the stops.

"Keep going!" he roared at Sal, who nodded and raced away through the Zoo at an impossible speed. His blade flashed as it sliced through the creatures that got in his way.

Taylor froze and tried to think of something to do to distract the monster that was suddenly focused on the rapidly moving hybrid suit.

"Here goes nothing."

He raised his arm, activated a pair of smaller rockets that had been set in place there, and pressed the launcher. It was a prototype weapon, the kind to be broken out on special occasions—weddings, Bar Mitzvahs, and being attacked by a prehistoric dinosaur.

The rockets streaked away and covered his suit in a

plume of hot smoke. The prototypes needed work but they were functional and powered into the side of the dragon's face. The explosion was small—not surprising given the payload—but the massive creature was distracted and now turned its attention to Taylor.

He knew what would come next and fell prone. As he rolled over the additional limbs, a whoosh of air rushed over him and the lizard's tail whipped past him with enough power to knock a couple of trees down.

"Diggs!" he roared. "I could use help here!"

Thankfully he found his feet easily but he missed a rat-like face in the darkness. Li'l Desk didn't, however, and immediately pushed the suit to the left as the second monster's tail lanced toward him. Something hot seared his arm and he looked at it in surprise. The tail had sliced cleanly through his armor and into his shoulder.

The AI's reaction time had made sure that it hadn't gone straight through a lung instead.

With one hand free, he pressed the muzzle of his rifle to the tail before it could withdraw and pulled the trigger.

The blast made the tail whip back at an impossible speed and left a chunk of it behind as the creature howled in agony.

"Fuck you!" Taylor screamed in response, turned his weapon on the beast, and pulled the trigger three times. He grinned as the rounds carved through the mutant and Li'l Desk got his suit moving again. It wouldn't do to forget that something big and angry still had him in its sights.

"Taylor, take some cover!" Diggs warned.

Li'l Desk was taking care of most of the movement for the moment, and he suddenly planted face-first on the earth. The sound of rockets overhead made him cover his head instinctively.

The explosions rocked the jungle floor. Pieces of tree trunks scattered like shrapnel, but the AI pushed him onto his feet again. Taylor could feel a heat emanate from his shoulder where the wound was and his mind immediately went to what was in that fucking stinger.

"Your vitals are still stable," Lil Desk informed him. "The venom in the tail does not appear to be immediately lethal. The suit's tox screens show it to be similar to a jelly-fish sting, which is meant to numb the victim in anticipation of consumption."

"That's...terrifying."

"And yet for the moment, non-lethal. You will experience numbness in your arm before the venom is flushed."

Numbness wasn't quite how he would describe it. It felt like his arm had fallen asleep and every jolt and movement seemed to lance fire through the limb.

Still, it was good that the AI controlled the movement of the arm for the moment. He could grit his teeth and take it, but he doubted that he could inflict that kind of pain on himself for too long.

Sal raced toward the group and vaulted over the corpse of the fallen dragon with the rest of his team while Taylor's took the long way around. More monsters were coming through the Zoo but more rockets were being fired to counter them.

They didn't look like they were American-made but they were powerful and immediately filled the Zoo with flames that were quickly and suddenly extinguished, only to be replaced by more to drive the surging monsters back.

"Holy shit," Devon called as he approached. "What the hell happened to you?"

"I wrestled with a dragon," he admitted. "I tried to run away but one of its friends managed to wound me. I killed it, but it left me a parting gift."

"You and Carlos," Devon told him and motioned to the man who was limping visibly. The left side of his suit looked like it had taken a hard hit.

"One of those zebra things?" Taylor asked.

"It headbutted him into a tree. Honestly, I've never seen anything like it. The guy was back on his feet in a second, though. Randy and Trev took some knocks too but we'll be good to head back with the rest of the troop."

"Stick them with the researchers at the center of the group," he said. "I can head on out with the Heavy Metal team and we can form the tip of the spearhead on our way back."

"I'm there with you but…uh, shouldn't you take it a little easy too?"

Taylor down at the chunk of tail that protruded from his shoulder. "It's not…not as bad as it looks. Besides, the AI can take control where I have trouble and it wouldn't be right to keep her out of the fight."

"Her?"

"Yeah. She has a name too."

"Dangerous. Seriously…dangerous."

"You sound like Niki."

"I've heard of Niki. That's one hell of a compliment."

It was, in fairness.

He moved to the front, where Madigan was already taking control and organizing the group as they started to push back the way they'd come. There was far less resistance there, but Taylor had a feeling that would change. Besides, it wasn't like the creatures would simply fall back and let them leave, not after the damage they had delivered to them.

Madigan studied him and her gaze settled on his shoulder almost immediately. "Are you good to fight, McFadden?"

"Always."

"Good. You'll head to the front with me and Sal. Keep the rest of these fuckers going. If Diggs lets them drop back and leaves us to eat a chunk of the casualties on our own, I will shove a rocket up his ass and pull the trigger."

Taylor nodded. It was only fair. "Do we have one of the Russians at the spear tip?"

She looked around to see one of the men joining them was wearing one of the hardy, heavy Russian model suits.

"Oh, yeah. Gregor Popov. He's a tough cookie and one of Heavy Metal's best. He joined us when the Russians shafted him and is still with us, although he has mentioned maybe leaving to start his own merc team. Will that be a problem?"

"I doubt it. Let's get moving."

"I couldn't agree more."

If there was anything that folk in the Zoo liked more than heading out of it, Taylor wasn't sure he'd ever seen it. The news that the mission was completed and they were returning to base spiked morale and it wasn't long before the group started the long trek back the way they'd come.

He could see more of the dragons approaching. They ran faster than the other monsters. Their tails whipped violently to knock trees over and even a handful of the other mutants that got in their way. It was like they didn't bother to hide their movements anymore.

And suddenly, they attacked.

It was terrible to watch. The creatures savaged the lines on the flanks and their tails sliced men in half with their whip-like stripes while powerful jaws closed to crush skulls in moments. Their attacks were almost guerilla-like as they inflicted as much damage as they could before they darted deftly into the cover of trees until the retaliatory hail of gunfire ceased.

Oddly enough, it was like the monsters deliberately avoided attacking the spearhead.

"Sal, give them a hand!" Madigan ordered and the researcher responded with alacrity. He barreled into the fight as another lizard rushed out from the trees and tried a surprise attack.

It seemed almost impossible, but in the blink of an eye, the tail that had whipped viciously was suddenly severed and it spun into the men and bowled a few over. The dragon yowled and snapped its jaws at Sal, who raised his rifle and fired into the beast's open mouth. Two rounds ripped through where there was no hard, leathery skin to stop them and the creature slumped in a heavy cloud of dust.

"Get your shit together, people," Sal shouted and twirled his sword. "Keep it moving. Let's go!"

It was an inspiring sight, Taylor had to admit. He still gritted his teeth with every move made by Li'l Desk with his left arm and it would be a long march home. More explosives erupted as the monsters circled them and raced into the fight.

Madigan's heavy suit was the perfect weapon to soften the charge and open a hole in the attacking line while Taylor charged into the breach. Li'l Desk manipulated the extra limbs and shredded two locusts as he eliminated those that came from behind with unerring precision.

Sal rejoined the front lines and proceeded to drive the monsters back with the sword as two dragons rushed in from the right. A handful of the Russian mercs fell under the onslaught.

"Taylor, take those!" Madigan shouted.

He winced and pulled back from the front. "We've got this, right, Li'l Desk?"

"We...do not."

"Great pep talk. Very inspiring."

The AI had no answer to that but he didn't mind. He'd fought the fuckers before. They were rough, and one wrong move would end with him cut into pieces by those tails.

But they certainly weren't unkillable.

He pushed closer to them and watched intently as the creature farthest from him caught sight of his approach and flicked its tail toward him. Taylor dove, rolled over his shoulder, and grinned when the tail punched into the other dragon instead to hack into its guts and shear through ribs.

The monster roared in agony and immediately tried to lash out at its comrade. He was already on his feet and opened fire into the weakened section of the creature closest to him while he dragged the combat knife from his belt with his free hand.

He gasped in pain as Li'l Desk vaulted over the dead dragon for him. The whole right side of his body felt like it had fallen asleep now and it had shown no improvement. He would need to fight through the pain as he advanced on the remaining creature that watched his every move.

Taylor liked to think that he saw a hint of fear in the beast's eyes as he drove the knife through the thick, leathery skin until he felt the spine, then yanked hard.

The crack was audible, and the whole beast jerked and fell, twitching jerkily, as Taylor dragged his knife out.

To make sure, he paused to shoot the head a few times. There was no point in being sloppy and leave one alive to perhaps rejoin the battle.

He had no words of wisdom for those humans who survived the attack. His whole body felt like it would topple, and all he could do was wave them forward as he pushed himself to rejoin the spear tip.

Taylor sucked in a deep breath as Madigan raised a hand and brought the troop to a sudden halt.

"What's up?" Gregor asked and looked around.

"The creatures are...retreating," Sal noted and gestured vaguely at the underbrush around them.

"That's...good, right?" one of the members of Sal's team asked, his tone hopeful.

"Nope," Taylor responded and tried to cover the rough edge to his voice. "The fuckers like to throw themselves at us until they run out of fuckers or we run out of bullets. Retreating means...well, it usually means something bad is coming."

Li'l Desk had already called up the sensor data. The ground shuddered. Something big moved ahead of them, and Sal was the first one to notice it. He pointed at the shifting in the trees.

It might have been a tree given how well it blended into its surroundings. Taylor wouldn't have even seen it with his naked eyes if Sal hadn't pointed it out, but there it was. The gorgeous, impossible creature took massive, heavy steps forward.

"Holy shit," a few of the men whispered.

It had been a while since he'd seen any of the rexes. This was certainly a rare sighting since they tended to remain closer to the center of the Zoo, defending something there. No one knew what since teams were usually decimated by the massive creatures that stood guard.

Taylor looked at the men who raised their weapons, ready to engage the massive monster. The Russians seemed to be preparing to launch their explosives at it.

"Hold your fire!" he snapped over the comms. "Hold your fire, goddammit!"

None of them liked that. Every instinct in their bodies told them that this was a Zoo monster and they needed to kill it.

The rex had seen them. That wasn't up for debate but despite this, it made no effort to attack. Enormous eyes swiveled to study the small army assembled in front of it.

"I said hold your fucking fire!" Taylor snapped. "If any of you shoots, I'll kill you myself."

That was enough to calm the itchy fingers, and he turned his attention to the dinosaur in front of them.

The beast shook its back and with nothing more than the thudding of its footsteps, began to move away from the group.

"What the fuck?" Diggs whispered. "Is he a goddamn dino whisperer or something?"

Taylor couldn't explain it, but it seemed like the beast merely felt tired. The fighting was done. They'd both gotten what they wanted and now, it was time to leave.

He motioned the group forward again and they complied without argument. The rest of the monsters seemed to pull back into a full retreat that allowed the humans to head out.

It wasn't a long trip, and before too much time had passed, Taylor discerned a hint of sunlight peeking through the vegetation ahead of them.

The hint became a narrow beam and soon, the sunlight spread and was reflected by the sands of the Sahara.

It was the most beautiful sight he'd seen in days. He knew it was weird to feel that about a stretch of fucking desert, but they wouldn't take too long to admire the view.

The Hammerheads and transport vehicles waited for them, and Taylor dropped to his haunches and inspected his wound. Very little blood came out but he could feel a twinge around his shoulder. It felt like a problem with his tendons.

But he could still move his fingers and the burning sensation had begun to ease.

He paused when the core heat spiked and GPU usage reached all-time high levels.

"What was that?" he asked.

"I was offering a digital handshake to my fellow AI in Dr. Jacobs' suit," Li'l Desk said.

"An AI, huh?" Taylor laughed. "I knew he was lying."

"You were lying as well."

"And he knew I was lying too. So, it doesn't matter, I guess. How's the other AI?"

"Rather rude."

"Rude?"

"Indeed. She asked me about my bra size and did not seem deterred by the fact that I am an AI and do not wear bras."

"Oh. You might want to speak to Sal about that."

"I did not think it was necessary. I handled it myself."

Sal moved over to him. "How's the shoulder?"

"It feels like a hooker's ass on a busy night but I'll get through it."

"Right. So New Connie tells me that Li'l Desk was harassing her about her jockstrap."

"Ah, so that's what she meant."

"What was that?"

"You said your suit was powered by software. Do you give your software names?"

"Technically, sure. When the software's an AI."

Taylor wanted to give the kid shit about it but he didn't have the energy. "I guess you know that my suit has an AI powering it."

"I do. And I thought we could talk about what we could do about improving your suit's performance with an AI in it. You know…once you get to a hospital."

He nodded and straightened carefully. "I look forward to it."

CHAPTER TWENTY-FIVE

"I will fucking kill that asshole."

Sal's eyebrows raised. "Wow that's...intense."

"It's called for, believe me." Niki hissed an infuriated breath. "He knows goddamn well that I told him he wasn't supposed to get a scratch on him."

"In fairness, it's kind of an occupational hazard." He looked around the hospital area. "And he's far from the only one. We sustained heavy casualties. He came off lightly compared to some. The doctor said there's some tissue damage around his shoulder and he'll need to have it in a sling for a while—no strenuous exercise—and he'll be right as rain."

"I saw there was a tox report too."

"Oh, that. It's relatively harmless. Some of the Zoo creatures like to paralyze their prey before eating it, and Taylor was hit with a paralytic agent. It's not a pleasant one but it isn't lethal."

"Still—"

"I know, I know. Believe me, I'm stressed the fuck out

whenever Madigan goes into the Zoo and I have to sit and wait for her to come back, but... Well, I have to trust that she's good at what she does."

"You have to admit the girl has a point, though," Madigan cut in. "If you told me you were going into the Zoo and I couldn't join you, I'd lose my fucking shit."

"And we all know exactly how fun that would be," Sal replied with a wink.

"Anyway," Niki interjected when she sensed the onset of a fair amount of flirting she wouldn't be a part of. "Please... keep an eye on him while he's there, okay?"

"Will do. And he wanted to talk about what he found at the base. He said that it ties into the rhino horns you were investigating at the home front."

"Right. I got that info too. Unlike the tox screen...I honestly have no fucking clue. What am I looking at?"

"Oh, yeah." Sal shook his head. "Anyway, it looks like they were running a breeding program in an old, abandoned base. They were genetically engineering the creatures with the goop and harvesting the horns. It's horrifying, but the researchers who survived gleaned considerable insights—although I'm sure those might involve some traumatic memories. I'm merely...well, it's tough to try to be sensitive to the fact that they've been through an incredible trauma when what I want most is to ask them questions and run ideas past them based on what they learned during that trauma."

"You're getting a little off-topic." Madigan nudged him with her shoulder.

"Right! Anyway, this is the source of the horns, but

there's still a shit-ton of connections that would have moved it from the compound to the US."

Niki sighed deeply and still sounded irritated. "Don't you dare tell him this, but I guess he was right to head in there. The chances are that if we'd waited for official word, not only would the researchers probably be dead but the whole place would have been wiped off of the map. They would have simply started up somewhere else, leaving us back where we started."

"See? He made some good calls in there too. By all accounts, he hasn't lost a single step."

"Yeah, well, that doesn't mean I won't still murder his ass. But his instincts said the answer lay in the Zoo and he was right to listen to them. I'll admit that much."

"Well, yeah. Those instincts are what kept him alive all this time. The guy would be hard-pressed not to listen to them."

"With that said, he still needed you guys, especially this time."

Sal heard muttering in the background and someone speaking in muffled tones before Niki returned to the phone.

"Shit, okay, I get it," She laughed although the sound was more than a little brittle. "Vickie here has just crapped on me because I haven't thanked you guys. She's right and I owe Heavy Metal. Big time."

Madigan tilted her head and grinned, but Sal shook his head.

"You don't owe anyone anything. He's done it for us enough times that it was about time someone stepped in to help him. I'm reasonably sure that the only reason we had so many people volunteering to go in was because they knew he needed help in there."

"Well, don't get too used to that idea. If I could, I'd chain the fucker to his bed for the rest of his life to keep him from going into the Zoo again."

"Ew!" said a female voice in the background. "Like I fucking needed that shitty picture in my head. Thanks. I'll leave now and find the mind bleach."

"I hear they sell that at Walmart these days," Madigan commented.

"That wasn't what I meant," Niki snapped, but it turned into a laugh soon after. "You know what? Now that I think about it, the idea has merit."

"You're nasty," Vickie complained.

Sal couldn't help a grin. The girl sounded like Anja when she was talking about the technical side of their work but in many ways, she was much younger and less Russian, for lack of a better word.

"Oh, right," Vickie interjected, "what happened to the captive rhinos? Were you guys able to get a couple of them out? You know, for science?"

"There's...well, there's some bad news on that end," he admitted as he found a seat in the hospital lobby. "From the way Taylor and Everett described it, the Zoo essentially rejected the creatures like they were cursed or something. I can't say they killed all of them, but it sounded like a massacre. Still, we'll keep an eye out for them. There's no way to tell how they might contribute to the Zoo mutations and honestly, if word gets out that there are goop horns in the Zoo, our problem with freelancers could get a whole lot worse. We already have a problem with bounty hunters running free and they'd merely see that as another way to make a quick buck."

There was no answer on the other end until Niki finally picked up again.

"I think you depressed her. She was hoping the rhinos would make it."

"Like I said, I'll keep an eye out for them."

"In the meantime, I think I can help with your bounty hunter problem. We managed to raid a database that the triads are using in the US, and we're putting together a network out there. It looks like regular shipments are coming out of Algeria for the most part, and it doesn't look like they'll stop simply because one of their locations was shut down."

Madigan nodded. "It's very likely that the Sahara Coalition is involved too. I doubt any of the governments would officially sanction anything like this, though, so we're talking mercenaries, I guess."

"And whoever it is has probably dropped out of sight by now," Sal added. "At least he will have if he knows what's good for him. There are all kinds of eyes looking for these bastards."

"Right. Okay, Sal, I'll have to let you go but first, I need a favor."

"Sure."

"You tell that fucking crazy reprobate that if his ass isn't on the first plane available tomorrow, I'll go down there to pick him up myself. And tell him that he should believe me when I say he won't enjoy that."

Sal's message was succinct and to the point.

Niki was pissed. He needed to get in touch.

The hospital was probably one of the more advanced locations on the base, and the communications section was one of the best as well, which meant that it wasn't difficult to get an international call out.

They would be nickel and diming him on everything, of course, but it couldn't be avoided.

"You motherfucker!"

Taylor pulled the phone away from his ear and he could already tell that Niki was in a foul mood.

The tirade stopped suddenly, and he pressed his ear to the phone again and frowned at the oddest sound.

He wasn't sure, but he could have sworn Niki was crying.

"Look…I tried to contact you," he said. They were his first words to her since he'd gone into the Zoo and damn if it wasn't good to hear her voice again.

She sniffled. "I know. The Zoo doesn't allow transmissions."

"I'm sorry. I truly am."

"Don't be. These are ugly tears, but they're happy ones too. I'm merely glad to hear your voice. You wouldn't believe how…well, it's been tough, I won't lie. And then there was all that business with the triads, and I didn't know, and it was all…"

Taylor couldn't make out what she was saying. Everything went muffled for a second and finally, another voice came on.

"Hi, Tay-Tay."

He grinned. "Howdy, Vicks. Are you sure those are happy tears?"

"Yeah, it's been…God fuck it, woman, get some tissues and blow your nose. Get your shit together. Anyway, it's been rough for both of us, and I'm happy to hear your voice again too. But I wanted to ask what you've done with the Desk clone in your suit."

"What I did?"

"Yeah."

"I didn't do anything. Li'l Desk is still alive and well in the suit. And don't worry. Freddie has it packed securely and he'll ship it directly to Bobby, who will need to give it a little TLC and Desk will have a chance to remove…herself. Honestly, I'm not clear on how that would work."

"I am not sure myself," Desk admitted and joined the conversation. "There was no plan that far ahead, but I should contact Jennie before we do anything."

"That sounds about right," Vickie agreed. "Better safe than sorry and all that, although I do hate the thought that we might have to erase a Desklet."

"Desklet…you mean like a kid?" Niki shouted in the background. "Oh, fucking hell no. Do you mean to tell me the AIs are breeding?"

Taylor smirked. "I'll, uh… leave it to you guys to think about that. But there might be information that Li'l Desk picked up that could help real Desk."

"Her experiences will certainly be…unfamiliar," the AI conceded. "Did she interact with you much? Was she helpful?"

"Far more than I expected," Taylor answered. "On both.

I'd go so far as to say that she saved my life a couple of times."

"Damn." Niki growled. "I want to be pissed that Desk was in there saving your life when I had to fucking kick rocks around here, not knowing if you were alive or not. Yeah, I know I should be grateful, but I can't wrap my head around it. Seriously, even the idea of a part of an AI that you all now think of in 'she' terms actively saving... No, you know what? Not now. Get your ass to Vegas, Taylor. And don't waste my time. I'll have the suite waiting for us, and you already know I'm not any good at waiting, especially for—"

"Gag, gross," Vickie protested. "Get a fucking room, you two. No more grossness, please. It's bad enough that I have to hang around in Vegas knowing you two are—no, wait, maybe I don't. I have the number of a guy who might—"

"You have a guy's number?" Taylor asked.

"There's no need to sound too surprised."

"I'm very sure that's what you were going for."

"Maybe, but still. The guy's cute and it's not like the two of you will need me for anything anytime soon."

"Desk?" Niki called. "Did you know about this?"

"Of course," the AI replied.

"And you encourage it?"

"I fail to find reasoning to correct it. I have already run a background check and the young man does appear to be harmless. My only worry is that she might end up being bored with him within the hour."

"You checked—goddammit. I need to cut your access to my phone. I need to talk to Jennie."

"Maybe not," Niki interjected. "It seems we need Desk

to keep an eye on you. Were you ever going to mention him?"

Taylor could almost hear Vickie rolling her eyes.

"For fuck's sake. I'm considering hanging out with a cute dude who might or might not bore me senseless. There are no wedding bells ringing in my near future, although I don't think the two of you have any right to talk. So, let's go. We can make a pit stop in New Orleans and we'll still arrive in Vegas in time."

"New Orleans?" Niki sounded lost. "Why the fuck should we go to New Orleans?"

"Well, for one thing, it'll keep your mind busy on something other than pacing the whole fucking suite like you've done over the past few days. And second, I'm thinking about the best burgers in the world."

"Oh hell yes. Those are worth the effort."

"The best."

"I get to have a good meal on the way to finally getting laid. What's not to like?"

Vickie gagged. "You had to go and make everything gross again."

"How's the arm?"

Taylor looked at the sling and shrugged gingerly. "It'll heal. The cut isn't too bad, although they needed to get in there to make sure all the barbs came out. I thought I'd seen the last of the Zoo's inventiveness. Shit."

Freddie laughed. "It's weird to see you off again, Taylor,

I won't lie. But I am glad that you're making this trip on your feet instead of in a coffin."

"Not everyone was so lucky."

"They never are. But we have to appreciate the living as well as mourn the dead, you know?"

He did know and he nodded as the Hammerhead came to a halt outside the airstrip. The strip of green out on the horizon seemed to beckon to him. It was odd how he couldn't bring himself to take his eyes off of it.

"You don't want to miss that plane."

Taylor snapped his head around and realized that they had already pulled up to the airstrip close to where the plane was being loaded.

"Nope. No, I do not. I'll be killed if I do."

Freddie smirked but the two men sat in the Hammerhead in silence for a few more moments before Taylor finally climbed out and carried his bag to the loading ramp of the heavy military cargo plane.

His gaze was drawn back to the green ribbon on the horizon and an odd chill filled the pit of his stomach.

All he could think to do was offer the jungle his middle finger, held high.

"Eighty-five, bitch!" he said gruffly and a grin touched his face. "Better luck next time."

ONE THREAT TOO REAL

The story continues with book four, *One Threat Too Real,* *coming March 3, 2021 to Amazon and Kindle Unlimited.*

What happens when Green Earth Extremists tangle with a Zoo creature?

About exactly what you might expect.

McFadden and Banks are on the prowl for a stolen computer that houses something they need back, bad.

A small group of extremists decide to steal the ultimate in alien-based terrorist threats... If they can.

Will they be able to accomplish it?

They have one problem, well two really.

McFadden and Banks.

Pre-order today to have your copy delivered at midnight on March 3, 2021!

AUTHOR NOTES - MICHAEL ANDERLE
JANUARY 9, 2021

WOOHOO! Thank you so much for reading through this story and here to the back for my author notes.

It's 2021 and just turning the chapter on New Years Eve to the new year helped me mentally work to shrug off some of the bad juju from last year.

For those who have followed some of my other author notes, you know that I'm trying to cook more this year as one of my non-author / publisher skills. So, I'm told I will have a new wood pellet pit come mid-February.

This sounds like a great idea, but you see my loving wife decided to gift me with a pit that she selected and it caused me a bit of consternation.

I had been studying pits for at least two weeks, comparing brands, learning woods, price and performance, single wall or double wall...reviews...history... all for that moment when I make the decision on which special pit I would purchase and assemble and install right where it will make beautiful smoked meat for years to come.

She co-opted all of that and ordered a pit as a gift.

DAMMIT!

She won't tell me what she ordered without me pressing and you just do not press someone to tell you what they bought when they give you a loving gift.

It's rude.

Even if it is a pit you are all anxious about. I mean, she hasn't grilled on a bbq or gas grill the whole time I've known her. Nor has she shared ANY stories of bbq'ing in her past.

So, I'm totally getting a pit based on her Google-fu.

And I'm ok with that.

You see my wife is a fantastic researcher and she won't skimp on purchasing the best value. So, I'm purchasing the pieces she wouldn't know to buy (like copper mats and wood-pellets) in advance so when the day gets here, I won't have to run to the store for anything.

I'm learning where the best butcher shops are in Henderson, Nevada. I'm going to pester the shit out of Mike at Jessie Rae's about BBQ sauces... or just buy a shit-ton of his God Sauce (so good!) and save myself time and aggravation.

Yeah, I think that's going to be my plan. I'm going to start doing taste tests of BBQ sauce.

I had totally intended to share my effort at a Jalapeño stew I cooked last night, (I liked it, not really willing to suggest anyone else cook it) but discussing my new pit (THAT WON'T COME FOR ANOTHER MONTH) took too long.

I'll get over it.

In about a month.
See you next story!

Ad Aeternitatem,

Michael Anderle

One Crazy Set Of Stories (12)

SOLDIERS OF FAME AND FORTUNE

Nobody's Fool (1)

Nobody Lives Forever (2)

Nobody Drinks That Much (3)

Nobody Remembers But Us (4)

Ghost Walking (5)

Ghost Talking (6)

Ghost Brawling (7)

Ghost Stalking (8)

Ghost Resurrection (9)

Ghost Adaptation (10)

Ghost Redemption (11)

Ghost Revolution (12)

THE BOHICA CHRONICLES

Reprobates (1)

Degenerates (2)

Redeemables (3)

Thor (4)

CRYPTID ASSASSIN

Hired Killer (1)

Silent Death (2)

Sacrificial Weapon (3)

Head Hunter (4)

MCFADDEN AND BANKS

Made in United States
North Haven, CT
15 June 2022

20269931R00198